# WHISPER MAMA

Protect Your Heart...

M.

"Lift your feet."
—Evelyn Castle

# Whisper Mama

a novel

Linda Haas-Melchert

Published 2017

Printed in the United States of America
ISBN: 978-0-9989087-0-0
E-ISBN: 978-0-9989087-1-7

Cover and interior design by Tabitha Lahr
Front cover photo © Ashlie Lee

For information, contact Linda Melchert at whispermamawhisper@gmail.com.

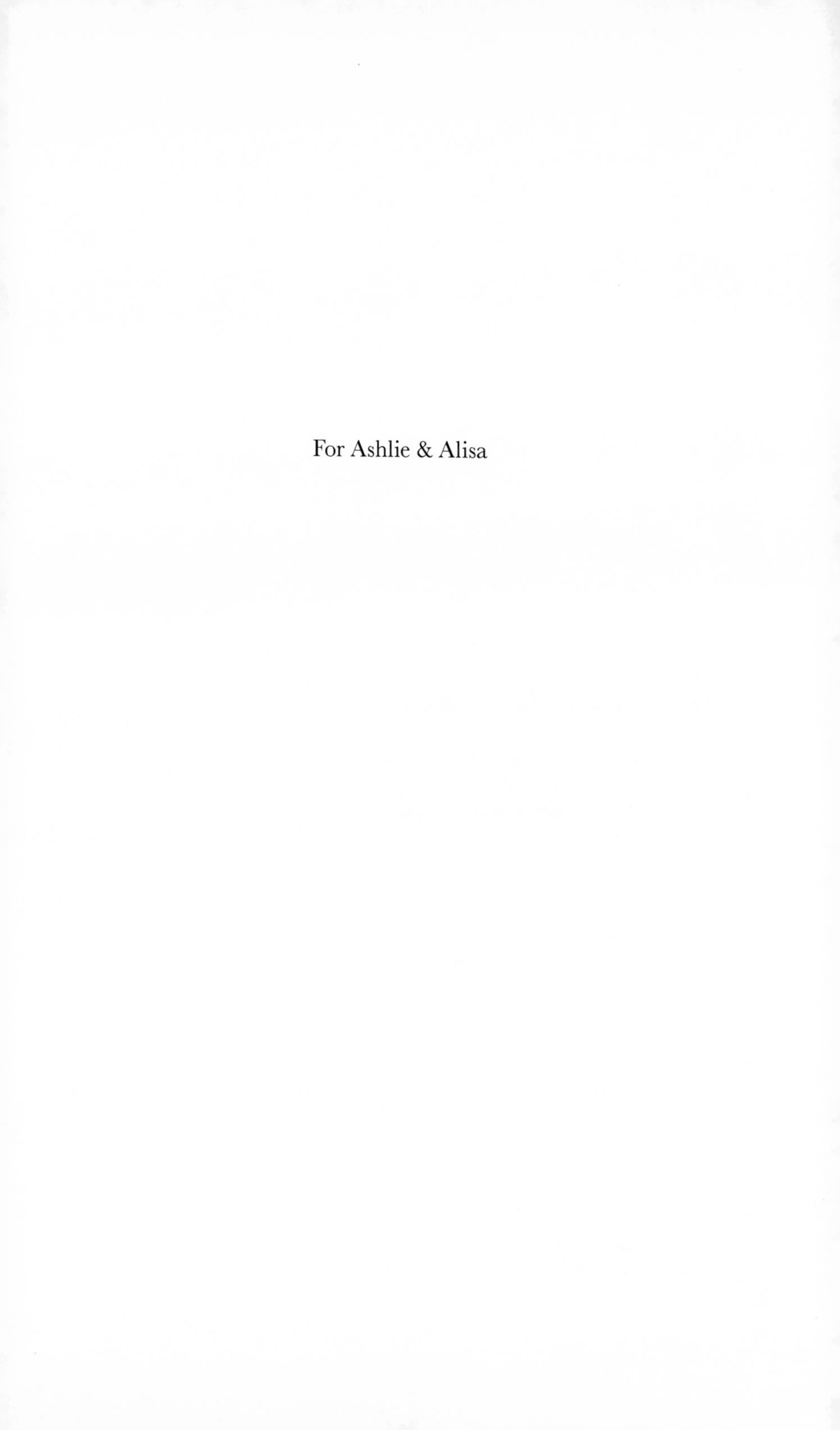

For Ashlie & Alisa

# PART ONE

*Ripped from loving arms, she flies.*
*Cold slams against her cheek, as pain cracks through her bones.*
*Shaken, she hovers.*

# Evelyn

## Harrisburg, Oregon
## August 1925

It's the biggest sound she's ever heard, and the brightest light she's ever seen. She's heard adults say there's a bright light when you die, that sometimes you get a choice. Should she go?

There's a train man. He's busy finding pieces of the Model T, her mama, her papa, and her two sisters; their bodies are broken, gone. Next, he finds her. She's thrown across the front point of his train, twisted, as if puppet strings have been cut, letting her limbs fall as they may.

The train man climbs up; he leans in, holding his breath so as to better hear hers. He's careful not to touch, his hands tremble above her instead.

She moves; he jumps, then turns quickly on his heel. "Here, over here!"

A sudden lift takes the bright away.

*Her name is Evelyn. She is nine years old. A crash with a train has just shattered her world.*

# HOSPITAL

EUGENE, OREGON
HOURS LATER
EVELYN

My thumb rubs across my itchy nose. The sound of moving curtains and stepping shoes has stirred my drowsy interest. My arm and leg ache with deep and throbbing pain.

"She's moving!"

"Good morning, Evelyn. Can you open your eyes?"

They seem stuck, like they've been glued that way—I don't know the voice. Again I try, opening my one eye, then the other, I blink.

"Well, there you are. Are you thirsty?" Her nurse's hat tips slightly to the left above her tight, blonde curls. She quickly pours a small cup of water. "How's your head?" Her face shows worry and pain. She looks porcelain, like a doll. "How's your arm? Are you hurting?"

High on her toes, arms held wide, a blanket pulls over me from the other side. She tucks, then leans to crank the bed. It seems a nurse's dance practiced over and over—she knows it by heart. Her free hand lifts hair from my brow, gently placing it at my temple. More questions follow: "Can you say your name, sweetheart? How old are you?"

The shape of my name is all she gets as it silently crosses my lips.

"Say again?" She's searching my face.

The room is clean; there's a water basin, white and blue blankets, it smells like medicine. There's no question I'm in a hospital—but, why? Where's my mama? The room grows heavy—my eyes give up.

—

*Hot, falling stars visit me in the dark; they fall fast and too close.*

*Are they embers or angels?*

*They almost always follow the most pounding thunder I've ever heard. There's a thrust too, where I float, then fall right alongside them—my settle to earth always much harder than theirs. Time after time, my eyes snap open, wondering what is causing my heart such flutter and pain.*

—

A drift of baked bread moves about. My eyes are low as the room comes clear. The fog of creeping ache returns—this is not a dream.

I notice the light cast across the crisp, white fold placed neatly across my chest. I'm alone. My head is listing. A twinge here, a strain there, every muscle is stiff. I decide moving is not an option, just as talking is not an option. And so I lie still, pushing my mind to think.

To the right of the bed sits a tray of food: a flour-dusted roll resting beside a covered bowl, a sweaty pitcher sheds water, drop after drop joining the pool that hugs its base—sunflowers glow gold in the corner. I'm not hungry, but cannot take my eyes off the roll.

Mama makes rolls all dusty with flour—is she here?

Blonde Curls steps in, her arms stacked tall with linens. Shocked, she steps back,

"Vivian! Send Dr. Haven, she's awake!"

"Hi, Evelyn," she beams. Her smile lives under cheeks rosy as cherries. She looks like lemonade, too, light and fresh. She's too much for my eyes right now.

"It's great you are able to join us for dinner this evening. We thought maybe our soup might raise a sleepy little girl. Our kitchen has a way of raising just about anybody out of their deepest sleep." She reaches for the pitcher.

"You must be thirsty," she says, pouring, then moving on, busy, twirling herself about the room; she's more than my head can handle.

"Well, well!" an older gentleman interrupts. He peers over glasses that hold on for dear life at the end of his nose; a smartly trimmed mustache hangs heavy on his upper lip. I don't know him, but he acts like he knows me. I can tell that he's trying too hard, like he needs to make me his instant friend. Rocking back on his heal, he strolls forward.

"Little Miss! You sure have this sleeping thing down pat. Good, though, makes for proper healing."

He has gray hair and wears a white coat. He's a big man, but looks like he's made of comfort. "Now, let's have a little look-see shall we?"

Blonde Curls catches my eye, still flitting about the room, placing, replacing, pampering.

Dr. Haven pats my hand. "How are you feeling, Evelyn?"

I'm sore from the inside out, but I keep it to myself. He reaches for me, tugging at my upper eyelid. His hands smell of soap; a scent of coffee and hints of sweet pipe loom near his sleeve.

Like Papa's pipe—where's Papa?

Dr. Haven reaches back, blindly swatting at a light switch. Aiming his flashlight, he skims brightly across my one eye to the next, then back again. I flinch. I wonder how much broken can be seen from the outside in? He steadies my forehead with a firm press of the side of his hand. His light then peers deep, so deep it throws a punching flash—a sick whirl of hurt from my head to my heart.

What is that—the hurt?

The doctor steps out for a bit, then returns with more light. Again he skims, this time in reverse. My stomach flips sideways as the punching flash returns.

How is it that a simple light can make such a sick feeling in my tummy?

Can he see a secret in there? Something so secret, I keep it from myself?

I want to cry.

I want my Mama.

Closing both eyes I reach for answers. Nothing. Opening them, I study his face for clues; he's doing his job, looking for what's out of order inside my body. I'm guessing he can't see nor fix this flash of confusion or my aching tummy.

"More rest," says Dr. Haven. "Close those hazel eyes and mend, sweet darling."

Fading again, I sleep, trusting my answers will come.

—

Dr. Haven enters quietly. He's quick and thorough just as he's been the many times before. He checks my face, my eyes, then the temple of my head and cheeks with the back of his hand. He follows with a glance at my foot attached to my injured leg.

Satisfied, he pulls a chair in tight. He then lowers his large frame, settling us face to face.

"Evelyn? Do you know the reason you're here?"

I move my head from side to side, showing him "no" as my answer, my eyes all the while fixed on his. Blonde Curls tinkers with the chart at the foot of my bed.

"Well, you were in an accident, you and your family, a difficult accident to explain." He clears his throat. I can already read a little of the story as it settles across his face. Blonde Curls stops her movement; she stands frozen, watching him struggle with his words.

"Evelyn, it's important that you understand that you are going to be okay," he says, pausing a moment to collect himself. "Your mom and dad are not able to visit you here—I'm sorry to say." He swallows then searches the room; he's looking for something gentle, I can tell. "And, your sisters have passed on with your parents."

Wait—Mama, Papa, my sisters? Passed on? Does he mean . . . they've died?

I can't breathe.

The doctor's eyes hold on mine. Sharing his sorrow, he confirms my confusion with a saddened nod.

"They didn't survive the train," he explains.

How is this possible? All of them? My heart tightens, it hurts.

Taking my hand in the most caring way, he exhales his final, crushing words, "It all happened so quickly."

Blonde Curls has placed her hand on my good ankle. She slowly rubs my foot and squeezes my toes. Pools of water sit above her lower lashes. I look away—I can't bear to watch them fall.

Dr. Haven runs his hand along my cast from the top of my shoulder to my barely exposed fingers.

"This arm is broken, Evelyn. And, you'll have to be careful with your leg." His tender hand steals a tear at my chin. He goes on speaking in his doctors' way. "These cuts, scrapes, and contusions should heal perfectly," he says.

I'm lost in my head, trying to catch up with his words.

Contusions? What's contusions?

They're all gone? It can't be. The tightness in my heart has spread across my chest; I can feel it finding its way up into my brain. I put my eyes toward the ceiling to steady myself.

His deep voice booms past something tight in his throat, "You, sweet Evelyn, will heal just fine. We are all here for you, my dear. It may take a great amount of time, but let's be patient. Time, and lots of these hearty dumplings will heal just about anybody good as new."

Again, he swallows, sends a serious glance toward Blonde Curls, mumbles a suggestion for night medicine, and leaves the room.

---

Moving shadows become my only sign of passing time. The days blend slowly into nights and then into other days—it's all a tearful blur. Blonde Curls, all the while, humming, nurturing; like air, she's always there for me. Without her, the quiet is too quiet, and every noise is jumpy and uncomfortable.

There are the days I pull the blankets over my head leaving just a small opening to breathe through; it's my way of disappearing. Blonde Curls doesn't mind, in fact, she carries on, chatting in the room like I am sitting up normal, happy, and well. Like I'm her little sister waking, getting a late start on the chores or school. She hides her concerns. They show up, though, in moments when she thinks I'm not looking. There are times that I watch my problems run right across her face. Even so, she just carries on: collecting my tears, dirty laundry, dishes—one by one, she carries my problems straight out of the room.

How does she do that?

She's there when I'm out of my mind thrashing, moving to

and from heavy sleep, she watches for my slightest movement or need. I trust her, I think as much as I've trusted anybody, ever.

Many an evening she hums throughout, she's a vocal butterfly—floating, delicately landing on her decided spot.

"Evelyn, I'm going to sit a while. Maybe we can attempt a few bites?"

She leans her hip onto the edge of the bed. Cradling the spoon, she gives the broth a swirl, scooping salty liquid over fluffy white dumplings.

"After you've had a bite to eat, Dr. Haven would like for me to give you more pills to help mend your arm and leg." The sunset slips through her ringlets—she's glowing.

"Also remember, he mentioned sleep is good for proper healing. The pills will certainly help with that." She reaches for a pillow. "Here, let's prop you." Lightly blowing, she dips and raises a steaming spoonful. "This is the first of many, sweetheart." She offers the second.

"One spoonful at a time."

# Broken and Blonde Curls

Most days I'm between tears and wanting to throw something. Anger, frustration, broken bones, and a broken heart is more than any one person should handle. But, somehow in this mess, I've made a friend. A dear one, that's willing to live through everything broken right alongside me, no matter how much it hurts.

Dazed, day in and day out, my body doesn't feel like moving, and I'm tired of thinking.

People say that I'm in shock. I am not sure what they mean by that word. Does it mean a jolt so strong that it snaps your life away? I wonder: Can shock make things disappear right before my eyes? Can it keep me in the dark even though I'm wide awake? If so, then yes, I'm in shock—I think I'll always be there.

Sometimes in the middle of the night I refuse to believe any of it has happened. Or, I imagine, one or all of my family, greeting me at the door to my room. Maybe they're also banged up by the train, just like me, but still breathing, even smiling, because they've finally found me.

Inside, where my heart beats, is just as shattered as my outside. My body might be getting stronger, but my heart feels like it breaks more and more every day. I think it may be broken beyond repair. Will my pieces ever be put back together again?

There's talk that I am making news across our whole nation. That I am called "The Miracle Child." They say that I'm a "blessed little girl," surviving such a terrible crash 'only to be left behind by those that are closest to her.'

I don't feel blessed. How could I? Safe, in the back seat of the Model T, held in Papa's arms one moment, then ripped from them the next?

What happened? Why couldn't I have gone with them?

Through tears, I glance at my cast and then toward the blanket that warms my aching leg. All that I've known, in my life, is the love and care of my family. How can this be?

I WANT my mama—I need her strength and her words.

Lifting my one ear from the puff of the pillow, so as nothing can block her, I concentrate.

"Mama?"

Bowing my head, with all my might, fists balled tight, "Please, Mama, I'm begging you—I would settle for a whisper."

---

Quiet words move about the hospital. Like a mouse in the corner, I listen—unnoticed. As they clean and prepare for the day, the nurses gossip. They think I'm asleep.

"These fatal accidents are terrible!" says the dark-haired nurse, placing her hand on her chest. "The ferry incident, last spring, and now this?! Wasn't that horrific enough? That poor family slipping right into the river. And, now look!" She gestures toward me. "Another family devastated, hit by the train just a few months later? It's heartbreaking!"

"Don't you wonder how she survived? It's like the train scooped her up, shoving her away from harm, to a safer place." Skinny Nurse shakes her head; she looks like something you would find hanging on a clothesline after a hot day of drying—thin and droopy.

They both turn to look at me; I keep still, eyes low.

Skinny Nurse then raises her hand, pointing it, aiming it toward the wall, like the walls are glass and they can see right through them, "Did you see it out there this morning? The press is arriving from all over, they are desperate for details." Her hand finds the cloth in the pocket of the apron tied around her hips. She looks me over adding, "They ALL want to know more." Skinny continues, "They tried to get me to talk, to tell them what's she's like."

Dark Hair takes one last swipe, cleaning the doorknob. They rattle on, their voices fading. I strain to listen as long as I can, but only the hallway walls get to hear the rest of their gossip.

Blonde Curls soon greets my morning. Although she hesitates with her usual routine of throwing open the drapes, inviting the warmth of the morning sun, I can tell her eyes still want to go there.

"Don't these people know that you're all ours?" she says, forcing her grin in a crooked way.

She knows I won't talk in a conversation full of words, that she's lucky to get a nod, or one or two words at a time. She goes on, though, pretending like I'm sharing my opinion.

"Evelyn, people just keep showing up, one after another. They want to know *all* about you." Snubbing the outside world, she gives the heavy drape an extra yank, then pulls limp flowers from the vase nearby, replacing fresh ones in their spot.

Hearing something outside, she returns for a peek. Pointing through the stiff, rose-printed fabric, she tips her head.

"Some just camp themselves *right* there, outside the door thinking we will change our minds and let them in."

Closing the curtain she walks toward me, shrugging a chuckle.

"As if that's ever going to happen; you're safe here with us, sweetie."

"Keep them OUT!" I hear, pulling my curiosity toward the door to my room.

The hospital staff sounds angry, like swirling worker bees guarding their hive.

That's all well and good, but I can't help but think that they may be shooing 'my' people away?

Is my family out there? Surely somebody will show up. Maybe someone from back home, family, a friend?

"This little girl has suffered enough; move along!" the good doctor commands.

Who are these strange people, and why do they want to see me? If it's about my mama, papa, Bertha, and Sylvia, what's the point? There's really nothing more to say—they are all gone.

"What about him?" Blonde Curls asks, poking her head outside my door. "He's not the press; he's okay right?"

"Of course!" shouts Dr. Haven.

"He seems the only sensible person amongst this brash bunch. Let him come and go as he pleases. Regarding anybody else, well, just watch her closely and protect her diligently!"

Him? Let HIM come and go as he pleases? I knew it! It's not my imagination. Maybe someone from back home has come to collect me? Come to think of it, I have felt it all along—something, someone protecting me. Not right here inside my room, of course, but just steps away. There are times when I see Dr. Haven forehead to forehead with a mild mannered gentleman type, flowers in his hands. I see him leaning over a shoulder spying my medical chart, sharing a murmur. He's there, and then he's gone. He's not another doctor, the press, nor a family member. Who could it be?

Still, day after day, I lie here listening to swirling hospital bees, gossiping nurses, and gentlemen murmur. Those around me, 'those' that are checking on my well-being, seem bothered by the drama of people showing up unannounced, by the deadly accounts reported in newspapers and radio broadcasts. I hear them, and I see them shaking their heads. They have little patience for the twisted stories told by word of mouth: A wrong date, the wrong time, misspellings of names. But in all reality these things don't matter to me. I haven't a care in the world about twisted details; I just shrug it off with my one good shoulder. After all, nothing changes the heartbreaking outcome: my precious papa, Sigel Wylee Castle, my mama, Edith Mary Chedister, and my sisters Sylvia Mae and Bertha Irene have suddenly left my world. In my opinion, nothing else matters.

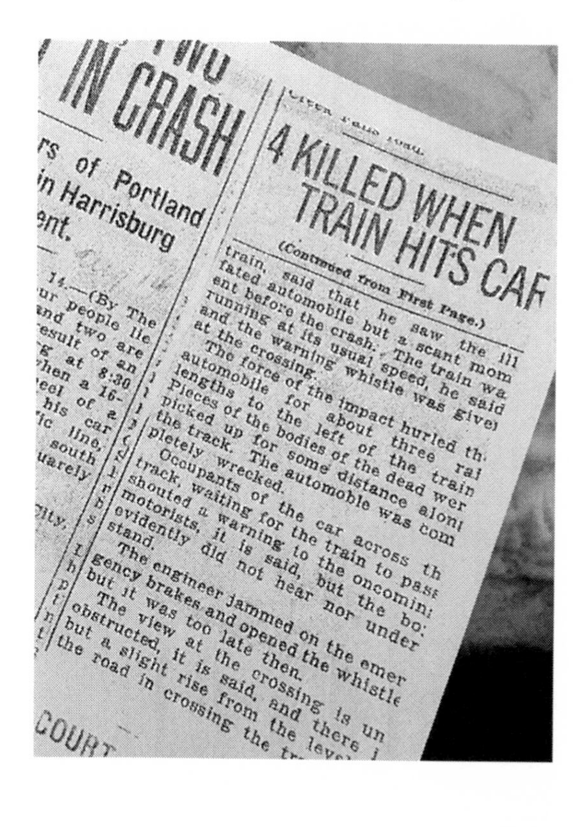

IN CRASH

...rs of Portland
...n Harrisburg
...ent.

4 KILLED WHEN TRAIN HITS CAF

(Continued from First Page.)

train, said that he saw the ill fated automobile but a scant mom ent before the crash. The train wa running at its usual speed, he said and the warning whistle was give at the crossing.

The force of the impact hurled th automobile for about three rai lengths to the left of the train Pieces of the bodies of the dead wer picked up for some distance alon the track. The automobile was com pletely wrecked.

Occupants of the car across th track, waiting for the train to pass shouted a warning to the oncomin motorists, it is said, but the bo evidently did not hear nor under stand.

The engineer jammed on the emer gency brakes and opened the whistle but it was too late then.

The view at the crossing is un obstructed, it is said, and there i but a slight rise from the level the road in crossing the tr...

# Of Mind and Movement

Eugene Hospital
September 1925

There are many a day and night that I question this painful stroke of hard luck.

Was our trip worth it? Our grand plan to move to Oregon from the Black Hills of South Dakota, has exploded into a thousand pieces.

I am sure if Papa could reverse things, he would. His decision for change, for a big move toward a new life seemed logical at the time. The thought of work and a new beginning was even a bit exciting for us all.

South Dakota, filled with family, friends and the beauty of our beloved Stagebarn Canyon, will always hold our roots. But, even I could tell, it also held struggle after struggle and family health challenges. It failed to provide the basic comforts in our lives. Papa's dray delivery service, his business delivering barrels, containers and crates from town to town by horse carriage, hardly provided enough to live on. He wanted and needed a fresh start—he wanted more.

—

I find the deepest, darkest nights the hardest. Sometimes even worse than my nightmares of hot falling stars and thunder. The restless nights, where I'm forever stuck in the stillness just before sleep, where it's blank and dark. I try and think of something bright and good—I think of my sisters.

Oh, how I miss Sylvia Mae. She was six years older, she had dark-brown hair, blue eyes, a heart-shaped face, and a turned-up nose. She was my constant companion, quiet and thoughtful. She used to read to me. We went after the cows together and rode Old Jetty to school from our canyon in South Dakota to Piedmont. In the winter we made snow angels.

She loved to ride horses. She even tried her skills on Lightning, who wasn't 'broke in' yet.

This was scary for me. I remember hiding behind Papa, shouting his instructions from a safe distance. Sylvia Mae was, in one word, brave.

My sister, Bertha Irene was a picture of grace; she's music for my head. Nine years older than me, we shared the same features of red hair and freckles. People used to say, "She's six feet tall in her stockings." She was great fun and could play any musical instrument. She played for dances and for our family and friends. There was always excitement when she was home.

She had beaux calling on her, tall, handsome boys, one after the other, at our door. I was fixated on her, watching her primp her hair; the curling iron heated by our wood stove. Many a night I let the memory of her music play, hoping for a deep remedy of hibernation. Bertha Irene was, in one word, happy.

Keeping Sylvia and Bertha near and dear helps heal me.

—

This morning I begin to tally the days. Most have been blurred by my struggle to feel better. Chances are, I'll be off a few in my count. I'm thinking it's been around three weeks, or more, since the accident. So surely, I'll run out of fingers to count, maybe even my toes. A light tap of each finger on the top of the blanket helps me do the math. Just as my pinky lands, the room suddenly fills with the brightness of Blonde Curls, and by the looks of what's piled in her arms, I realize I have a big day ahead me.

Before I know it, Blonde Curls is helping me dress.

"Today's the day, Evelyn. You're going to have a nice outing. You need to take a ride in your wheelchair, and it's about time you had some fresh air, don't you think?" She reaches for clothing neatly draped nearby.

"I brought a few things from my closet just for you. Here, this sweater is one of my favorites." She wraps the plush, peach fluff over my shoulders. It's beautiful. It reminds me of something I've seen in one of the fancy store windows that lined the streets back in Rapid City. I can just hear my sisters now, and can see them being silly. "Ooh, look. It's crowned in a jeweled neckline, trimmed in a collar of lace." Sylvia would say. Bertha would bend a sarcastic curtsy, and break into laughter. Soon, they'd be sharing giggles and funny faces, knowing this kind of luxury to be way out of our reach. Oh, how I wish they could see.

I smile up at Blonde Curls and touch it adoringly. It feels special and rich. I think only bunnies compare to the softness.

Blonde Curls completes my outfit, slipping a delicate chain around my wrist.

—

Surprisingly, the clumsy transfer from the bed to the wheelchair goes better than expected; I must be ready to use my muscles.

"Here, Evelyn, you hold the parasol."

We find our way outside.

A sudden air pulls through me. A breath so automatic that it doesn't seem my own. The last time I felt fresh air against my skin I was surrounded by my family. As sad as that makes me, I've yearned for all things outside for days now. I think there are times when nature mends you even better than doctors, nurses, and hospitals do.

I take in the air, the sights, and the sounds; I let it fill me.

There's a light, cool breeze against my skin. Tumbling brown, orange, and yellow leaves lift free from busy tree limbs sweeping clouds across the sky. I can feel winter crouching just around the corner.

Blonde Curls leans near my ear, "It's a big world out here, Evelyn. You can handle it. You are one of the strongest people I know. Just look how far you've come."

She kneels at my feet, slowly lifting the foot rest. Moving it aside, she lifts the laced parasol from my lap, then offers an assisting arm. A bench collects the both of us.

Our outing continues throughout the afternoon, resulting in some of the most healing hours of my stay.

"Look!" Blonde Curls says while tucking me in for the evening.

"You've been kissed by the sun, my dear." She smiles while

sliding a pillow under my leg. "Could it be that I see a few more freckles?"

—

I know that I have to leave the hospital soon, though I can't imagine where I might go.

Every day, I try to find my balance: sitting, standing, even lying the correct way—I push myself. I am moving about, on my own, but not with much success. Even so, it's time to be brave, to work at this wheelchair.

I tug at the stubborn wheel—it kicks in, glides smoothly for a bit, then it comes time to turn. Left, right, or all the way around, it doesn't matter; this chair seems to have a mind of its own.

Uhhh! Why always the wrong direction? Help me, my Sylvia Mae, to hang on, just like you did on Lightning. It's all very frustrating. Clearly, I need more practice.

I've come to realize how much I rely on Blonde Curls; she truly has been an extension of me. I need her. I can't help but well up at the thought of leaving. Chances are, wherever they send me next will be far from this place, far from her. I do know this much: no matter how far and how hard my life changes will be, I'll be forever grateful to both Blonde Curls and Dr. Haven, and will give my best effort to get better because of them.

# LOST

EUGENE, OREGON
OCTOBER 1925

I'm nervous.

The butterflies feel more crowded than usual, flitting around inside. I sit up a little taller so as to give them some room. I don't know why I do this, as they just seem to spread up into my rib cage inviting others to fly in.

Why is it that people never ask ME what I want?

They ask if I'm hungry or if my arm and leg feel okay, but, they never ask about anything else: my mind, my bleeding heart, or this belly full of butterflies that are now crawling as high as my throat.

They say that my presence has been requested by the owner of the Harrisburg Hotel. Something about "closure and acceptance."

Some lady is picking me up, I guess she's the owner?

At first, I wonder what she and the hotel have to do with closure and why it is they insist that I go there. But, now I know more than I did before. I've learned that the hotel is located very near the location of the crash and also not far from where they've laid my family to rest.

I try to put my finger on how I feel about all of this. I begin with the fact that most certainly there will be a machine, a car, involved in getting me from one place to another, as the hotel is located miles away from here. I don't know what bothers me more: the machine, being forced to go near the very spot of the crash, or the fact that this trip takes me far from this hospital and from those that I've grown to trust and care about so deeply.

I understand, they want me to get better, to fully recover, but, don't they know this is all that I have?

"Hey, it's just another bed," Blonde Curls says, sensing my worry. She lightly swipes her finger on the tip of my nose, sending me a wink.

Again, the very idea of leaving her makes me upset, almost angry.

"In our minds we are within easy reach," she insists. She gives my bracelet a spin.

"I'll keep you in my thoughts every day, Evelyn."

Feeling lost and afraid, I wonder how it is that I go into a whole, new life all by myself, without my family—without her?

All I want is to surround myself with every person that I've ever known and cared about—dead or alive, it doesn't matter. I want to wrap myself in each of them, use them as a cloak for my head and my heart.

"I feel like you saved my life, I'll never forget you," I say to Blonde Curls as she sets a travel bag on the bed beside me. It feels like a crab apple is lodged in my throat.

"I feel the same about you, Evelyn."

Pushing away these newfound problems, I try to reason with myself. After all, surely, others are in need of hospital beds and the healing powers of Dr. Haven and Blonde Curls.

But, still. Here I sit, facing one problem into the next.

I have to get into this car. . . . Will it hit something?

The thought makes me weak in the knees. I'd rather take

a wagon; one like we had back home, or walk for that matter, if I could.

Placing a trembling hand onto the side of the machine, I close my eyes and wish it to be safe.

While loading my things, again, I shift my thought toward Papa. Of his shouting wild horse instructions to Sylvia Mae. Only, on this day, he changes his words a little. “Evelyn, hold tight, you’ll be okay. Pretend you’re stronger than the machine you ride in.”

Stealing one last glance, I turn to look through the back window. Seeing and hearing Blonde Curls and the staff shouting good wishes, I can’t resist the urge to cry.

Facing forward, I brace myself.

Will every change come with this shattered feeling? I refuse to crumble—I can’t.

But, where will I go; where will I live?

I suppose this is not the time for me to know the details of my future, nobody seems to know. I see my same questions all across their faces no matter who they are.

I want to get out of the car, change my mind, but I can’t. I have no choice in the matter—it seems not one thing has been my choice! So it will be that I’m forced to leave behind big pieces of my heart, two very special people and one mysterious visitor.

The motor cranks. There’s a sputter, *POP,* then a full-on rumble.

The sound doesn’t startle me, but brings a flutter of sadness instead. It strikes an image of the last time I sat in the back seat, nestled in Papa’s arms, drifting off in a happy sleep, hearing Mama talking in the front seat, Sylvia and Bertha sitting close by, all without the slightest hint of what would take place next. If only I’d known right that minute, I would’ve studied each of their faces, their movements, stamped them in my memory forever. I would’ve told them how much I cared.

# Earthly Slumber

Alford Cemetery
Harrisburg, Oregon
October 1925

This feels awkward, certainly not right. I hardly know this woman, in fact I don't! Yet she's proudly pushing, wheeling me through this maze of plotted dirt.

She runs a hotel—a hotel! Not graveyard tours.

I'm not even sure that I like her.

So what is this? We find ourselves together, looming amongst headstones big and small and mounds of messy earth? I want to kick something, hard! If only I could, I would kick and kick, till I couldn't kick anymore.

She's wheeling me toward a grave site.

THE grave site?

"All four of them are together, Evelyn," she explains.

"They're over here somewhere." She flicks her hand to the right and then shoves my chair in that direction. Bumping along, we forge—my wheels now caked and damp.

I know what she tells me is true, but I don't want to believe her.

They just can't be here—not in this place. It's positively dreadful!

"Oh, here we are, Evelyn."

My urge to kick till I bleed turns into a growing fountain of tears; I push it down. Then with everything I have, I try shoving it down even further.

"Here it is, Evelyn." That's all she can say? "Here we are. Here it is?"

I look at the paper marked Castle 4 held up by a stick, crooked and soiled by the weather. My tummy lurches. My face runs stone cold.

I feel the sun spread over my creamy, freckled cheeks. I tilt my head back, my face angled upward, begging tears to run the opposite direction.

"Inward please!" I say to myself. Haven't I cried enough?

Eyes sealed shut, I focus on sound rather than sight; it's just easier this way.

I hear the hum of birds, grasshopper wings, and the flitting click of dragonflies. My heart swells as I embrace the thought of each of them.

"I should be with you," I say, drawing the deepest of breaths; I let it escape without desire for its return. Head down, my chin and the world sits heavy on my chest. My throat responds, hollow and tight.

Why should I be the one still filling my lungs with air? The one who has to go on living?

I just want to scream, to push my shout through the mounds, the stones, and the earth, "WHY?!"

Yes, I've survived, but I am dead inside.

I look at the ground, confused. I'm still not fully convinced they are under there. It just doesn't seem real. I try picturing them huddled together, their arms wrapped snugly around each other, for if it's true, that's the way it has to be.

Lady Inn Keeper says, "I'll leave you alone for a minute, Evelyn. Go ahead, say a few words if you like," I shift in my seat.

I watch her as she strolls back toward a tall, bent tree. It looks like a hard wind caught it during a weakness of growth, throwing it off its intended course—like it just got stuck there. I watch her rip a leaf from the closest limb, then twirl it; she's spinning it between her fingers.

I sit a while, still heavy in my chest, bewildered.

"Now what am I supposed to do?" I ask them under my breath.

A chilling train whistle blows in the distance.

I don't understand—why bury them so near the tracks?

Lady Inn Keeper returns. "Come now, we need to get back to the hotel and get ready for tomorrow. Mayor McGrath would like to meet you, Evelyn." Midsentence she lands a pity pat on the crown of my head and then fidgets with my chair, her jerky motion pushing harshly over the bumpy path. She could take some lessons from Blonde Curls in how to best move a chair with a sore body sitting inside it.

"Seems everyone wants to meet you," Lady Inn Keeper adds. My mind is distant from her chatter, though. My head still lingers with the train sound and my napping family. The sound just hangs there; it repeats itself. It might as well be calling our names one by one.

I try to shake it off.

Turning back, I decide to memorize their surroundings: the field they are lying in, the grassy cover of earth and shining sun, the traveling moss crawling along trails, up and over wooden props, statues, and tree roots. All of it seemingly touched by a misty brew of sap, damp pinecones, and fallen leaves.

As the path comes to an end, a squirrel stops as squirrels do, all frozen and wide-eyed—fixed on us, busily turning something in her small grip.

I want to stay here, with my family and with this busy squirrel.

Please, just leave me behind. I need to figure this out—to pick up my pieces.

To find something of my own to grip.

I lean to brush the earth with my hand. The squirrel spooks, then scampers up the tree. My family will always have each other. I, like this spooked, little squirrel, must make my way through life collecting, gripping anything, when and where I can.

# The Mayor's Gift

Harrisburg Hotel—Harrisburg, Oregon
October 1925

Lady Inn Keeper, like at the graveyard, stomps and swirls in a fit of nervousness. Her hands are choppy, swiping at tablecloths in the cafe, then lighting candles under glass at the guest register. She quickly reaches back to set a loose hairpin behind her ear, yanks at her collar, then briskly settles the front of her skirt.

While she fusses, all I can think about is Mama. She was a small woman, her dark, red hair piled high on the very top of her head. Her skirt dusting her ankles above her scuffed, tightly laced boots. My whole world revolved around her. If she were here with me, in this moment, she would be pacing. Her limp from a childhood horse incident notably less exaggerated than before. She would find this gathering, this amount of attention a bit overwhelming—in her words "a nuisance." If she's with me now, she's reaching for my hand, all the while willing me her strength. Nothing could budge her without her allowing it to. She's a rock, even on the other side, no doubt, just as she was here with me a couple of months ago. And so here I am, taking Mama's imaginary lead, my hand cupped in hers. I'm quiet, soaking it in. Okay, Mama, here we go. I feel as if I'm a spectator rather than a nine-year-old miracle child—the latest object up for grabs.

The community has gathered in my honor.

I see him, Mayor McGrath, standing there. You can tell he's someone important just by the way he stands, the way he moves his hands.

The Mayor bellows his hello. His arms outstretched, open wide, his palms turned up in a grand gesture. He's addressing 'his' people—the front step of the Harrisburg Hotel is his stage. There's just a small crowd, but large enough for him to make an all-important gesture; they all seem like his friends. His small town is showing interest, at pause for me. In his words: I'm a "Little girl hit by hard times." Onlookers across the street break their stride to listen.

"On this day we gather for Miss Evelyn Castle," the Mayor lifts his voice. He looks my way. "Evelyn and her family have experienced a terrible accident. Unfortunately, one that has taken place right near this very community." Mayor McGrath humbly prepares his throat. "The City of Harrisburg would like to extend our deepest condolences." He glances my way again, then out of his shirt pocket he pulls an envelope. He bends to shake my hand and presents his offering.

"Evelyn, this won't begin to fix what has taken place, but I can only hope that it brings you a little bit of pleasure."

Tucked inside the envelope, I realize it's money. Wow! A lot of money.

I now hold in my hand more money than I've ever seen in my whole life—a ten-dollar bill! Ten dollars just for me? I can't believe my eyes! As I try to process the amount, something is nudging me.

Oops, maybe it's the spirit of my mama making sure that I

show my appreciation? No, I realize it's Lady Inn Keeper keeping me in line with my manners. Unbothered, I take my gaze back toward him. Mayor McGrath can see the gratefulness in my eyes and in my facial expression.

"Thank you," I say, blushing at his generous gift.

---

The afternoon and evening falls calm, but I am feeling restless. I'm still taken aback by the mayor's generosity, such kindness, but all I want now is to leave this place. There must be some way to sneak away. I'm pretty good at moving my chair now, and my ten dollars should give me a good start.

So that's exactly what I plan to do. Sliding my one arm into my coat, which is now layered over my dress and my favored sweater, I reach for a leftover dinner roll and tuck it in the very bottom of my pocket. I'll rest a while wrapped in my layers. Then tonight, I'll slip away once the Inn is fast asleep.

Dressed and ready to go, I think about my future, about everything that I've been through, and I'm realizing something: There are kind people in this world—someone will surely come along and help me find my new home.

Fully dressed, waiting for the ideal minute to escape, I'm gripping my ten-dollar bill. It's tightly curled, snug, inside the fold of my fist.

I wait, and I wait. And my eyes grow heavy.

After what seems like only a minute, my eyes roll open. The smell of fresh bread and coffee is cause for me to sit straight up. My small bag, still packed, is close by—perhaps now is the time? I listen.

I check my hand for the money, it's gone! I look down on the floor, I search under the pillows, then carefully bend to look under the bed.

Where is it?!

I quickly feel my wrist for the bracelet—still with me, thank goodness.

Did I tuck the money away in my sleep?

My hand slips under the roll in my pocket. It's not there.

The smell of bread and coffee now filling the room, it dawns on me that it's morning.

Have I accidentally slept the night away? And, where is it?

A quick, heavy step halts just outside my door. After a moment or two the door swings open.

"Good morning, Evelyn," Lady Inn Keeper announces her entrance. Balancing a heaping tray of breakfast, she gives it a twist as it lowers, like she's done it a thousand times before.

"I see that you're already dressed and ready for the day. Well good for you!" She says, placing the tray on the bed stand.

"Anything else, darling?" An icy smile spreads across her face; the door is already squeaking its way shut.

"Ummm, yes." I hesitate, building courage. She steps back in, hand on her impatient hip.

"There is one thing—I can't find my money. Could you help me find it?"

Her quiet shrug isn't the answer that I'm looking for.

I look directly at her. I'm slightly uncomfortable, but now I want her reply.

"Did you find it?"

My chest is pounding. I can tell by her stiff, silent way that yes will be her answer.

"Do you have it?" I ask again, needing to know for sure.

Her icy smile melts away.

"Well, Evelyn, somebody has to pay for your keep. Now eat!" She shouts, then turns her stingy self and slams the door behind her.

# Say Uncle

Portland, Oregon
October 1925

A man named Clemmett is here. I understand that we are blood related. We've had a few visits, but I don't really know him very well. He's a distant uncle. My clearest memory of him was during a family visit, upon our arrival in here in Oregon, just before the accident. Then followed a couple of hectic visits at the hospital. I paid little attention to him. I think Papa just meant our visit with him and his family only as a necessity. Strictly a cordial, brotherly visit to catch up, then collect means for getting around this unknown place. I sensed at the time, some quick directions and a driver is all we really wanted from him.

Clemmett's sixteen-year-old son, Mervin, our loaned driver, proved a grave decision. For it was his pause on the tracks that evening that caused the loss of my family. He was distracted, busy talking with Mama in the front seat, and looking for the detour, due to newly laid pavement in Harrisburg. What baffles me is the fact that he was thrown free, that he escaped without a scratch. Furthermore, he's allowed to move on with his life, hardly touched. Of course, it's not that I've wished him any hurt; but, how is it that I am the one that ends up harmed and alone? Such is the unfairness in life, I guess—I suppose that I'll never fully understand it.

Uncle Clemmett has arrived at the Harrisburg Hotel to collect me. I'm told that he was the person that arranged the hotel visit in the first place. I watch and listen as he thanks the Lady Inn Keeper for her "kind hospitality." He repeats his words, saying them slightly too loud. He has a wink in his voice.

"Let's go, Evelyn, before it gets dark outside." He reaches for the back of my chair.

Uncle Clemmett is taking me to his home in Portland. Although I'm relieved to get away from the selfish, cold-hearted lady, I haven't made up my mind as to how to feel about this new situation. What does this mean?

During our ride he goes on and on about the nonsense of doctors.

"The Lord shall heal you. Look, Evelyn! How he saved Mervin. He hardly let the train touch him—he protected him."

I keep my eyes on the road in front of us.

"It's not for us to know why God permits us to go through such trials of hardship, he knows best, and we must trust him."

I quickly understand how he feels about his lord. There's a small part of me that wants to feel the same way, but I just can't—besides, I'm a little upset with the Lord right now. And on the subject of Mervin, I can hardly look at him. I've never wished him harm or pain, but he's the last person I want to see or be around.

Uncle Clemmett continues, "See the land? Those buildings, the people and pets walking by? The Lord made all of it. Everything. He made you, too. And, his plan is to keep you here with us."

He stops in thought, then adds, "Evelyn, cast thy burden

on the Lord and He will sustain thee." Nodding my way, he moves his head up and down as if to convince me. "He saved your life, and he'll make you feel better soon. NO more doctors, Evelyn. They're a bunch of quacks!"

Clemmett preaches on.

I'm lost in my own thoughts of generous, caring Dr. Haven: his strong and supportive nature, his healing hands, and his expertise. I don't ever remember hearing him quack, not even once.

Uncle Clemmett is without his wife; they say she's been 'hauled' away for some reason. That she lives in a big building somewhere, locked up. Something about a lost mind. So without a wife on hand to take care of me, he finds sufficient help amongst the people of his church. Still, the house looks like just men live here; nothing's been washed in days, maybe weeks. We eat, but mostly what the church people feed us. They either drop a dish on the doorstep, or we are given something when we go to church in the evenings.

We are expected to attend church every night of the week—*every single night.*

I wouldn't mind attending every night if it were fun or even peaceful, but it's not.

Churchgoers know me as the Miracle Child, and I am held in the highest regard. They think I'm an angel meant for Earth, left behind for bigger purposes: to save them, make good on their prayers, or to deliver His message.

Being praised by this church frightens me. They prop me up, they chant, pray, and as my uncle puts it, "speak in tongues."

When they talk in their tongues, I don't know what they're saying; seems more like noises to me. It sounds more like a hum than a language. Some people fall to their knees and just stay there, stricken with a power that makes them drowsy.

"Please, no," I say, begging them not to put me up there. They make me sit in a chair on top of a table. They reach, wanting to touch me—quick brushings of fingers, sometimes a full-on palm press, their heads low. Night after night, I cry and beg them not to. The choice is not mine, nor theirs; it's the same reason over and over, "It's the Lords plan."

I can't shake my nightmares—the hot embers. I'm constantly waking in a cold sweat, worried.

Why is it that I wake so tired? I've just slept.

Uncle Clemmett forces me to talk to his lord, to thank him for my life. He's quick to suggest that more terrible things might happen if I don't.

---

On this evening I seek out a safe spot in the church. One blink of a moment when no one is looking, I quickly move about on my own. I take a hasty dive out of sight. My shouting body still finds it hard to scoot in a crawling way, but I push myself and settle for the space under a skirted table—uhh, my arm hurts. It's throbbing, but I don't care. Quickly I shuffle myself farther back, safe and secure between sacred benches and pews. There's no amount of coaxing that will result in me giving up my safe spot. A hand pulls the table skirt aside ever so often, checking on me, I suppose.

My arm is still very much in pain, there's a constant lingering itch and ache. My cast is frayed and dirty. Eventually, they give up and toss a blanket inside, leaving me there.

Shortly thereafter, there's a sudden flurry of motion and a set of new sounds.

I hear hushed voices through the table skirt, "Evelyn! It's the man that killed your folks, stay there."

WHAT? The man that . . . ?

They have my curiosity now, enough to make a brave move forward. Scooting again, I crawl and lean out to take a closer look for myself. I pull the table skirt aside. The lights are bright—too bright. Seconds later my eyes adjust. I see him now—a tall, familiar figure standing near the door. His face is kind but holds a look of shock and disbelief. I know him—it's him!

A frantic pull yanks the table skirt shut at my nose. The churchgoer hushes her shout, "He saw her!"

# Clean Getaway

Portland, Oregon
November 1925

A lovely lady, proper and friendly, swings the door open. Holding it there, she uses her other hand to motion me in. The room is big, white and bright. There's a mixture of pine and cinnamon in the air. The whiff of pine is no doubt coming from the oversized, open window, framing the tree limbs just outside. There's a small plate of what looks like oatmeal cookies cooling on the table in front of it. My mouth waters.

She leads me to a bed and a smaller table with a lamp on top. The bed is clean and well tucked. My dirty cast has been removed. I've had a bath and for the first time in a long time I feel nicely put together under my combed hair and neatly pressed clothing. My clothes are all one color—that is, if white is a color. Everybody here wears white, even the lovely, proper lady.

The Boys & Girls Aid Society has taken me in. This is yet another place for the pieces in my tummy to get used to, but for now, I'm doing okay.

Most days I'm tired, and I find it hard to walk, so I spend a lot of the time resting, practicing moving my body as much as I can.

During the mornings the other girls go to school. I am left behind perhaps to fully heal or find peace in yet another place—I'm not sure of the reasons. There's just me and the tiny girl. She might be tiny, about half my age, but she carries a big personality. Definitely big enough to pick at me.

"Crybaby!"

Her shouts are so near my ear, I can hardly stand it.

"Dummy!" Tiny Girl yells at me most every day, always shaking her head, showing me some kind of little-girl disappointment.

"You're big enough to go to school, so why don't you?" she says, poking at my chest. She stomps in circles around me, ponytail swishing; she pokes me from the other side.

"If they'd let me, I'd be at school in two shakes, but I'm only this many, so I'm stuck here." She throws her five fingers across the front of my face, then drives her point home by waving them back and forth for way too long. Leaving the room doesn't help much. She follows me everywhere. She's annoying, like a pebble forever stuck in my shoe. I wish she'd just leave me ALONE.

At my wits end now, after a morning of her stepping on the back of my heel. I turn to her face to face, "Stop it! Leave me alone. I'm doing my best!" Finally, squaring my shoulders above hers, with everything that I have, I go on shouting at her, "I Don't Have a MAMA or a PAPA!!"

Tiny Girl stops, steps back, and looks at me surprised.

"So?!" She says, her face in a scrunch, "Don't you get it?" She looks around the room.

"Neither do I!" She raises both arms as if showing me the room for the very first time, "NOBODY DOES!"

I take a moment to look for myself. Seeing now: this large

room, the rows of beds, white sheets, nightgowns, and nightcaps. She's opened my eyes; she's right.

The unbearable thought that other children are faced with such hardship as my own tugs at my already-ragged heart.

We are orphans. . . .

# A Carpenter's Love

Portland, Oregon
November 1925

Lovely Lady takes my hand again, it must be bath time or time to learn a new chore. But to my surprise, this time, she leads me into a special room. It looks like a room where business is done.

"Evelyn, this is Mr. Harvey Carpenter."

It's Him. Harvey Carpenter is his name? Finally! I know his name. Mr. Carpenter . . . Harvey Carpenter . . . Missssster Carpenter.

I set his name to memory where I used to set my words in spelling practice at school, right near the top of my brain behind my forehead. Keeping it there, I say it to myself over and over.

We take a moment to look at each other, there's something behind his eyes. Something good and noble.

Yes, it's him: the protective presence that has been there all along. The gentleman that leaned over shoulders to look at medical charts and the man responsible for glowing my hospital room with flowers every day.

Mr. Carpenter—the person that was daily, forehead to forehead with Dr. Haven. And, the very man that peered at me, shocked, through the table skirt at the church.

He's the Train Man, the engineer of THE dreadful train, the man that my uncle and the church insist has killed my family.

He kneels to take my hand. He smiles, a cluster of daisies in his grip. I notice the neatness of his hair, the crisp of his shirt, the way his eyes turn up along with his smile.

"Hello, Evelyn, this is Mrs. Carpenter." He turns in her direction. I say hello to both of them, but then I'm at a loss for words.

He hands me the flowers, his blue eyes turn up, again. I decide right here and now that I like him. It's about the feeling that surrounds him—there seems a hug of goodness in the air that he stands in.

He rises and returns to his chair.

"Are you feeling okay, Evelyn? Are you comfortable?" he asks.

"Yes," I say, tugging at the bottom of my clean, pressed dress. I lightly run my hand down the front of it.

"Good then, we've been thinking about you quite a lot these days." He places a warm touch above Mrs. Carpenter's resting hand, near her wrist. She angles her head and nods in agreement. She's put together head to toe: every hair in place, her makeup is just right, her nails are clean and shiny. She too has a crisp collar, it lies flat against a shapely, light-blue jacket. Her matching gloves lay across a clutch purse, propped on her lap.

Mr. Carpenter adds, "We would like to make arrangements for you to come visit our home one day, would you like that?" Before I know it, my head is bobbing in agreement. Something tight in my stomach loosens a bit; a mixture of relief, but, still, there's a flutter of sorts.

"Alright then, it's settled. Next week we will collect you for the day."

I make my way back to the main living area, to my favorite corner where there are built-in shelves holding books inside. I love how they made the corner of the room the exact middle of the bookcase, how it stretches higher than can be reached. It's like the walls have more than one purpose there: to entertain you and to hold up the ceiling at the same time. Most days, I like to get lost in the stories and the overstuffed chair that sits next to them. Today, I'll leave the books alone, and just take some time to think in my chair—to lose myself in the possibilities ahead.

While getting ready for bed, this evening, I think more about what took place earlier; I know this has been one of my good days. Laying my head to the pillow, I wonder about a train engineer's responsibilities. How it probably begins and ends with: running his train, stoking fuel, shuttling people and supplies, maybe some paperwork here and there. So why is it he has taken such great interest in me? Does he want to fix his bad feelings? Maybe he needs to turn a wrong into a right? Could it be that my well-being might help heal his wounded heart? Maybe he too is unable to close his eyes at night without seeing my family broken along his tracks.

---

Mr. Carpenter and his wife have regular visits with me over the following couple of weeks. I find our time together pleasant. After plenty of comfortable conversations, he and his wife have taken me to visit their home in Portland. The home is pleasant. It has a light and clean feel to it, but as bright and new as everything looks to me, there are hints of past times. On corner tables, a touch of lace under colorful, stained-glass lamps. A large rug, designed in pastel ribbons and roses, cushions the clawed feet of a dark, polished dining table. The floors are shiny, too. I remember Mama always scrubbing our floors back in Stagebarn Canyon. I'm just sure this must've been the shine she was searching for in that old worn-out house.

Could I live in a place like this? Would she want me to have such shiny floors, pure white lace, all this clean and comfort? I think so.

I take another look around the room, my mind on my family, still constantly seeking their approval. But, then I stop myself. What if this time I were to make this decision on my own?

My hand glides over an ornately framed picture of a young girl. She's pretty. Sitting proper on the edge of a chair, her ankles crossed, her fingers laced together at her knee. I haven't even thought of asking if Mr. and Mrs. Carpenter have children.

Mr. Carpenter enters the room, takes my hand, then leads me through the kitchen onto the back porch. There, tucked into the warmest corner, hangs a swinging bench. We decide to sit awhile. He shares with me that this is his favorite spot—my feet dangle, his foot is pushing the sway of the swing.

"Do you have children?" I ask.

"Yes, one daughter, but she's much older than you," he says. "Her name is Annette; she has a baby boy, his name is Jack."

He talks about the critters that live in the backyard. How he keeps an eye on the birdhouses, making sure that there's enough seeds for the birds that visit there, and for those that decide to live there, too. He points out the trees, bushes, and the last of the season's flowers leaning under the birdbath—daisies intertwined, hanging on, protected there. He goes on about how he likes to grow them. How they grow best in the warmth of spring and summer. That he enjoys most the hardier types that grow through late fall and hang on to edge of winter—the strong ones.

"What do you think, Evelyn? Would you like to have a backyard like this?"

I look up at him and smile.

There's something peaceful in the idea of living with the Carpenters. Although unusual, there's a forever connection shared between Mr. Carpenter and me. The eternal bond of a tragic time together. He and his family just might be the answer to my future.

# The Train Man and the Orphan

Portland, Oregon
December 1925

These professional people talk in a language I don't really understand.

They say stuff like, "Petition for legal adoption is underway."

Even when I see it all on paper, their words always seem too big and out of order. I guess it all means that somebody has to get permission to keep me.

Mr. and Mrs. Carpenter have made up their mind. They've decided to share their home, to welcome me into their world of comfort. That is, if they get permission to do so.

It goes without saying that there will be trouble, though. My uncle hates the idea of my life with the engineer and won't give up easily. Understanding my desire to even stand near the man, let alone live with him, has stumped my uncle to no end. The fact that I could consider living with the very person that took my parents goes beyond his imagination. You can see it in his eyes, the worry—or is it *worry*?

Does he want me for me? Or for his own benefit with the 'Lord' above?

Even I can tell that the judge sees right through him.

Like all of us, I suspect the judge thinks Uncle Clemmett is fighting against anything that has to do with losing his gift from the Lord. It seems selfish on his part. Sure, he's wrapped it in the fact that there are plenty of relatives afar that would like to take me in. But, something tells me he's lost his grip.

A heated trial fills a great big room. Uncle Clemmett talks fast and nervous, with moving hands and shifty eyes.

Mr. Carpenter is respectful. He shows concern for me, and he shares the fact that he also lost somebody important to him at a very young age. That he may understand some of what I am going through.

It's been an eye-opening week to say the least. Officers take the stand describing the awful conditions of my uncle's home, the piles of dishes and dirty laundry. The doctor talks of my appearance and lack of physical care noted as he carefully removed my filthy cast.

Other's take the stand, one by one.

"He used her for personal gain with our Lord," one woman says.

A man refers to the day that I was found under the pew, "She looked more like a crippled animal rather than a child." He adds, "It was a sorry sight, this poor, little girl."

Uncle Clemmett sits stern in his chair, stiff and furious. There are moments where his stare goes right past me, as if God were standing over my shoulder—he glares long and hard. I think, if he could, he would march right over, step behind me and give God a good peace of his mind. He throws his head the opposite direction. A pout sits heavy around his chin. He's lost his big chance, his fate.

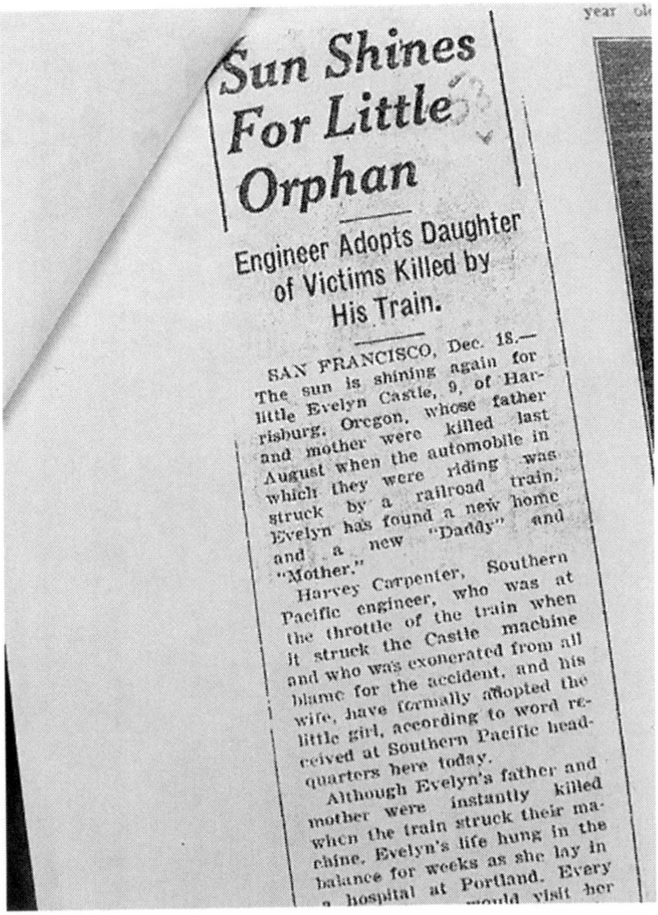

# Sun Shines For Little Orphan

## Engineer Adopts Daughter of Victims Killed by His Train.

SAN FRANCISCO, Dec. 18.—The sun is shining again for little Evelyn Castle, 9, of Harrisburg, Oregon, whose father and mother were killed last August when the automobile in which they were riding was struck by a railroad train. Evelyn has found a new home and a new "Daddy" and "Mother."

Harvey Carpenter, Southern Pacific engineer, who was at the throttle of the train when it struck the Castle machine and who was exonerated from all blame for the accident, and his wife, have formally adopted the little girl, according to word received at Southern Pacific headquarters here today.

Although Evelyn's father and mother were instantly killed when the train struck their machine, Evelyn's life hung in the balance for weeks as she lay in a hospital at Portland. Every ... would visit her

January 11, 1926 my adoption is finalized.

People say that this will secure my future. That I should get along just fine now. They suggest, in their actions, that it may be time for me to put my thoughts into some sort of order—a memory checklist, all neat and tidy. Maybe a list I can set in the corner of my mind and dust from time to time? Their idea of my list might look something like this:

- Horrific Tragedy
- Sadness
- New Life
- Gratitude

But no, my list, as it turns out, is quite different than the one they imagine. Mine is a personal list. One that's too important to set aside and dust when the urge comes over me. And, I will add to my list and carry it along with me, proudly, out of order, and beautifully messy:

- Kindness
- Strength
- Bravery
- Happiness

These words float in my head along with my families' faces. My papa was kindness; my Mama, strength; Sylvia, bravery; and Bertha, happiness. Together, they become me, they are me. I've decided as my family nestles deep in their nap of eternity together, I will adapt their strong and loving ways and make them my own—I'll take them with me.

# Hiccups and Magpies

Painful months slip away, there's a slow sense of relief as I find myself growing and settling into a new life.

I'm fascinated with freshly pressed, folded blankets and sheets. The intricate patterns of lace, china, and silverware—everything in its proper order. All of the fuss over the timeliness of set schedules, manners, and behavior. There's a comfort in it, and I'm truly grateful. But, I often wonder of the importance of it all. Time ticks by, and life seems practiced, even fake at times.

I struggle to find happiness. Just when I think I have it, it escapes me. There are times that I have to shoo the butterflies away, to force them to settle. I have days that I want to crawl under something, to pull the table skirt shut or stay under my blankets with just that small opening to breathe through.

Sometimes when I'm quiet, my mind has to sidestep my heart. It takes a quick shift to the left or right, but then it lands in another world. Here and there throughout my thoughts I allow my fingers to unfold and sneak up across my lips; it is there that they cup and hold my expression. I let the memories flow.

I long for Stagebarn Canyon, near the Black Hills of South Dakota. I can smell the summer's day—it weaves dreamlike throughout my mind. I feel the afternoon sun giving into the evening coolness. I see the warm, vivid sky as it settles across our deep valley high along the tip top of the rim rock; you can see for miles. Red, rust, pink, and golden hues hang in the distance, glowing after our hot summer day. There are sounds of life: our playful dog, Shep; and extended family and friends, including Eva, her husband, Doc Harvey, and their four children, Roy, and his wife, Mary. Nephews, nieces—some older, some younger—and my precious immediate family. The leaves flutter in the breeze; there's a nearby creek. I hear the ribbons of water meandering, finding its way. I take a deep breath; life is humming.

My mind still in our canyon playground, when suddenly I'm amused. My hand slips up, cupping, catching my smile—I can't help it. I'm recalling 'The Man on the Hill.' We don't know his name; we've never known it, though, we do know of him well. We instantly recognize this man by his robust, echoing hiccups! Our playground instantly turns into a listening chamber for a funny man full of bodily noises. There's seldom a more amusing moment, as his hiccups are so loud, they echo throughout our entire canyon. The boys are dramatic in their mimicking. They exaggerate his sound adding their own obnoxious bodily noises and movement—walking, extending their heads forward like a rooster on a hunt for chicken feed.

'The Man on the Hill's bouts of hiccups tickle many a funny bone.

I entertain the thought that hiccups naturally echo; that what air comes in, must come out. Add the hiccups to the echo of a canyon? Well, you can't get much better than that! I catch myself laughing. These memories are forever treasured, held tightly. I let my mind visit there often.

My smile and canyon surroundings are intact. I think of magpies. Mischievous magpies, they are comical in every way. My love for birds is everlasting, especially birds with personality. Magpies have more than personality, they are beautiful and ornery at the same time. I remember their white feathers and striking contrast of their black and bright-blue markings. Yes, instantly recognizable by their look and beckoning banter atop a fence or a tree, they seem to argue with all sorts of life, but mostly with my dog, Shep. Taunting as they can be, there's something wonderful about them.

A group of us kids had heard that if you slit a magpie's tongue, you can make him talk. Curious, we set out to catch one. We scattered corn, baiting the social birds, for days. Finally, one gray day, success! Feathers flying, squawking loudly, the bird is in a panic under our grip. We can hardly keep control of it. It's angry and loud!

In the middle of our triumph, great big, redheaded Roy came around the side of the barn. Nobody had planned on an adult joining our efforts. Everybody took off, leaving me holding the fluttering bird. There's just me, my magpie, and big Roy. I'd been caught 'bird-,handed'!

Well, this certainly wasn't part of our brilliant plan and I had no idea what to do next. I held the magpie at arm's length, then decided to drop it. Wobbling at first, it regained itself and attempted flight. Startled, I threw my arm across my face, shielding myself from its quick, dodging getaway. Waving away the dust and feathers, I looked up. Roy locked my eyes in a glare. Using a puff of breath, I pushed away the hair and feather stuck to my lip. He tried, but couldn't hold back. First, a faint smile crinkled his eyes, then appeared his full-on toothy grin. A big belly laugh soon followed. I realized there was no explanation necessary and turned to leave with red cheeks, chin held high.

To this very day, I still wonder if magpies have tongues.

Living along the Belle Fourche River in the grasslands, or prairie as we called it, held its mysteries. At times we found Indians in the area. The Sioux Indians liked to camp at the mouth of the canyon. Us kids were told, in a scolding manner, never to go near them. "Stay away," our parents would say. "The Indians sometimes swipe children, and then they're lost forever." Not always "good" little children, we crawled through the tall grasses, blue belles, and shooting star blooms to sneak a peek at them. Quietly, we hid behind trees to spy on them. We soon tired though; they seemed harmless, as all they ever did was cook over their fires, talk, and walk around. I'm not sure what we expected. Maybe big feathers? Or, a dance around the campfire? Disappointed, we crawled backward slowly, then ran safely out of their sight.

Braving further into the past, comfortable enough now, relaxed, I remember our simple way of living. Natural, earthy, far from my current modern home and surroundings of clean fluff, social engagements, and indoor bathroom facilities. Surrounded by cupboard after cupboard stacked high with fine china and sterling silver. Further still from the sleek, modern societies, dazzling as they are. I used to long for it all, for the fringe, glitz, and glamour. I remember catching glimpses of these lifestyles on our Rapid City visits, being dazed by window displays, the printed newspapers and magazines, where they featured glass chandeliers, velvet furniture, and the most modern lines of art. We lived the opposite life in our canyon of outhouses, carried water, laundry done by hand, then pinned and hung in the wind to dry. We lived a life of limited means and work. Lots of work. Play would come only when the work was done.

Sometimes Mama and I would find time for a morning stroll. We would talk, collect fallen apples, or pick and savor sweet, wild strawberries together. One morning, during a lazy walk, we were met with a darkened sky. The sky groaned under heavy, black clouds. Before we knew it, what started as pellets of hail, turned into hail as big as hens' eggs!

"Run, Evelyn!" Mama shouted taking my arm. Her limping gate accelerated to something between a jog and a run. I stayed with her, running beside her, dropping apples along the way. Finally, after leaping onto the front doorstep, laughing and relieved, we were safe under our crooked eaves.

I recall one of our last family outings; it makes me smile, but also tugs at my heart a little. It was another warm evening. The family climbed onto the carriage, all bundled up and ready to go. Others scrambled onto another carriage trailing behind us. Heading up toward the top of the canyon, we could feel excitement was in the air.

"We need to get there just before dark!" Papa shouted back toward the others. "Up the canyon, yyyyaaahhhh!" He snapped the reins, *chk, chk.*

"This must be something special," said Sylvia Mea. "We never wander into the hills at night." She pulled me close under a corner of her blanket.

Just as the sun slipped behind the cooling walls of the canyon, to our amazement something very special did happen.

"Keep your eyes peeled," Papa said, pointing toward the city. "Watch!"

Right then, Rapid City lit up in electric lights! Tons of street lights turned on, joining those that were already glowing in individual's homes and public buildings. What a beautiful sight.

"The city streets are shining with electricity!" Papa explained. "Now people can see, and they'll be safe in the streets at night."

Although Rapid City is miles away, a full-day wagon ride there and back, we felt as if we were celebrating right alongside those that lived there. For, in a way, this was our victory, too.

In this special moment, somehow, all of our futures looked a little brighter.

After returning home, I remember helping Papa stoke the wood stove. His quiet manner then sinking, relaxed in a chair nearest the light of his oil lantern. He then went about the business of collecting his papers; he was always working. Even so, it was there in his chair, where he would shake off the stress of his day. I remember many an evening, this one no different, lifting the pocket glass from his shirt, holding it near my eye, "I see you, Papa," I would say. Then quietly handing it back to him so he could peruse his letters with ease. It was something playful he started with me when I was just a baby girl. I remember his laugh as the magnifier grew my one eye bigger than the other.

"I see you, too." He would say, smiling.

My haunting, yet precious memories are clear and fresh. I realize, though my physical body has mended, both my mind and my heart still have a long way to go. I know this: they will never be the same.

I've decided to allow myself these daydreams, these moments. I'll steal a laugh here, add sweet memories there. In the black of night or bright of day, I will allow myself to reach out to each of them. To continue sharing my life with my family—all of them. This will be what saves me.

# DALLAS

DALLAS, OREGON
1927

Soon after my eleventh birthday, my new father and his wife, Alta, set me down for a talk. They explain that Father has received a position on the Dallas Line, that this new train route requires us to move from Portland to Dallas, Oregon. Again, I stir inside. I'm unsure of myself, of a brand-new place, and of being uprooted once again.

My first impression of our new town is how pretty and simple it is, how it takes only a minute or two to get from one side to the other. It's small, much smaller than Portland. The one main street has most everything you need. All you have to do is go down the road a spell, or around the block to find the rest of it: the post office, the newspaper office, and the Majestic Theatre. A huge, ivy-covered courthouse sits proudly in the middle of it all.

We live on Jefferson Street in a house with large picture windows. The windows are so big that even though we stand inside, behind them, it feels like we live outside in the neighborhood. I lounge on deep-blue and green, velvet cushions for hours, the side of my thumb rubbing over the green stitching of leaves, watching the dogs, the people, the world stroll by.

The trees in this town are unmatched. Some sway long and blossomed; others are thick and stable. I measure them by wrapping my arms around them. Often the trunks are too big, my fingertips just shy of touching on the other side. Sometimes they only reach halfway.

Father and Alta fit well within the Dallas community. Father belongs to the Masonic Lodge, and Mother Alta (as she's now asked me to call her) has social gatherings. She is happiest there, flitting amongst her peers at her weekly Women's Club or her bridge club. If her day doesn't include a social affair, she can't be dealt with; her moods are abrupt, even abrasive at times. We gladly give her space.

Due to the year of the accident, recovery and adoption, I still find myself slightly behind in school. As time goes by, though, I get better at catching up. I try and stay focused. Distraction happens mostly when my mind is quiet—too quiet. A mind can wander back easily if it is not kept at task. So keeping busy is the secret to staying on top of things. I am very good at staying busy these days.

When not deep in my book studies, I work on a scrapbook for myself. I cut pictures I find wonder in. Perfectly snipped from magazines, flyers, and newspapers, I cut and then paste them with care, giving them their own space in my book. Things, full of life: flowers, babies, dogs, elephants, mountains, and rivers—birds, too. Creating something of my very own keeps me centered and fills me with hope. With every day that goes by, I'm beginning to see myself and the world around me in a different way.

# Sister

## January 1928

There are times where I surely could use my sisters, especially on the days I feel my body change. I'm sure if I lie still enough, I can feel the changes happening that very moment. I had no idea it was possible for a chest to grow so fast, or that all women find themselves once a month in a "delicate way." I remember Mama talking quietly with Sylvia and Bertha about "big-girl stuff." That's exactly how she would put it, "Big-girl stuff." She would quietly escort them to a private area of the house to have a little discussion. Oh, what I would give, right now, to be a fly on that wall listening to Mama and her instructions on how to go about becoming a "big girl."

One time, I overheard Bertha say to Sylvia, "All this fussing and changing is about having our own babies one day."

A sadness comes over me as I realize neither one of them came close to becoming a mama themselves.

Annette, Father's daughter from a previous marriage, has returned home. We've met a few times before, but I've never had the pleasure of spending any length of time with her. Her relationship has fallen apart, and her and her little boy, Jack, need a place to stay. They live with us now. We instantly take to one another despite our eleven-year difference in age. She's shorter than me, but she also has red hair. People see us walking together, and they just know we are real, true sisters. She has the warmth in personality of her father. Eerie, as she seems yet another piece of the puzzle. I'm convinced Father must have seen a bit of Annette in me as he reached, lifting my lifeless body.

My new sister will never take the place of Sylvia or Bertha, but I can't resist her draw. I enjoy, listen, and watch her every move, word, and action. And, I can't get enough of little, Jack.

"I'm happy my daddy found you," Annette confides in a quiet moment, while combing my hair. Jack wiggles in my lap reaching for his stuffed bear sitting on the vanity. I look up and smile at our reflection in the mirror.

---

After months in the crowded Jefferson home, Father has found us a house with more elbow room. We live on Birch Street now. This house sets slightly above it all, notched in a hill. It's even a more spectacular home than the others we had before it. Sprawled below us, are tennis courts and fields full of blackberry bushes, with paths cut through them—each path a shortcut to the main part of town. There are homes every few blocks or so. The rail tracks lead near the center of it all. The train stops just a block or two from our courthouse. Every time I see the courthouse, I'm amazed at how it demands attention. Impressive, as I hear it holds both the courts and the prisoners alike. They say, there's not another like it for miles.

Grandma Leet, Mother Alta's mom, has also moved in with us. She might be built small, but she is grand in every way. She shares stories of her past, running the Embroider Department at Meier & Frank, in Portland. Day after day, I enjoy coming home to her after school or weekend play. Her little body is full of energy, but shows every bit of her ninety-plus years. She's always cheerful to see me and anxious to hear what's new in school. We have our very own tea parties. She drops two sugar cubes, spins my cup three times, then tells my fortune.

"You are going to have a great day tomorrow, Evelyn," or, "You're about to make a new friend . . . might be a boy . . . might be a girl," her finger tapping on the sharp of her chin, her eyes locked onto a high corner in the room. She smiles, then adds, "Either way, Evelyn, a friend is a friend—always special."

How does she know these things? Quite often she's right.

I ask her about my future sometimes. About who I will be with and how many children I might have. She smiles, "A husband and children are a lot of effort. This is the time you should play, Evelyn. Pay no mind to setting your future so quickly."

Of course I have the urge to ask her about my lost, broken family, but I never go there.

Sister Annette seems a little out of sorts with our move. She's had eyes on a delivery boy that she could easily flirt with from the large, porch-level windows at the Jefferson Street house. She'd wait for him there, seated behind the glass in her best outfit, her face framed in shiny curls, her breath held—caught in her throat as he dropped his ice blocks near our front doorstep. You can tell he likes her as much as she likes him. I just know it's a matter of time that he will find her and they will reconnect.

I find the holidays the hardest. It's the little things that get to me. Grandma Leet, simply setting a cup of hot apple cider in my hands, sends me straight back to South Dakota. The smell and warmth of it takes me there. The hot liquid seems a magic elixir, as it brews up a memory of a cozy Christmas Eve, our family together around the firelight. If I close my eyes, I can reach out and touch them.

There other things, day to day, that bring the past to the surface: Father's hat on the stair banister post, his train smells, and his soiled shoes. There's the whistle three times a day announcing the train's arrival, downtown. Then of course there's the screech of a blue jay or a magpie, their ornery banter and play. All of it nudges my heart, but my new sister, little Jack, and Grandma Leet keep my hard feelings at bay.

---

I'm growing tall as a teenager—five feet seven inches. I have wavy, dark red hair, and hazel eyes that lean toward golden brown; my mood blends them green with emotion sometimes. Teen life is good, I feel well accepted. The kids and teachers seem to like me, so much so that I've been voted in as secretary of the student body. All things considered, we've come a long way. I've come a long way.

Since my sophomore year I've wanted to become a nurse. I'm sure that the events of my past lends a push toward this desire, but I suspect that Blonde Curls, her compassion and natural healing abilities have most to do with it. Her influence sunk clear to my bones when I found myself fragile and broken under her care. Her calming way stuck with me and fixed everything in my eyes; especially while in my early years of recovery. If I could offer even a fraction of her talents to somebody in dire need, I would be honored to do so. I know firsthand how it is that a gifted nurse can breathe life right back into somebody. Even in someone that seems has not a breath left inside them.

There's very little Annette and I won't do together, which makes this sisterhood even sweeter. With her, I get to confide private things. Ask the questions that sisters need to ask each other. It's undeniable, our bond, and the fact that our age difference disappears as we grow deeper in our friendship. Our only challenge is who is washing and who is drying the dishes from night to night, but it works itself out. Family, church, fashion, rouge, fingernails, and costume jewelry make up our world. She helps me style my hair and make decisions on the latest trends in clothing. We try and keep up with the featured models in high fashion magazines. We swoon at the boatneck, shin-length dresses—a sash tied about the hip. We imagine draping a string of long beads, accentuating the colors of the sash. But then, page after page something better shows up. A bow tie plumped at the collar of a long, slim coat, topped off with a smart, matching hat. And the shoes! Oh, how we want it all. Ladies' high fashion can be expensive, though. We decide that some extra money on hand could help, so us girls set out to make some.

We decide on a work/camp trip, outside of Dallas, near a town called Independence. Thinking this just might be the answer to our fashion financial needs, we quickly gather some things, make arrangements for baby Jack, and then we hit the road. Word is, this opportunity could be profitable. There's money to be made there in the hop yards. On our way there, I gaze out the car window, taking in the awesome fields and big, blue sky. I can't help but notice the rail tracks alongside the road, how they're structured, the way the sun catches the length of their stretch. How, once in a while, the wheels of the car clamber over them, knocking at my heart. It feels a bit disrespectful, to just run over them like that, without a care, without a second thought. Of course nobody else could know something as simple as crossing railroad tracks could cause me such discomfort. How, since that split second in time, getting from one place to another has never been the same. I decide lifting my feet ever so slightly, without anybody noticing, might give my loved ones the respect they deserve. Besides, it feels better; it makes my heart lift, too. And so I raise them each time we clunk over the tracks. After a while, Annette catches on and joins me.

—

Father has caught wind of our plans three days in. The fact that we've traveled outside of town, with a tent and a camp stove has angered him. The idea of two young ladies on their own makes him furious. What we think is a grand plan to make fast money, turns out to be a bust. But, not because of low hop yard pay, because Father is spitting mad. Out of nowhere, he has shown up agitated, quickly yanking our money dreams out from under us.

"You two get back home THIS INSTANT. Let's go!" he shouts, angrily tugging at the tent stakes.

Our adventure is short-lived, but one I'll never forget. I glance at Annette and cringe at our hasty decision.

So, picking prunes in a local orchard it is. Closer to home, under Father's watchful eye, where he can see us sisters, tucked safely, in our own beds at night.

# HENS

DALLAS, OREGON
1931

It's been six years since the accident. Every fall I feel it in my bones—the heaviness. The holidays get easier; it seems spring and summer is when I grow best. Life feels right when I throw myself into my book studies and physical activity. I am taking more piano lessons and dance lessons, and I spend a lot of time on the tennis courts. I've been involved with Camp Fire Girls, also Rainbow for Girls, and I love to swim—I'm even winning lifesaving awards.

Alta only tolerates me. As time passes, I see her and understand her more. She seems most interested in just being Mrs. Harvey Carpenter, not so much my mom. After all, that was the life she had signed up for in the first place, certainly not a life where it suddenly springs a new family member in an instant. Thinking back, it would've been hard for her to say no to Father's heartfelt, generous offer to save and raise me. On some level she was forced to go along with the idea—I'm sure of it. There have been times that I've needed her, if only to hear some motherly guidance, as I stumbled along, finding my way.

It's not like she closes me out, but, she's not open to me either. Father on the other hand, loves me. I know this. I can see it and feel it. He didn't hesitate to pick up right where my precious papa left off before him.

Since the accident and the adoption, I still often wonder the reasons behind Father's need to watch over and rescue me. I overhear talk around the ladies' gatherings. They round out the room, clucking like yard hens, often poking for more of my story. They watch me come and go as they cluck over their flavored steam.

One of the loudest hens, the one that has hair stacked way too tall on the crown of her head says, "Alta, how is Evelyn getting along?" She goes on, "I can't imagine how she's felt all these years."

"Very well," Alta shares, sashaying across the room, offering butter cookies from a silver tray. Of course, I wouldn't expect her to say anything else. God forbid anyone see her, and the life she lives in, in any other light than perfect. And then I hear it. "Yes, he was also nine when he lost his mother," Alta says. There's a collected gasp as the hens lean in to hear more. Alta continues, "I think it was the final straw in his decision to adopt her."

What?

My mind spins a little, then stops. She goes on to explain, "He agonized, but then one morning he woke knowing it was the right thing to do. There was no looking back."

I remember his words now, with the judge. During the adoption proceedings, there in the courtroom, he said, "I know what it feels like to lose someone dear at a young age."

Now it makes sense to me. Someone had left him early in his life—but his mama? I had no idea! He was nine just like me?

This explains quite a lot. In fact, what may be the biggest piece of the puzzle has fallen into place. It's yet another thing that Mr. Carpenter and I have in common. My heart goes out to him, and if it's possible, I respect him even more than I did before.

# Through the Looking Glass

I've just lifted my hands from the piano keys when there comes a knock at the door.

"I'll get it, Evelyn. You go on practicing." Grandma Leet says, setting her embroidery hoop aside. She then gets herself up from her chair to see who's there.

She finds Mr. Caffin at the door. He was the train conductor working with Father the night of the accident. He is a very nice man. Usually, when he visits, he brings me candy and good conversation. He's kept in touch, dropping by a couple of times a year to check in with us. I always enjoy our time together.

We decide to sit in the sun-flooded dining room. It seems a good place to catch up with some nice conversation. Grandma Leet shuffles off toward the kitchen—she must be after some tea.

Today Mr. Caffin seems a little more serious about our talk. Not serious in a bad way, but in a soft way. He's mesmerized by the fact that I landed on the train. He expresses thinking of it often, and tells me he feels that I'm old enough now to understand the exact events that took place that night.

"You know, Evelyn, you landed right there." He hangs his head, attempting to reason, carefully collecting his words. "It was like something reached out, plucking you out of the chaos. I still can't believe it."

Grandma Leet has set a pot of tea between us, she then slips out of sight.

"I know, without question, that you're in the right place here with Mr. Carpenter," he says; his round, pudgy face softens with emotion.

"Evelyn, when Mr. Carpenter found you, he hesitated at first, he called out for help, but then turned, gathering you up in his arms, running you toward safety." Mr. Caffin holds his arms in a cradle way. "It's as if your kind papa set you there, placed you onto the train, purposely. Quite honestly, it seemed a direct hand-off from your papa to Mr. Carpenter." Mr. Caffin's eyes grow bright. "It was the most heroic thing I've ever seen."

I understand his message. The thought that my papa, somehow in that flash of confusion, decided to lift and place me out of harm's way. That very thought has given me night after night of comfort. Could it have happened that way? Papa helping me stay alive? Maybe, Mr. Carpenter's mother helping, too?

He goes on, "Evelyn, do you remember? How we scrambled to find help? I know it's been years, but I remember it like it was yesterday. All of the squabbling between professionals, motorists, and passengers alike, standing there shouting orders at us, each of them looking out for your best interest. That shortly after all was discovered and accounted for, Mr. Carpenter realized there was no one available in Harrisburg to help you."

Mr. Caffin takes a deep breath; it's like he's reliving it.

"So then followed his urgent decision. Mr. Carpenter quickly reloaded you onto the very same train, collected the assistance of a kind-hearted, Harrisburg woman; a teacher good with children, to sit by your side. Once you were settled, he then demanded the train to move on. Mr. Carpenter rolled farther down those dreaded tracks to get you the help you needed; all the while urgently wiring ahead for the nearest doctor."

I dig deep and think hard, but all I can remember is a flash of light—nothing else.

My hand reaches for the teapot. Angling it his direction, I look up at him. He nods yes for a warm-up, then continues with his story.

"A Dr. Love answered his wire and boarded the train at Junction City—still, at least twenty minutes from the nearest hospital. After a series of frantic whistle blows, followed by a heated flag stop, the doctor climbed on. He quickly looked you over, giving us the go ahead, assuring us that you were in good enough condition to reach Eugene."

"Dr. Love?" I say.

"Yes, Evelyn. I thought his name was interesting, too. It was like the world was looking out for you, surrounding you, protecting you."

"The whistle blew, again, long and hard. The train barreled on, soon meeting the ambulance waiting in the Eugene area. It was then and only then, after Mr. Carpenter handed you off to the medical professionals, that he completely lost himself."

Mr. Caffin paused a moment, then said, "I watched the ambulance leave, but then noted that Mr. Carpenter was suddenly nowhere in sight."

He took a sip of his tea, looked toward the window and added, "I soon found him, up against his train, crumpled in tears."

Processing the experience leaves me deeply touched. It's very emotional. I do know this: I can now think of my life as a gift.

"I've wanted to share these details with you for quite some time now," Mr. Caffin added. "But, up until recently, I wasn't fully convinced you could handle it. Most importantly, you deserve to know just how brave you are, and have been all of these years."

Mr. Caffin leaves me with something other than his gift of words. He leaves me holding a soft, brown pouch with a golden leather drawstring.

"Evelyn, I found something along the tracks that night." He explains, "I'm not sure if it holds any significance, but I thought you might like to have it anyway."

I can feel the slight weight of something inside. Loosening the strings, I let it slip from its container. Papa's smooth pocket glass lands comfortably in the palm of my hand.

I'm speechless.

—

I've decided it's time to write letters back home to Stagebarn Canyon. I'm feeling the need to touch base with those that I tromped, played, and did chores with—those I loved before. I've waited purposely to give myself a chance at this new life. There is also the matter of a recent confrontation regarding old letters found, hidden by Mother Alta.

It all began when searching for a hat and gloves to borrow for a special occasion; I pulled open a drawer I shouldn't have. Seeing a corner of a letter, I recognized the name, Roy. I wondered. Could it be from big, redheaded Roy? The Roy from back home? Yes, there it was, the top of a stack, peeking at me, hiding amongst her things. I couldn't help myself—I had to read them.

The letters, one after another, written many years ago, told of how desperate my Castle family had fought for me. How even months and years after the adoption, they just kept trying. The letters went on about how they couldn't imagine how cold someone could be to keep a child from all that they've known and from those that cared for her the most. About the fact that these people are able to provide luxuries, but beyond that? They questioned: would I be taught the important things in life? Would I be lonely? And finally, expressing their worry at holiday times, my birthdays, and whether or not my teachings, both academic and religion, would be to their liking.

Quite honestly, I had no idea anybody had been in touch. Outraged, I felt betrayed.

As angry as I was, I wondered, was Mother Alta protecting me? I was so very young.

Getting caught on the floor, letters all around me, was a bit uncomfortable to say the least. But, deep down inside, it was worth it. These treasures are too important to keep tucked away.

Mother Alta no longer keeps letters from me. I can imagine Father had a lot to do with that decision. His jaw was stern with her, when we spoke of it later that night at the dinner table.

So now, in my quiet time, I flip through the most recent envelopes. I get to read of their lives moving on. Of loved ones growing—my aunts, uncles, and cousins, now older; new babies of their own . . . new life. It's clear that I wasn't left out. I see their thoughts were with me all along, it's right here in my hands, written so beautifully and with love. I like to slide Papa's pocket glass over the top of the letters to magnify them closer, to spring them to life; use it as a crystal ball, not to look at my future, but to grasp a glimpse of the past. I see big, redheaded Roy even traveled here to collect me right after the accident, but was turned away because I was too fragile to move at the time. My heart warms with joy knowing that they kept me alive in their world.

# Graduate

Dallas, Oregon
Spring 1935

There's the promise of all things new.

Day after day, I watch the sun-wrapped trees, the warmth enticing the tiny leaves to uncurl. Daffodils and tulips have unfolded in all their glory. I can relate to each of them, having blossomed into something somewhat bright and vibrant myself. I'm not one to flaunt my physical blessings, but am fully aware of them in a quiet way—I think much like the trees and flowers.

Today, I graduate from high school. There are times I didn't allow myself to think about reaching this goal, it just didn't seem possible.

"One day at a time," I would say to myself.

We stride proudly under flowered trellises held high against the bluest of sky. I can't believe I've arrived at this moment. For years I couldn't imagine this accomplishment as there are plenty of young ladies, back home, that never make it this far. I narrowed it to one conclusion: if I dare believe in angels above, they must have shoved me forward, as a lot of it flew by in a blur. I can hardly take credit for some of the effort along my journey. But then I'm also quick to turn my gratefulness toward my lost parents and sisters, for they surely have had a guarding hand in all of my successes. The fact that I've excelled in the activities they would've chosen for themselves is not lost on me. I spent a lot of time making music, studying English, and staying busy with anything active.

Our Dallas is bustling in celebration. There's an extra pep in everybody's step, both young and old. This feels less about individual accomplishments and more about our town as a prideful community, where all are celebrated in reaching their life goals. There are the announcements by radio, the newspaper features of graduates, and shiny well wishes splashed across business windows. The pride and energy is palpable.

# Plum Delicious

## Prune Orchards—Dallas, Oregon
## September 1935

There are shakers, truckers, and then there are the pickers—we are the pickers.

Using buckets or crates, we pick up fresh prunes soon after they've been shaken to the ground. We fill our buckets, then we fill our crates.

"Plums or prunes?" A shout comes from a few rows over. "Prunes!" I look over at Annette; she bends to see who's talking. The answer comes from a row behind me. We try looking through the trees, but can't see either of them. "These are Italian prune trees, grown for dried fruit." One of them explains. I work quietly, listening as they go on talking of war history, and how the soldiers needed them in the trenches for nutrition.

—

As far as the eye can see, there are shades of lavender and patches of blue below each green tree. Leaves and limbs stretch over, protecting their fallen fruit. The contrast in colors is striking, so much so that I have to take pause—the efferves-cence of the morning pausing with me. Already mesmerizing, then there comes the morning light casting through lines of trees and trunks, laying shadows, changing colors in the rise and movement. It takes your breath away. My bucket half full, held tight at my hip, I take it in.

As the shaker's shake, the cooling September adds urgency to getting the delicious fruit picked up before fall and winter set in. We work our early mornings, the crisp air and bright sun pinching than warming the tips of our noses; extra sleeves are a must till around noon. Famished, we then tear into our lunches. Soon after, we shed our extra layers, the physical labor along with the sun above, having warmed us nicely. At the end of the day our labor proves rewarding. We take a nice, long stretch then drop into bed at night, exhausted.

---

There is something about the truckers this fine morning. One in particular makes my heart stop. I can hardly breathe around him.

Today he shakes our trees and collects our crates. His gor-geous brown eyes are sharp; his dark, heavy brow is raised in my direction.

Is this my imagination?

He has thick, black hair that behaves no matter how hard he works. I notice his long-sleeved shirt, the folded cuffs, pulled high above his elbows. They pause there, strapped, keeping each muscle in place.

More prunes drop to the ground for my picking. He and his buddy shake, lift, and load.

While wiping fruit stain from my fingers, I hear him say, "See that redheaded girl? I'm going to marry her." I look behind me expecting to spot a beauty loading buckets or filling crates—someone leggy, statuesque. But, there's no one there to be seen. Could he be talking about me? I flutter at the thought, then clumsily get back to work. Those beautiful eyes, they follow me. It must be me; there's no one else in sight!

"Here, let me get that for you," he says, reaching for my crate. "What's your name?"

For a moment, I dig deep for the answer.

"Evelyn," I say.

What is wrong with me? It's my own name for goodness sake!

"I'm Perry," he says with a wink. "Sometimes I forget my name, too."

There's an ease in the way that he moves and talks, like he's never known a stranger. I watch him with others. Everybody is drawn to him. All of them appear spun, wrapped up, each of them looking as captured as I feel.

It's been days since I first saw him. He and his friend keep on with their work, but are never far away from us. On this day he puts a little more linger in his watch.

Just before lunch he steals a kiss, pushing me up against a tree. Like the fruit, he's delicious. Afternoon whiskers have shown up early, along with his intoxicating smell. It's okay, though. He pulls me in, his masculine features are irresistible.

We drag the afternoons into evenings amongst the trees. Sometimes we throw a blanket near the back of the orchard to watch the sunset. Other times we sway dance to his whistle or quiet music in our heads. My hand curled in his, my head on his chest, snug in the space under his chin.

There are moments when I wonder about his story, where he comes from, and how it is that I get to be "the one" for him. How is it possible that he hasn't been taken by another girl?

When I playfully poke about his past, he simply says, "They can't handle me, honey." Or, "I've been saving myself just for you."

Weeks go by and work feels like play. I can think of nothing else.

I've fallen, hopelessly. There's no turning back now.

---

Annette looks on as love blooms in the orchard. She has fallen for her own handsome man—the delivery boy. The one she playfully lured through the Jefferson Street windows. Come to find out, he's a busy young man. He delivers ice blocks to front steps, grocery stores, creameries, and the local dairy truck businesses. On top of all that work, he joins us midafternoon in the orchard. His name is Hank.

In the evenings, we girls float in dream clouds comparing flirty notions and stories of romantic rendezvouses. I have Annette for my girl time, but sometimes I still need to talk about my sisters. I'm reminded of Bertha Irene.

"There were so many at the door, tall boys, one after another. All of them very handsome and cordial," I say.

Annette looks over at me. She knows I rarely bring up my lost family in conversation. She calms herself, settling to a quiet; I can tell she wants to hear more.

"I wish she were here with us," I say, running my fingers across the arm of the chair. "Bertha surely could give us some sound advice regarding matters of the heart."

Annette's sweet smile lights up the night. She has a sisterly look of content in her eyes. She knows she's the one and only person I can fully be myself around.

"Let's see if she'll help us," I say. "Bertha? Give us a sign—maybe a shooting star?" I coax her quietly.

We give Bertha a moment or two.

There's plenty of sparkle in the air, but no shooting stars from Bertha on this night. She gave us just one sign: a gust of wind, low to the ground, sweeping pine needles under the hedges.

—

Father is putting an end to our efforts in the orchard. We knew this was coming, that it was just a matter of time. Maybe he or Mother Alta have caught wind of our frivolity, our flirtatious activities amongst the trees. Or, maybe he just rejects the idea of his daughters being field workers. There's a part of me that agrees with him, but I want him to understand. Setting aside the idea of the boys, if only he could accept the fact that I'm most comfortable working with my hands, running them through the fruits of the earth—our earth. There's something about this kind of work where I feel a deeper connection or purpose. I often think, in some odd way, it makes me feel whole. I can't and won't attempt to explain it to him.

After a few curt lectures from Father, we now understand his concern and opinions. He wholeheartedly believes all of this is beneath us in terms of class, and so are the boys. There is a side of me that feels Mother Alta has a lot to do with his lectures and decisions. That she may feel her social reputation is at stake. So we follow his wishes and immediately stop filling buckets in the orchards. But, if his plan is to distance us from our handsome heartthrobs, he is greatly mistaken. Things have come too far for nonsense such as that. It's too late. Our hearts are no longer ours.

Despite Father's disapproval, Annette and I carry on with our relationships and endless hours of boy talk. Always, after dinner and dishes, we lounge in our spot, draped over outside furniture under dark, clear evenings on the porch. Our starry-eyed gaze on the vast sky above. Gushing and giggling, we pick over what we like and dislike about them, verbally listing what we expect in the future from the men that we so desperately love.

"No hitting."

"No cheating."

"And, never EVER go to bed angry!"

We say it strong and together, knowing this is the secret to a long-lasting, happy marriage. No question about it. We also know that we've found the perfect men for each of us.

I have heard about men that treat their women harshly, how they are abusive. Annette has shared stories from her past relationship, the fact that she feared him. Other friends talk of their relatives. I have witnessed a few heavy hands, back in South Dakota. A neighbor man having his jerky way with loved ones, grabbing an arm or a shoulder of his wife. I've seen men sour faced, demanding, even dismissive of their women from time to time.

Out of all of the men that I've encountered throughout my eighteen years, I've never been ill-treated myself, at least not in a dangerous way. Sure, my Uncle Clemmett had some odd ideas, but he never struck me or called me dirty names. Both Papa and Father have been great examples, showing their frustration or irritation in brief episodes, always resolving them responsibly.

---

"Evelyn? I need to speak with you," Father says, stepping toward the front window of the living room. His eyes fixed on the last sliver of light before evening. He places his foot on the sill and leans his elbow onto his knee. There's a fireplace glow at his back. He has no idea he's interrupted one of my favorite, romantic daydreams.

Or does he?

"Yes, Father," I say, scooting to the edge of the golden, silky, wingback chair.

"Who is this man that you've been getting about with? And, I say man, because you know, Evelyn, he is one, right?"

Tipping his head forward, he draws a puff from his well-stuffed pipe. The sun has slipped away to dark, so it's just Father, me, and the fire.

"Yes, I know." I hesitate to say more.

I note that he won't look at me, which usually means he's not fully comfortable with the subject.

"He's not a boy, he's a man with some history and hard life under his belt. This concerns me," Father says.

Mother Alta moves through the adjoining dining room, one ear on the conversation. Father glances over at her. She quickly leaves, heading into the kitchen.

Realizing now that this is not meant to be a casual conversation, I brace myself for a planned, serious talk. Doesn't he realize it's too late for this?

"You've come such a long way with your life, Evelyn. Do you want to take the chance of a life of discomfort?"

How can he say this? Perry makes me feel like the universe has stopped—that it finally knows me.

Father turns my direction. He's a bit surprised, as he's met with a puzzled look on my face.

"I'm worried, Evelyn. And, um . . . I want you to be careful," he says.

"But, I don't understand," I reply.

I can tell he's holding back. He seems suspect and reserved; he's biting his tongue.

What is this? Is he being overprotective? He saved me, now he wants to keep me forever?

"You're not ready for a serious relationship, and you certainly can't expect to handle the world on your own, at least not yet, Evelyn. And, not with . . . ," he stops, leans to tap the ash from his pipe into the fireplace, slips it back into its holder on the hearth, and says no more.

Scooting myself back over the silk, I kick off my shoes and pull my feet up under my skirt. Leaning my head against the wing of the chair, I watch the darkness dance with fire, and I wonder, does Father know more about Perry than I do?

# Two Years Later

1938

# YES

## Portland, Oregon
## August 1938

I wake foggy this morning. It's the weekend.

There's something blurry in front of my nose, silver and flashing. I realize Perry is flipping a lucky fifty-cent piece, gliding it, then rolling it between his knuckles and his fingers. He does this, always one-handed while flexing a well-defined muscle in his forearm. I'm surprised he's up before I am. He's wearing yesterday's T-shirt, which smells like his day of work and night of play.

"Mornin', honey."

His mischievous grin takes over. I know there's no getting around it, that's where he keeps his charm. Once he turns it in your direction, there's no choice in the matter: it's simple—he has you. If Perry wants anything in his life he just motions for it. There's no such thing as a formal request.

This time he motions for me while giving his half dollar an exaggerated, two finger drop into the pocket of his T-shirt. My lax response isn't quick enough for him, so he leaps at me, landing on his knees.

"Shhhhhh, Perry, you'll wake her," I whisper.

Little Niecie is sleeping in the corner of the room.

"Come 'ere, you," he says, "I have an idea."

He lays his head sweetly beside mine, his hands grabbing, pulling me close.

Still checking my breath and sweeping the sleep from my eyes, my hands block him, my elbows high in the air. He gives up, but then buries his face in my neck.

"Let's get married this week, let's get it done." He muffles his words right there, in the soft spot where my neck meets my collarbone.

Pulling my hands down over his head, he slides himself up to get a better look at my answer. I feel his puckered lips at the end of my nose.

"Come on, I promise to make us right. To take care of you and to put our family in order. Nobody has to know."

I'm not surprised at his suggestion as he's been talking about this for quite some time now. I knew eventually this would be the plan. Something last minute, quiet, even a bit sneaky. After all, Father could hardly look at us the last time we visited the Birch Street house. He was spitting angry with both Annette and me for choosing and keeping our "lower class" men.

Thinking back to that clammy Oregon day, I had swung by the house to collect some things. Then I sprung last-minute travel plans to Portland, with Perry, on Father when he least expected it. Looking back now, I think I may have purposely handled it that way, so we could take the least amount of grief for my decision. We claimed a visit with Perry's family and a possible job for the reasons.

"Go then!" Father said.

It stings a little—the memory, the combination of irritation and sadness in his stature and expression. Despite his disappointment, I said thank you and then told him that I would see him soon, hoping with all of my heart that he would feel better about our life decisions by then. As we pulled away,

Grandma Leet caught my eye. She kissed her fingertips, then placed them on the window.

Sneaking over to take a peek at Niecie, I can't imagine my life without her. The perfection of her tiny fingers, her delicate lashes. Father would love her, I just know it. I realize it's a hopeless dream to share her with him now. He'd never accept the way things have turned out. We've made our bed, and now we're forced to lie in it.

—

Perry doesn't want anything fancy and quite frankly neither do I. We can't afford it. Counting our dimes and nickels, including his lucky half dollar, we don't have enough money for a wedding license, a service, let alone some fancy gathering. I've never known what it was like to be truly broke, to live in a depression. I had no idea that the word depression meant anything more than the simple word itself, or that adding the word severe means no jobs or pennies to live on. We just lived normal lives in South Dakota; Papa kept us going. Father's position at the railroad certainly provided all of the comforts needed, so how could I know? I was busy healing and catching up with myself. Perry certainly doesn't talk about such things, he just hops from one job to the next.

We set out for a visit with Hank and Annette.

They've come a long way, now married and settled together, with Jack and their youngest boy, Teddy. They are quick to lend us the five dollars needed to go forward with our plan. We appreciate their generous offer allowing us our very own future of marital bliss. They recognize our undying love for one another, but most of all, our situation. Above anybody else, they understand and can relate to the hurdles we've faced along the way. They know asking Father for the money will result in nothing but a stern talk. All four of us have taken lecture upon lecture on the subject of marriage. He and Mother Alta have gone so far as to threaten forced annulments and have practically disowned us for even thinking of planning lives together.

We've decided to get married across the border, in Chehalis, Washington. Perry and his mom say things may go easier this way.

"Surely there won't be any verifying of names, places, and back history," I hear his mom say. She's busy tossing a few lunch supplies in a basket for the road.

Of course, Portland certainly would be the most convenient place to tie the knot, but Perry has convinced me that we would then take the chance of knowing somebody in the courts. Concerns about his past, hushed words about a divorce, and records of petty theft could derail our plans. He also mentions the possibility of running into others that may know Father or Mother Alta.

Our plans are nobody's business. This is our future, our life.

Patting a final touch on the bow under Niecie's chin, I pull her up close for a nuzzle near her ear.

"Today, I will marry your father." I say, relieved that she's too little to understand. But, in this moment, she's the only other person I can confide in.

---

On this day, August 12, 1938 at 11:30 in the morning, we marry.

An air of sweetness has come over us—all of us. Finally, we breathe a sigh of relief knowing we no longer need to live in secret, for now, we're officially a family. One, from this day forward, we can be proud of.

Of all the many challenges I've faced in my life so far, the marriage license and battle to get here, has brought out a rebel in me that I never knew existed. So much so that I've felt as if I'm meeting myself for the very first time.

This morning, when completing forms, a rush came over me. Perry helped, but for the most part, I'd already done the damage. I fed him information on top of what he'd taken upon himself to answer on his own. Correct or not, I went along with him, knowing that soon everything would be okay. I didn't care about the consequences. I just wanted to get married, raise Niecie, and carry on with our lives.

It's as if the pen, Perry, and I had one big mind of our own.

We claimed to live in Washington, listing Portland as my birthplace and my last name as Castle rather than Carpenter. All of it untrue. But I think the most rebellious move, made on this day, is listing the odd Uncle Clemmett as my father. Why would I do this?!

I know that all of this effort is to move things along without disruption, but to deliberately disregard both Papa and Father? Rebellious, yes; it hurts a little, as I love them both, dearly.

Maybe this is my way of lashing back at the world for pulling everything out from under me, then forcing me to conform to a whole new life; none of it my decision to make.

The one thing I refused to lie about, is the name of my mama. I list her proudly as Edith. I'll admit it. I spelled her last name slightly differently, (Chester rather than Chedister), but I held strong on Edith. Even to this day, I hear her in my ear, and feel her limping beside me.

# I'll Miss You

Dallas, Oregon
September 1938

It's been weeks since my most rebellious act of all time, but I know what it is I have to do next. I'm losing sleep at night even thinking about it.

At this point I'm not even sure if Father and I are on speaking terms. I just need to face him, to square up my past, collect my things, and look toward my future.

We pull up a block away. It's morning on a Sunday. Niecie is sleeping, snug in my arms, wrapped tightly.

"Perry, could you take her while I do this?" I say, sliding our baby girl across the front seat.

"Sure," he says. "Come 'ere, squirt."

"Please wait here; I'll be back soon."

I open the car door to step out. Pine needles and leaves crunch under my foot. Everything is covered in maple pods, seeds wrapped in wings—they've always looked like angels to me. I kick a pinecone up a dirt slope.

Walking along, drawing the deepest of breaths, I fill myself with some much-needed clean air and courage.

A squirrel catches my eye, as my hands slide over my head settling my hair. I quickly nudge a test at the silver barrette securing a curl above my left ear. Standing taller than I have in months, I pull my shoulders back and give a final tug at my dress.

Now begins the practice in my mind of how a conversation may go between us. A familiar rumble in my stomach joins me in my walk. But, then comes a settling thought; a brief moment of hope that the house may be empty. That I've missed the chance to see them because they've gone to church or have taken another kind family up on a Sunday visit.

I slip through the side door, walk down the hall, then head up the stairs. Hearing the clink of rose-embellished silver against precious fine china coming from the kitchen, I scurry a little faster up the steps and then quick slide through the door to my room. I let it lightly click shut behind me.

I know the first thing that needs to be done, I've been thinking about it for months now.

Minding a carefully balanced, one-footed stance on top of a wooden step stool, I reach up toward the corner of the highest shelf in the closet. There's a special place there, built in a way that best protects the dearest of objects and bobbles.

My hand locates the soft, brown pouch with the golden drawstring. Inside holds the familiar weight of my most-prized possession. As I loosen the strings, my head takes a reminiscent turn. I realize that it's been a while since I've held it.

Papa's pocket glass slides easily from the pouch landing snug in the palm of my hand. Holding it firmly there, I take a moment, then slide it under the soft hem of my dress giving the glass a much needed polish. It never fails to stir memories as it catches the light across the room. A punch of bright hits me as I raise it—it's okay though, time has softened glaring and punching lights. I raise it higher toward the ceiling. It makes me smile. I find myself quietly mouthing the words, "I still see you my papa."

My heart is tender, wrapped in pangs of guilt as I finish gathering my things.

This room has seen me through night after night and many a day of pain, growth, health, and, yes, finally some happiness.

While tossing my sweater across my box, I realize the hard part now follows. Facing Father, his family and his home hurts more than I expected it to. Am I strong enough?

I decide to pull one last bit of strength from my long lost Mama. I finish straightening the room and building my nerve. I'm a bit shaken. I'm realizing my rebellious shell may not be as tough as I thought it was.

Under my breath, I whisper. "Mama, please help me say good-bye."

While descending, more mixed feelings join me on the stairs.

How dare I feel the need to disappear; he's done so much for me.

Who do I think I am?

Setting my things on the floor near the front door, I step lightly, approaching the kitchen. Stopping just short, I take in one last look. I'm surprised at my reaction. My glossy stare lingers on the amazing father before me. The divine train engineer sipping his coffee and tapping his poached egg, the morning sun beams through the curtain highlighting the very hand that hovered in my rescue and that reached for mine as we left the courtroom the day of my adoption. There's little doubt that his hand, along with his open arms, are responsible for saving my life. But, as much as he's done for me, as much as he's fulfilled these past years, I know that I don't belong here anymore.

Today is the day that I'm forever changed.

Toward a train I flew from Papa's arms, straight through Father's into Perry's. The pieces of my past, present, and future have fallen together. I feel strong; my tummy is solid and, again, alive with life.

The floor cracks below my foot. Father looks up. His face is drawn in a bland way—not angry, nor hurt, not elated either. He's hiding his disappointment, of that I am sure. But, there's something else. I can see it; I always have. It's a glimmer, right there, in the outer corner of his eyes.

I tilt my head to the side and send him a loving nod. He nods back.

We both know, it's time for me to go. . . .

# PART TWO

*Whipped by his hand, she cries.*
*Wail after wail; it runs through her.*
*Shamed, she cowers.*

# ELIN

## AGE EIGHT
## 1949

The salty air is thicker today. She can taste it.

"Hurry up, Elin!"

Her stomach runs thick—her dad's voice makes her sick.

She's running. But, running and crying at the same time is exhausting. And so she slows down, crouching low to see better.

"Where is it? Hurry King, where is it?"

King sniffs alongside her. Zigzagging, poking his nose at her legs, helping her to look faster.

"Move it!" her dad echoes through the trees. Ashamed, for taking too long, she clenches her jaw to concentrate. She knows the longer it takes, the worse it gets.

Her feet trip along, her woods, her playground now one big blur of switches of every size. So why is it so hard for her to choose one?

She quickly scoops up the closest two, one in each hand. Looking them over, she drops the thickest, because her dad likes them thin.

She hurries back to him, her chest pounding, her head down. She wonders, *why now? Why here? Why always?*

It doesn't matter. She doesn't matter.

She hands him the chosen switch.

"What is this, a joke?"

He slings it to the ground, then shoves his hand against her head.

"Get your ass out there, find a better one. NOW!"

Her audience glances off—there must be something more comfortable to see out there; their eyes shift back, cast low, focused down at their feet.

She asks herself, "Why do they just stand there?"

"Mom?"

Low, from his gut, he warns, "Do it right this time or else!"

She scampers off to find the perfect one, the one that will hurt the most.

*Her name is Elin. She is eight years old. Does she belong in this world?*

# PARADISE

## Bayocean, Oregon
## 1949

We live in a place where people vacation. They may think this is their paradise, but it's not—it's ours. We are the people that get to live here all the days in the year. Sure, we don't have fancy lives, but who cares, 'cause we have the ocean, the bay, and the freedom to play all over the land in between.

My mom's name is Evelyn, and my dad's name is Perry. I'm the youngest in the whole family. First there's Niecie, then Bubby, Carp, then me. Oh, there's King, too. He's our dog.

Us kids live most days outside, only going home at night to fill up our tummies.

Mom is a good cook. She makes everything out of just about nothing. Mostly she uses powdered stuff, food and milk in cans, along with what we can pick, poach, fish, or dig. We just bring it home, and she cooks it up for all of us to eat.

Our family moves a lot, always looking for work and a way to live better. The roof over our head is never for long, and mostly kind of rough around the edges. Us kids share rooms, sometimes, a log in the backyard, a really nice Mom, and a very scary Dad.

This misty morning started out fun enough, an adventure, like most days. A nice morning spent with King and Wayne, my three-year-old friend. We took off into the forest to check on some things.

Wayne has been staying with us for months now. His mom needed to take care of some big-person things. My mom said yes to taking him in, as, she says, 'cause that's just what friends do for one another, besides, he fits in. He bumped our family number up to seven, for a while, anyway.

Wayne walked beside me, just like any other day. I could hear him talking to himself, saying his words out of order, my ears only half listening. He always stops to look at everything, and then changes his mind about what to look at next; this day was no different. Something catches his eye and then he wanders. I remember reaching for him, saying, "Come on, Wayne. Here, take my hand. Let's go check the trap."

Wayne moved his feet like he was trying hard to keep up with his chest.

"Maybe today's the day I'll find a new pet chipmunk," I said. "This trap is one of the best I've built so far. It should work." Getting a better grip on his arm, we turned off the trail. "Here it is, Wayne!" Sliding onto one knee, ear angled toward the trap, I listened.

Wayne knows how this works. He's been watching for some time. He even pounds tacks into boards pretending to build his very own traps.

He reached for the top of the wooden box. "Wait, wait," I said.

Pulling his hand back, he put his knees on the ground just like I did, then matched the angle of my head so he could hear better. His big-boy moves made me smile. He's been a good, little chipmunk trapper in training.

Leaning down to listen for myself, I wondered, will it be

a chipmunk or a rat this time? I opened slowly for a peek. I do this mostly for Wayne, 'cause normally I just rip it open for a quick check, always ready to slam it shut if something happens to be in there.

"Neither. Darn!" Dropping the lid shut, I picked up the trap. "Okay, time to move it, we need a better spot!"

Wayne used both hands to push himself up from the ground, then wiped the dirt left on his hands down the front of his shirt.

I stopped, giving it some thought, tapped my finger across my lips—hmmm. . . . If I were a chipmunk today, where would I be?

It was that very moment when I heard my name called in the distance.

"ELLLLLIN!"

And that's just how it happens: one minute life is good, the next it hurts.

How was I supposed to know that this would be the day that little Wayne's family would return for him? Or, that I would be whipped for taking him along on my adventure. After all, bringing him with me has been happening since the very first day he got here.

My sinking chest knew I was in big trouble the moment Dad joined in the holler.

I quickly tucked my trap up against the nearest tree, then sprinted in their direction. Wayne's little feet shuffled along, taking two steps to my one. Out of breath, we found a collection of family standing there along with Wayne's mom. Dad, then proudly showed his power; a whippin' for all to see.

Even though I fear him—he shakes me clear to my bones and back, I take my whippings; I always do. This time was no different than all the other times. Drooping in shame, I just picked myself up, used the underside of my sleeve to catch the wet from my nose, and walked away. I managed to wave a melted good-bye toward Wayne, then went about trapping on my own. King followed, his tail between his legs.

—

My brothers, Bubby and Carp, and the group of older boys in our neighborhood, have been building their traps since long ago. I just knew that I had to make one of my own someday. At first I tried to learn right alongside them, but that idea always got me a slug or two, a fart in my face, or some name-calling. They don't like a little sister hanging around.

So, hidden, I watched them. Eventually, I picked one up and figured it out by looking at it.

With or without the boys, I knew I could do it. Wood and nails, string, and a tiny piece of bread are all that's needed.

My trap is set by crisscrossing two nails inside, near the back wall. I tie a piece of bread on the end of a string, then I run the string through the crisscross, up through and over the top. The door hangs there, giving just enough room for a pet visitor. The sniffer finds food, nibbles enough to free the string, then *bam!* You instantly have a new friend—a beautiful chipmunk.

Chipmunks are my favorite critters to catch, but stickleback fish, little crabs, and gray sand lizards aren't far behind—I love them all. My lizards are usually found under large pieces of old tin or boards; the bulging, rounded tips of their feet and bellies wrap and seal snugly, hugging my fingers when I hold them. Capturing them is always a thrill and keeping them alive near or on the front porch, in jars and traps, just makes sense to me. I try feeding them. They always manage to escape though, not happy with my bits of seaweed, bugs, berries, or grass—or maybe Mom just sets them free? I'm not sure.

I collect as many critters as I can, as they make me feel

happy. Each creature looks at me like I'm important—like I matter. They don't punch, whip, or scream so loud that I can't hear myself think. They don't have weapons or switches. They don't drink beer and hit people. My favorite time is with all sorts of animals, held face to face, eye to eye, and exploring our Bayocean with King.

I think of King as my dog. I know he belongs to the whole family, but I think he might like me best. Happy and playful, he always helps me in my hunts. He's just as surprised as I am when I catch something great.

Catching stickleback fish feels good, as I love the water. It's especially fun when it's warmer outside. On clear days, the sun reflects on our nice, calm bay. I lean over the water, steady, ready, then spring into action! King stands on the shore patiently waiting. Once in a while, he wades in. Sniffing the top of the water, he can't resist an outward sneeze, followed by a big shiver and shake. The wetness flies from his fur, as he whips up his very own rainstorm. He sends the fish in a scatter. I laugh at him. "You're in the water, silly. Shake when you get out!" I say, patting the top of his head. The darting fish panic and run, but then are quick to return nibbling at my ankles and toes.

"Let's try this again."

Timing is everything when catching sticklebacks, or anything else for that matter. The jar in one hand, lid in the other, hovering, over and over I dip. It's exciting when I catch three or four in one scoop. King is happy, too, as I twist the jar tight, he sits up to get a better look.

The Twitchell's Hotel is just down the way. I like to go there to look under the big rocks. Those rocks hold special treasures underneath. There's nothing better than finding a hidden treasure. Sometimes there's a pretty rock or tiny shell hiding under there, but most of all it's the crabs I'm after. I tromp over, barefoot, always barefoot, and squat down right up next to them. The biggest rocks are the best. Using both hands, I slide them way underneath. I get my best grip, then give it a flip! There are times I have to make noise to get it to move. But, that's okay; the gifts I find underneath are always sweet and well worth all the work to get them. Almost every time, I startle a crab right out of a nap! I have to be fast, 'cause if they wake up, they scurry away. They are lightning fast and light as feathers. King takes a sideways leap at them when they make a run for it, then he sniffs around, waiting, watching for the next one.

King weighs less than me, maybe forty-five pounds. He's gentle and protective. I can lift him easily 'cause I'm strong. If you know him, you love him. His soft, floaty black hair flows at the ends. He has a long, white patch that goes the entire top of his nose. There's also some white across the top of his paws and the very tip of his tail, sort of a final touch, like somebody painted it there to match the rest of him. There are patches of brown, just to break it all up.

I've heard adults call him a mutt, or "maybe a sheltie mix" they say.

Dad brought him home to our previous house, a year ago, or so, after Mom lost her dog, Corpy. We think he did it to cheer her up. Or, maybe King was a gift to make up for something Dad did that made her mad or sad.

I remember King, as a brand-new puppy, did bring all of us some much-needed joy. Soon after, though, something called "distemper" took over his puppy stage. Dad took him somewhere to get help. King survived, but now lives with a constant jerk to his head. His jerking never gets in the way of our play, though. He's a loving, friendly dog, always nearby. He sleeps on the porch of our house. Along with the rest of us, the only time King cowers is under Dad's booming voice. He's one of us, sharing our days and our Bayocean adventures.

—

This isn't the first time we've lived in Bayocean; there must be something special about this place 'cause we just keep coming back. At first we lived in one of the vacation cabins, all jammed in. I can hardly remember it, 'cause I was only three or four years old at the time.

We also lived in the brown house on the road between Bayocean and Cape Meares. It had a stone stairway that went up to the front porch, a small fishpond out front, and a tiny mouse that lived in the rafters. Before bed, Niecie read books to us up in the attic room. She read about Wooden Willie, Beloved Belindy, and their uncle, and about the old woman and a wooden king, soldiers, and ponies with wooden money. In their story, they find a box of golden pennies. A sign on the box says, "Help yourself. But remember: every golden penny will disappear unless you use it to bring happiness to others. I like that idea. I think the world might be a better place with magic, golden pennies.

Niecie also reads lots and lots of stories out of a big, red book. She still reads them to us, sometimes.

That house was kind of special, because it was there, in the window, where I spotted a great, big blimp hanging in the sky over the ocean water one day. Bubby likes to tell stories about blimps. About how he and one of his friends, Josh, would watch the blimps float over the ocean water looking for submarines and then over the beach for bodies. Like they were some kind of war police in the air. That they used to look for submarines, bombs, and dead people, but now they just look for live, pretty bodies sunning themselves there. He goes on to tell about a day that he and Josh climbed high on the hill with a bullhorn, waiting there for the blimp to go by. Josh, then shouting, begged the blimp for candy. Bubby uses the word "rations." I guess candy and chocolates were only meant for soldiers for a while. Now that the war is over, they hoped that they just might be ready to share some. Bubby tells this story better than me, but, sure enough, one day, the blimp guys hand made a tiny parachute and down came a whole package of Hershey bars. Bubby lights up when he talks about it.

I also think the brown house was extra special, 'cause it was there where we saw Santa in the air. I asked Niecie about the red light—sure enough, it was Santa flying by.

We've lived in lots of houses. There was the tar shack near Raineer, in a place called Apry. It was just boards, quickly pounded together, where all four of us kids slept on the floor in one room. That house was more of a wooden box than a real house, each room separated by blankets instead of walls. Dad threw it up in a week or so, using basic stuff. There was a toilet area, out back; a small log separated the clean side from the dirty side. When the urge came over us, we'd just grab a couple of catalog pages or maybe a leaf or two on the way back to do our business.

I remember Carp and Bubby made a hole in the top of our room just large enough so that chipmunks could slip through. The boys would chase them into a corner. Finally catching one, they attached a mini linked chain around the chipmunk's neck. They were the kind of chains that usually hold keys or toy trinkets together, but Bubby and Carp used them as collars for chipmunks. They would tie a string for a leash and then carry the chipmunk in their shirt pocket as they'd go about their day.

I'm not sure which, Bubby or Carp, named one of them, Chippy. The whole family got to know Chippy the chipmunk. He actually stuck around; he liked us. He had the run of the house. He had a cage, but was so smart, he learned how to let himself out. In the mornings, he would wake Mom by getting right up next to her face. He liked to take a bath in the sugar bowl, so Mom decided giving him his own bowl of sugar would be best.

Soon though, we had to leave our tar shack to live in a tiny trailer, in a park, under the cedar trees, in Forest Grove. One of Dad's jobs, driving a gravel truck, made us move there for a while. It was there where the six of us lived in a place with less room than a milk truck. I think sardines in their cans had more room than we did. I remember getting blisters. Mom said it was because our skin was too close. It was so cramped that Bubby and Carp would sleep outside, under the trailer sometimes. Before bed, we'd sit out under the umbrella and tell ghost stories. Wasn't too long before Dad finished that job, and then it was back to the tar shack. We returned to Apry and found that Chippy had moved in. And, he had invited all of his friends to live there, too. As angry as we wanted to be, all we could do was laugh. Not even one of the sugar bowls were sitting upright; nothing was for that matter. Everything that was small enough for a playful chipmunk to handle was tossed aside or turned upside down.

The house we live in now is called the Dew Drop Inn. It's nicknamed by an old, hand-painted sign that we found out front when we moved in. It's a white house, beat up and chipped away by our Bayocean weather. It has wavy floors. The bumps are called warps, I guess. It has a big bump right at the old fireplace where I lie to get the chill off from my day. The Dew Drop Inn is a little bit crooked, but much bigger than all of the other houses we've lived in before. I'm guessing we won't be staying long, though. I hear Dad is looking to buy a smaller house down the way, someday.

No matter where we live, I mostly like to keep to myself. Niecie is so much older than me, about five years or so, and the boys hate it when I hang around them. So, I like to be in my own world, my feet in the sand and the dirt, my dog always at my side. I don't care about much else.

Other than King, and my favorite critters, the closest thing to me is my stick horse. Stickhorse goes everywhere with me, it's like I have three arms and three legs when I take him along. He helps me walk and climb hills. His wood is a light-yellow color with some dark-brown ribbons running through it, and he's shiny, polished by my hands, I think. Maybe the dirt, water, and sand have rubbed him smooth? I pretend he's a real horse sometimes. I always wonder what it would be like to have a real, live horse.

One time Stickhorse disappeared. I lay awake at night wondering where he had gone. I tried to forget him, play with my doll, but it's just not the same. Dolls break, they get dirty if you play outside with them, and you have to be careful. I try to figure out how to fix them, but I just can't.

Our neighbor, Mr. Bigley, once showed me how to fix my rubber doll. Her arm kept falling off. No matter how hard I tried, I couldn't get the arm to go back in. One day he showed me all that I needed was some soap and water, that if I wet her arm, add some soap, and be gentle, it just slips right back in.

"Here you go, she's good as new!" he said, smiling. He added, "A little soap goes a long way, sometimes."

I knew it was his nice way of showing me how to fix things, but also maybe his way of telling me a bath might do me some good.

# MY OCEAN

Sometimes I hear the ocean; I feel it calling to me, but I'm not allowed to go there—it's dangerous. Mainly because it's rough and it pulls. It's just too easy to slip under the waves and never come back. Plus, I think, more and more of the houses and trees falling in worries my mom.

One day, Mom made it clear to me. She used her hands and a twig, drawing in the sand. Poking two big lines, she put an X where the Dew Drop Inn should be. She went on to draw a big wave on the ocean side, just outside the line, and then she placed a little rock on the bay side.

"This is you, this little rock," she said, tapping it lightly with the twig. "You can go anywhere but here, don't cross this line." She pushed the twig deep into the sand all along the ocean beach side.

I'm a little disappointed as I like to hunt for agates, shells, and glass balls—the Japanese kind. But, I'm happy that I get to have my bay water and the other usual kids' spots. There are plenty of other spaces and places to keep me busy. She said that I'm free to go to any other part of our paradise, but never the ocean without her or another adult. Even though I'm hopelessly drawn to it—the mystery, even the danger of it, I'm okay with Mom's instructions. Well, most of the time. I know myself though, I might not be able to resist it.

—

On the bay side, I get to go wading whenever I like. As Mom puts it, "There's less chance of it whisking you away."

I like to wade and swim at the pilings near the Bigley's place. I try to follow and outdo Bubby and Carp; they are always building something. I try everything they try, even making my very own rafts with pieces of rope, old boards, and driftwood. Again, the trick is to just keep my distance and watch them, or I'll check one out that they've thrown aside, fix it up, and use it for myself. If I get one to float along, I use Stickhorse, or even a bigger stick to go farther out or to paddle a little faster.

Mom laughs a little when company drops by. I guess when they ask her where the kids are, she points way out into the bay.

I can just hear her saying, "See those little black dots out there?"

I'm guessing she enjoys the look on their face when they realize what it is they see. Little, happy heads floating around on the water. It makes me think Mom might be as proud of our adventures as we are.

Sometimes I go to the Indian Graveyard—no Indians buried there, just a clever nickname and a place where the boys hang out or go camping. There's Nicky's Park, named after beautiful Nicky McVadden, a sweet girl that only visits Bayocean during summer vacation time. All of the boys share the same crush on her. And, finally Rabbit Hollow—some sand dunes with trees on the sides, which eventually leads to the ocean. I like to play there, but can only go so far.

—

The boys are allowed near the ocean. They and the older men like to fish for perch there. Dad fishes there, too.

It's a warm beach day, today. Mom sits with me on a log; King is lying on my bare toes. All of us relaxed, watching them string their poles.

The trick is to stay as dry as possible, but their pants always get wet from about the knees down. Their feet stay busy in the sand; their hands are busy too, so they use their teeth as tools to tie knots or break their lines. Some of their poles are made of bamboo with eyes taped on. They use spark plugs, old railroad ties, anything small and heavy, to keep their line down in the water for the fish to see.

Carp has a pole with three hooks. He and the others get ready for the big, white, lacy wave that rolls in and then out. I think it acts almost mean. A lot of times big waves look and sound mean, but they always leave a little gift behind. They bubble out shells and agates, dropping them up and down the beach. Or they leave a long stretch of seaweed, the kind that looks like it has a small head on the end, even some hair sprouting out the top. I like to step on them, watch the water squirt out. There's the seafoam too, sitting there, on the sand, fluffy. Or it tumbles away, pushed along in the wind. The ocean is always moving, doing something. It might sound and act mean, even ferocious sometimes, but it gives you lots to play with.

My top, top favorite gifts from the ocean are the Japanese floats—glass balls that get free from fishing nets and float around in the sea. Some bring a little bit of the net with them.

King nudges a tiny one on the floor with me in the evenings. Both of us on our bellies, eye to eye, nose to nose. His chin and paws lie flat; he's all flopped out. His eyes dart from me to the glass ball and then back again. You can hardly see his jerk when he plays like this. Somehow he knows to be careful. I give it a little roll, he lets it stop up against the flat of his nose, he gives it a sniff, then nudges it right back to me. I notice the ocean knows to be careful, too. There are times we can see the glass balls in the water before they get here, riding to shore inside the waves. We wait for them, and then grab them up as soon as we can. As dangerous as the waves can be, they seem always gentle with the glass. It's like the ocean cares about them, giving them a ride to shore, setting them down in the sweetest of places: in the sand, hidden in the seagrass, or gently on top of a log or piece of driftwood. It just chooses the very best spot, drops it there, then slowly pulls away.

Sometimes, the ocean sound and the sun make me sleepy. Closing my eyes, I listen for a minute. It rumbles deep like a big machine of some kind; other times, it whispers. I hear wave after wave roll in and then out again.

"GO!" My eyes pop open.

Carp and the others take off running, poles in hand, men tall and short going after the water. They chase the ocean all the way out, running so far, it looks like they might join the fish underneath. Then, just as the ocean stops, in that moment when it changes its mind, where it begins its return to swallow them up, Carp throws his cast with all his might! He quickly turns, running back, the waves chomping at his heels, the line trailing behind him, busy searching for fish.

With so many lines and hooks, the fish soon come in. Most are just pulled in, dragged right up onto the sand. The beach is covered in pink, as the hooked perch decide to lose their babies—tiny, baby fins ready to swim, hoping for the next big wave to come and pull them back out to sea.

Watching Carp fish makes me happy, but I cringe a little. I think of the time he rescued four or five goldfish from somebody's pond ready to fall into the sea. He knew the pond and the house beside it was going to slide in any day, and wanted to make sure the fish would be okay. He filled his bucket with water, then caught the fish. He added them to the pond in front of the Brown house and made sure they were taken care of. One day, Dad proudly brought home a twelve-inch trout and slipped it into the pond. Maybe he thought the trout could live right alongside Carp's fish? The trout must have been really angry and hungry cause it decided to eat not one, but all of Carp's goldfish. Carp was so upset with Dad's trout, he grabbed a pole, caught it, and killed it. Then Dad caught Carp. He didn't kill him, but Carp was sore for a very long time.

King is still lying near me, warm, soaking up the sun. Mom slides her light-brown cardigan off her shoulders, then drapes it across her lap. Her hair doesn't move wild in the wind, like mine does, 'cause she tucks it into a hair band. It rolls all the way around her face, like a sausage. The sun highlights the little bits of silver in it. Her dress hardly has a color. If it ever had one before, it has long since rinsed away. Or maybe the wind beats it out, when it hangs on the line to dry. The only real color Mom is wearing is on her lips; she dabs a little bit of red there sometimes.

After minutes of sitting quietly, I get curious. I try to look at things through adult eyes. They talk more and more about the power of the ocean these days. How it's stealing our trees and taking our homes.

I always wonder, how can something so beautiful be so dangerous?

I look to the right, farther up the beach, letting my eyes settle on the hill in the distance. The sliding houses live up there. Soon more will go off the edge of the cliff. The trees are breaking, too, roots and all. I have yet to see anything slide or break myself, but people talk about it all of the time. Turning to look down the beach, my hair whips across my face. I let it stay there for a second, then flip it out of my way. I squint to see the gap, Jackson's Gap, the space where the water cuts through, breaking the road between here and Cape Meares. It cuts every day making the space wider and wider between us and the bigger part of land.

Every school day depends on the ocean and what may be happening at Jackson's Gap. The school bus driver on the other side of the water only comes so far; he knows better. He either sits and waits a while, or simply turns around and leaves us kids behind, knowing that it's just too dangerous for us to cross that day. The gap where the water breaks through is too full, leaving logs and driftwood in its path. Many a time, the bus driver leaves us standing there, as he pulls away. Us kids celebrate, knowing the ocean gave us the day off to play. Joyful as that can be, we also know that it's cutting us off from the rest of the world. There are some days when we are all stuck in Bayocean, year-round families and vacation people alike; more and more, it's just too dangerous to cross.

On mild days we dodge the waves, counting them first. We know that after every seventh wave—the biggest, baddest one, it then calms enough to let us run across. And, so we hold hands, count together, and make a run for it.

"Ready, go!"

Shoes and socks in one hand, reaching for the person next to us with the other, we make a dash for it. Then off school we go, never really concerned about how or when we are able to return. It might take us a while, but we always get back.

We slowly but surely become an island. A town that feels like it's sinking. I try to listen and understand the reasons why, but the adults talk too big. I hear them during games of pinochle or canasta, sitting around talking, drinking soda and beer, smoking, tapping their feet under the tables. They go on about where the ocean meets the bay, where the "city people" built something there. Something that made the ocean push more water at us, and now the waves are eating away chunks of our land piece by piece.

# Stormy Gray

Bayocean
1950

Outside our front door, all people feel safe and friendly. It seems goodness is all around us. Kind, sharing people flock here, just like the birds do. Most go about their days happy, moving along like there's not a care in the world. They sound happy, too, like the seagulls that dance and laugh in the sky. Even strangers feel like friends; everybody's welcome. Our doors are never locked—a shell, a piece of driftwood, or kindling are used to hold windows open day and night when it gets warm enough outside.

In our town, there's only one bother each and every day, but especially on stormy, gray days—the days where the ocean rumbles harder than usual. Adults discuss the weather and "conditions" with the neighbors. Midsentence, they glance toward the sky over the ocean and kick at the ground, arms folded or jingling in their pockets. I don't know what "conditions" means, but after a while I catch on just by watching their eyes and their faces.

Us kids are never allowed in adult conversations—we are to be seen and not heard. But, in this case we don't need to take part in talks to understand something's wrong, maybe we are just built to know when things aren't quite right. Or it could be that we've crawled over every inch of this place, and we know it like the back of our very own hands. After a while, the reasons get to be too much and I can't be bothered by the big stuff. I walk away knowing this problem is way too big for me to fix.

—

Carp caught the sharp end of Dad's hand today. I wonder if this time, maybe he deserved it? Word is, he tried riding a house down the cliff. He knew it was just stormy enough outside to pull one down into the sea, so he sat and watched.

I guess one of the adults caught him in a dead run, just as the house decided to go over. They gave him a stern shout, cutting him off, just before he got there.

I watch Carp telling Bubby the details. "I could hear it snapping and popping. I just knew it was gonna go," he says, running his hand up the back of his head to the top. He holds it there for a moment, rubbing, his elbow straight out, his face flushed. I know enough, that this is his way of showing Bubby where Dad's hand had done its damage.

Bubby mumbles back, but I can't quite hear him. He's probably asking Carp what the heck he was thinking.

"I dunno, just wanted to ride it down, I guess," Carp says, his eyes at his feet. He kicks a clump of something out of his way.

"Thought it would be fun. Why not?"

Bubby just shakes his head and listens. I take off with King.

# Why Not Love

Mom seems worn out. I watch her and wonder how she keeps up with everything: us kids, Dad, and how it is that she can create a meal and keep our house going with almost nothing. She does it though, most days, without skipping a beat.

Once in a while I see a sparkle in her eye and some energy, but not very often. Maybe it's 'cause of Dad; I'm not sure. She keeps to herself a lot of the times, just like me. Sometimes I see a sadness. She never talks about sad things, though. I see her thinking inside herself, there at the counter, putting a pie together or stirring clams into pancake batter, and I wonder what she's thinking that very moment. She looks far, far away, like she's not even here. I know things are hard for her. She's not able to just pick up and leave; she can't—no matter what's happening or who's being hurt at the time.

Mom never hits us. Well, I shouldn't say never, but it has to be something really bad before she uses her hands on us. Once, she spanked me for hitchhiking when I was five. She caught me saying "Thank you" while sliding out of a great big truck. I took a ride with a stranger, from the local store to the tar shack in Apry. She made it crystal clear that I was in the wrong, 'cause not only did she spank me, she had a look on her face that I'll never forget. Not her angry one, but a cross between a you-scared-me and my-heart-hurts look. I never want to see that look again. We get to trust that the only time Mom uses her hands on us is when we've put our lives in danger. Otherwise, it's her other look that we fear. It stops us dead in our tracks. How do you make somebody freeze without even touching them? That's what Mom does. That look means one thing—she's disappointed. And, we HATE disappointing her.

It's a very different story with Dad, though. He can't help himself; it's like the urge to hit comes up from underneath his skin.

Every single night I'm seated at the dinner table next to him.

*Why?!*

I'm smacked or backhanded every single night. I'm never sure of the reasons, maybe I've said something stupid, or it's the way that I chew? I try keeping quiet, to sit very still, and I try to chew just right. Maybe it's my hair color? He picks on Carp and me the most, both of us having red hair and freckles; that could be the reason. He must see something different in the two of us. Maybe us two shouldn't have come along in the first place? I don't know.

Life surely would've been easier for them without us, being the last two born. Both Niecie and Bubby have dark hair and light skin, just like him—they hardly ever get hit.

There are the slaps, pinning and struggling of Mom's wrists, choking and fits of rage. He holds his gun sometimes—the gun in one hand, a cigarette in the other—upset, saying he's going to kill himself. I never think he's serious, though, 'cause he always hurts others, never himself. I think he must act like this to keep Mom in her place and us kids in line.

One time, he shot the floor and fell over it, tricking us,

faking his own death. I remember that day, thinking, could it be true? Is he really dead?

Us kids just looked at each other, stunned. We didn't dare celebrate, in case he didn't finish the job.

Why can't Mom just take us kids and run as fast as she can?

He is at times the darkest crazy; mostly he's drunk crazy. He really only wants or cares about Bubby. Mom protects Bubby, refusing to let him take him away, but he always talks about it. I see Dad, heavy in her ear, pulling at her arm. I'm not sure what he is saying to her, but I catch a word here and there.

"I'll tell them, all of them," he says. Or, "Fine! I'll just take him and go!"

I guess she's forced to stay with him for reasons my head will never understand. Even though things get hard from time to time, it just is what it is. We carry on day after night, enjoying the light moments in between the hard ones, just like all the other people, I guess.

I think the only difference between our life and other people's lives might be the words I love you. I hear people say that they love each other. Sometimes there's a story on the radio where children get to use the word love. There are books too, that talk about people that love each other and how important it is. Sometimes I want to say it, but, I guess those words make you sound weak—you get made fun of.

Sometimes, I get to see love, in moments, in something simple. I think, at our house, it means getting the basics: some food, warmth, or in learning something new. We never ever say it out loud, though. I think that the boys think that love is a stupid word. Some days I especially feel it in something Mom might do. I think my mom shows her love best in teaching us about the earth, food, and patience.

She takes us swimming in the bay, waist high in the water.

"Go under," she says, her palm held flat, just below my

ribs as I float there or dog paddle. She tells me that I can do it. That once I learn to swim, I can't unlearn it; I'll know it forever, then. I take to water like I was born to live in it. I find it soothing against my skin; warm or cold, it hugs me.

Now, if only I could see some love inside Dad. Maybe he doesn't know how? Maybe nobody taught him how it feels? I wish I had better thoughts about him. I don't want to hate Dad, but he gives me no choice. If only he would give me a chance. I just want to matter, belong with him, and feel free to be myself.

I know that Mom's afraid of him, too. But, surely she hasn't always been afraid. I'd like to think there was a time that they were so much together that they couldn't imagine hurt between them. I hear stories of how they met each other in the prune orchard, how much they liked each other then. Maybe sometime Mom could remind him of those times? If she could just be strong enough to talk to him, to stop him from pounding his family . . . It seems simple, but I understand that she takes a chance at getting hit just for bringing it up.

Maybe, she could wait till he sleeps? Maybe, while he's under his beer rest, she could whisper in his ear? "Perry, this is your family," And, in her gentle way, she might add, "I beg you to please find it in your heart to love them."

---

I see that Dad's home early from work today. The car is out front, and I hear loud voices coming from inside our Dew Drop Inn.

"King, what do you think? Is it safe?" King looks up at me, one ear higher than the other, then he turns to get a look at the house for himself. I'm hoping Dad's not picking on Mom. His voice sounds muffled though, like he's under a pillow. Opening the door, I see Mom in the kitchen, and I'm quick to know that he's downstairs in the basement. There are other voices there, too. Maybe friends from the neighborhood.

"Shoot it!" Dad says, laughing.

I think his laughter is too big for this time of day, like he's forcing it from the bottom of his belly where his beer sits.

I'm curious now, though, and I have the urge to peek in on them. I see Mom is busy, distracted by the stove. Sending King back outside, I slip onto the second step of the basement staircase, where they can't quite see me. The first thing I notice is the smell; it smells like the ocean up close. Also, the cracking and scraping sounds, shell against shell.

"Bet I can open three to your one," Dad says.

Leaning down, I see a pile of oysters sitting in the middle of the room, a couple of bowls and buckets beside them.

"You shucker! You're so full of shit!" I hear one of them say back.

"Oh, I can shuck with the best of 'em!" Dad shouts.

Laughing together, Dad looks pleased with himself. He then slides a big one right down his throat. It makes me shutter a little. He follows it with the longest swig of beer I've ever seen him take at one time.

"Shouldn't eat 'em as you go, Perry, you'll fall behind!"

Their hands and elbows fly around the room, knives and tools flying with them. It's a race to the bottom of the pile. Soon they're finished. All that's left is empty shells and bowls of goo. Kicking back, they relax. Dad tips onto the back legs of his wooden chair. He teeters there, his toes tapping, replacing the front legs. He balances in a rocking way, without a care in the world. The long sleeves of his plaid shirt are rolled up. His arms hang down, the beer bottle dangling from his fingers. Every once in a while, he jerks himself upright, catching himself just before slamming onto the floor behind him.

"They'll never miss 'em," he says.

"Nope, we're slick in the middle of the night," said one of the others. "Let's go dump the evidence."

Mom cooks oysters a few different ways, but mostly rolled or dusted in flour, then fried. It's important that she gets started right away, especially if there's a lot of them at once.

Many times the neighbors share their food. We especially have to share if someone gets a deer or something big, like after a hunt or maybe when a car hits something on the roadside. They just pick it up, throw it in the trunk, and bring it home, where it's hung, skinned, chopped up, and shared with others all within a day or two. Outside of the neighbors we've shared with, others shouldn't know that we have it, so we have to eat it up fast.

It's hard to make a lot of food last; there's nowhere to keep it. So we have to cook it as soon as possible, otherwise it spoils. We do have an icebox; it hangs outside the window. It's a wooden box that holds anything that needs to stay cool. It's small though, so there's not enough room for big things.

There is special food sharing, too. Like when Mr. Bigley goes out on his boat collecting his crabs. He then calls everybody together to eat some. My favorite thing that Mom shares is her pies—pies made of salal berries or any other kind of fruit she gets her hands on. My mouth waters as they sit on the counter to cool. Sometimes, I think they look just like the pictures in our books of rhymes.

Niecie reads to us a lot these days, mostly from the 365 Bedtime Stories. The book cover is red and blue and has a very happy family on the front. You can tell they're happy, 'cause they have yellow stars all around them. Carp's favorite story is the one about the hippopotamus. The poor hippo has a bad tooth that needs to be pulled. Once they pull his great big tooth out, he feels much better. The back of the book has a grinning half moon with the words "Good Night" circled all around him. Three hundred and sixty-five seems like way too many stories, but it's not; we like them all.

One time I heard a story about Robin Hood. He's a bad guy, but good when it comes to stealing. He only took things to help people that were hungry. Kind of like Dad, I think. He only steals what he needs for others: vegetables out of gardens, oysters out of the bay, deer off of the streets. Otherwise, he can be mean, but a pretty honest guy. A guy that would do anything for just about anybody. He never steals to get rich. When he was younger, in the army, he sucked gasoline out of a car, only 'cause he needed it to get somewhere. The army got mad at him for it and told him he had to go away. I guess they gave him some papers. Not bad papers, they just didn't want him in the Army anymore.

Dad whistles under his breath when he's in a good mood. It's the kind of whistle where your tongue floats in your mouth, not the kind where you pucker and blow. The air comes out over his tongue, just below the roof of his mouth, under his teeth. He's calmest when he's making that sound. It seems always the same tune, "I Wish I Had the Wings of an Angel." We think that's the name of the song, anyway.

The tune floats high in the air, whether he's inside or out. I'm not sure why he likes this song. I've been told it's a song about wanting to fly into the arms of a darling outside prison walls, and it's there he'd be willing to die. All I know is, we get to go about our lives a little easier when I hear him whistling it. He whistles between cigarettes while pulling his pocket knife out to clean his nails. If he happens to be sitting, his legs bounce up and down like there's a machine under them.

Relatives talk about his growing-up years. I guess it was hard. Lots and lots of kids, and they say that he also had a very scary dad. There's a story about a little sister that stepped into an apple fight. She was only two or so. A fast flying apple caught the side of her head, and she fell to the ground. She was okay for a couple of days, but then never woke up again. Nobody talks about who it was, exactly, that threw the apple that made her sleep forever. It's a secret between them. I think it would be hard to hold a secret like that inside you. Her name was Dorothy.

—

Some days I walk over to see Mom. She got a job as the Bayocean post mistress. She sits behind a window with bars on it. Even though Mom works now, she's always within reach. We can drop in for a visit whenever we like. I think her job makes her happy, as I see her smile at people there. She gets to know everybody, 'cause everybody gets mail. People go to send and collect their letters and boxes most every day.

My chin sits on the counter; it's just tall enough. Always happy to see us kids come by, she asks me what I'm up to.

"Not much," I say, shrugging my shoulders.

It's a post office and small store all in one, set up inside one of the Bayocean cabins. It smells like cats. There are a few shelves just inside the door, some grocery basics, and there's the glass case that holds penny candy. When we find a penny it's the first place we go.

Mrs. Glinn works the store part. She kind of looks like a witch, but she's okay, friendly. I never have enough money for a candy bar, so I get jawbreakers instead. It doesn't matter what color I pick, 'cause it turns all different colors when you keep it in your mouth. I just roll them around on my tongue and pull them out to see the color change from time to time.

Mrs. Glinn takes my penny and reaches in. There are ants and earwigs, but that doesn't matter, she just shoos them aside and picks two of the nicest. I pop back over, put my chin on the counter to ask Mom a question. "Mom, where's King? I can't find him."

Mom looks at me. There's really no big expression on her face. She just has that sweet comfortable look she gets. Mom takes in a big breath; her hands busy doing post office stuff.

"Well, I'm not sure at the moment," she says. It takes her a bit, but she finally settles her eyes on my face. "Maybe he had to go away for a while?"

Satisfied with her answer, I head out for my afternoon without him. Maybe our paths will cross—each of us on our own adventure.

# Twitchell's Dream

Time for more wind and sunshine; I step out the door of the post office and begin to shut it behind me when I see Mr. Twitchell. He is taping something on the outside window. He likes to hang stuff on the inside, too. Usually, he puts notices about upcoming events, but also things about history. I like to look at the pictures and try to read the papers on the wall that shows Bayocean in the past. About the times when the Natatorium was right here on our beach. I can hardly say the word Natatorium, but I kind of wish I could have seen it for myself. Judging from the pictures, I think the building looked like something out of a storybook. I guess, in its prime, it was a huge vacation spot. People came from far-away places to play in the heated wave pool. I've heard it said that it even had a special section for a band to play music entertaining the swimmers. The Natatorium was one of the first things that the ocean took away. All that's left now are a couple of big, cement pieces. Kind of odd when you think about it—those great, big waves, stealing away a great big wave pool.

I look up at Mr. Twitchell, and smile as I walk by. He's a quiet man, tall and skinny. To me, he looks like a coat rack under a hat. There's something about him that's dark, probably just his clothes though, not his personality. At first, when I see him, I'm kind of afraid. But that never lasts too long—I know that he's a very nice man inside all that dark stuff. I hear people say, "He's a business man through and through."

He owns Twitchell's Hotel and has managed the main, general store and post office over the years. He also sells other buildings in Bayocean area. There's a sign in the front window of his store that reads: Watch Bayocean Grow. I always wonder about that sign as I watch him wander about with a wheelbarrow, filling potholes in our rocky, paved streets. He fixes business signs, too—he fixes everything, in fact. I think as hard as he works at keeping our special town together, the ocean works that much harder taking his dream place apart. I wonder if he knows how fast it works against him?

"He's a dear man in denial," I hear people say.

"His entire life is invested right here." They go on, "It's crumbling though, along with his fortune and everything he's worked for."

Over time, as Bayocean takes its beating, somebody has crossed two letters off the sign on the front of his store; the 'r' and the 'w' have been slashed. It kind of breaks my heart 'cause his sign now reads: Watch Bayocean Go.

I feel for him and can't blame Mr. Twitchell for working so hard at fixing stuff. I don't want Bayocean to "go" either.

Recently, he and his wife have taken the back part of the Twitchell's Hotel as their home. The halls are empty, but they don't give up.

The hotel has a musty smell; the smell of old times and a kind of mildew. Its busy past now long gone other than a dance or two every few months. Mrs. Twitchell organizes the music and sets the mood. People come together setting a bowl or platter of food on a long table at the back of the room. It's there for everyone to enjoy. Feet move to live fiddle music or under polka sounds whining through the radio. Or, musical fingers tinker on the pump organ, filling the room with good times.

Us kids pull away from the big room full of big people. We see that the hallways and bedrooms are all very empty of day-to-day happenings. There are water pitchers sitting in bowls and bedspreads pulled tight. It's all very neat and tidy, except for a little settled dust, 'cause no one is moving around in there. We know that we shouldn't be wandering the halls but our curiosity gets the best of us.

---

Suzanne is my favorite friend. She's Mr. Bigley's daughter, and she's really nice to me. We play together sometimes. I get to be the leader; she doesn't get a choice 'cause she's a little bit younger. I hardly ever get to be the oldest in a group of kids, so this is my chance. She's the opposite of a tomboy, but she keeps up with me pretty good. Sometimes we strap roller skates under our shoes and roll around the front of the Twitchell's Hotel, or we go inside to explore.

"This way, Suzanne," I say. Using my hands to show her, we head down the long hallway, stopping just short of the end. There's a door there. It doesn't invite us in. It's curious and comfortable at the same time—kind of like Mr. Twitchell himself. But there's something more. An invisible feeling, like the door is absolutely none of our business.

Twitchell's store, across the street, also has a smell. A smell that sticks with you forever. I could be blindfolded, be turned around and around, and taken there, and would know exactly where I am just by using my nose. Even if you haven't been there for a week or so, you'd remember the smell. It must be a mixture of Grape Nehi, Pepsi, and Cracker Jack. Maybe also some Bit-O-Honey or Big Hunk—probably not, but that's what I want it to smell like.

In its past, it's been the only real store in Bayocean. Mr. Twitchell has always looked out for everybody's needs. He tries to collect and order things that make everybody happy. He does special orders just for the kids. He puts each of our names on a Milky Way bar, when the candy bars come in. Every child in Bayocean gets their very own name on one. They cost five cents. Us kids set out to find or make the money to buy the bar with our name on it. He saves them until, one-by-one, we show up with our pennies or nickel. If you have ten or fifteen cents, you're not allowed to buy anybody else's bar. According to Bubby, it's his very own "chocolate ration program" We like it, though. It makes us happy, and it makes Mr. Twitchell a very special friend.

# King

Bayocean
1951

I had a dream last night, one that told me that I might never see King again. It was almost like a whisper, right there in my ear, letting me know that he's moved on and will never come back. That he's perfectly okay where he is—that even his jerk has disappeared altogether. Honestly, where could he be?

I'm waiting patiently with the others for the bus this morning. Standing here, all I can think about is that dream—it was so real. It's been many, many days, maybe even weeks now since I've seen him. Anything that moves, up close or in the distance, catches my eye. Sometimes, when I see a game of fetch, I'm just sure it's him jumping and running at the stick.

Every morning I hope to find him flopped across the porch, or maybe sleeping, tucked up against the house.

I keep asking Mom where he could be. She keeps telling me that he might need time away, or that maybe he's sick and needs to be alone. She goes on to explain that sometimes creatures want to be by themselves when they are too sick to be around others. I can't help but think he needs me to help him get through it.

The bus is waiting on the other side, we are busy counting waves. "That's seven, go!"

My hand gets a firm pull, and we're off, looks like we're going to make it to school this morning. During our run, something catches my eye tucked up against a piece of driftwood.

*Is that? It is!* Letting go of the hand that holds mine, I dart over to grab it.

"Elin! Keep going!" Niecie warns.

I see that the ocean is on its way toward us, but I don't care—I need to get it. It's caked in sand, but I recognize the shape. I can be really quick on my feet, so I know I'll make it okay. Crouching down, I snatch it up and keep on with my run, joining the others with just seconds to spare.

"Elin! You know better than that." Niecie scolds me for letting go and trailing behind. I'm not paying attention, though. I'm wishing I had a little of that rushing water to clear the treasure that sits in my hand. I try cleaning it by rubbing and brushing sand away. Last in line for the bus, I shake it, wiping it off as quick and as much as possible, clearing the glass. The net around it is thick and wet. It's a good day when the first thing you find is a glass float! I would rather find King, but this will do for now. Besides, it makes me think of him. The times we nudged rolling glass back and forth between us. Even if I never find him, I've already decided that he'll be with me always; Mom says so too.

Holding it up by the rope, I get a closer look. It's not chipped or broken; it's all well and good. It's wet and gunky, but I stick it in my pocket anyway. It's bulging there, but that's okay—I'll keep it close.

# The Visitor

"Mom? What's in there?" I ask, running my hand across the wooden, gray chest. It sits in the corner of her bedroom, I never see her open it.

"Oh, some stories about my family," she says.

Using the soft edge of her brush, she gives her hair one last swipe, then lets the brush slip from her hand onto the dresser. Turning both palms up, she smooths the bottom curls below her ears, lifting them in an upward bounce. The curls loosen, then hold snug at her shoulders. She walks over to straighten the bed.

"Stories? I like stories. Can I hear them?"

"Well, these stories are for older ears, I'm afraid. Some people were terribly hurt. I promise one day to tell you all about it."

"Okay, It's about a train though, right?" I know that I'm pushing.

She throws her cardigan over the curve of a hanger, then finds a spot in her closet, near a smaller sweater, the color of peaches, with crumpled lace at the top.

"Yes," she says, following her word with a sigh. Not a mean or hurt sigh. It's more like a breath with a pause in it. Like she wants to add something, but maybe she's not quite sure which words to use.

---

Thinking back, I remember when the chest came to the brown house. I was much younger, but curious then, too. A man showed up, I remember his name was Mervin. He was nicely dressed in slacks and shiny shoes. His eyes were light green; his hair was dark.

"Evelyn, it's very good to see you," he said. He then turned to share a stiff nod and handshake with Dad. Dad then raised his hand in the air flicking it toward the front door.

"You kids get outta here—go play," he said.

We knew to scat right away, especially when there's adult talk and strange or new company around. I was the last one out and decided to stand near the doorframe for a minute or two.

Mervin set himself down at the dining table. He placed the chest on the floor, near his feet, between him and Mom. Mom set a glass of water near him and asked if he would like to have some coffee.

"Yes, thank you," he said. "As I wrote in the letter, you'll find it all here," He tapped on the chest. "I think it is most important that you have it, Evelyn."

Mom turns carefully with a fresh cup of coffee, "Thank you, Mervin, I appreciate you coming all this way to deliver it."

What is it? I can't help but wonder. Carp snickered, stepping off the porch toward the fishpond out front.

"What kind of name is Mervin, anyway? Merrrrrrvvvinnnn," Carp said, wobbling his head and rolling his eyes. I stayed close to the door for more.

They talked about a man named Clemmett and some sort of accident. There were quiet moments. Mom's hands rested on the table, placed inches outside her coffee cup, still holding them in a cupped way, but relaxed. It's almost like the cup may have been too hot to touch, but she still needed to feel the warmth of it. She was listening to him; her one hand pulling up to rest across her mouth every so often. It would soon find its place under her chin, her eyes toward a spot on the wall. I followed her eyes up, but nothing was there. I think it meant that there was more in her head than she's willing to say out loud.

Dad, busy strumming his fingers on the table, stayed quiet, but his eyebrows like to talk. They moved up and down along with Mom and Mervin's words—that's nothing new.

Mervin went on talking about how Clemmett cared deeply for Mom. How he tried harder than he'd ever seen his father try to help anyone before. How his father felt he let the relatives down when he lost her to the Carpenters.

Lost her? Does he mean Grandma and Grandpa Carpenter?

He leaned down and placed his palm on the chest. "Dad kept everything from the accident," Mervin said. He opened it.

Oh, how I wish I could see—to be a mouse sitting on the edge of it, peering down inside.

"In here, you'll find clippings and letters received from relatives all over, Evelyn. Most dated right around the accident, sent from Stagebarn Canyon and Rapid City, of course. But also, letters from California, Colorado Springs, Missouri, and Iowa. Everybody wanted you. You'll find responding letters from the Carpenters as well, mainly from Alta," he said, raising his hands up, like us kids do when we play cowboys and Indians—surrendering.

"Oh, I know, probably more than anybody could know, Dad's odd way of handling things, my dear cousin. But, I also know, clear as this very day, how much your uncle truly cared about you and your well-being."

Mom just shook her head in a nice way, like she wanted Mervin to feel okay.

Mervin went on, "He's gone now, and we can only hope that he's having a nice visit of his own with his brother and family. They might be having a fine time discussing us right this very minute," he said, tipping his head with a smile.

"As much as it hurts losing my father, Evelyn, I still can't imagine how you've felt all these years without your family. And the fact that I had a hand in . . ." His words trailed off quietly, his face finished the sentence with the deepest of meaning. She felt it. I watched it melt across her face.

Hearing Mom's words this morning and thinking back to the visitor at the table that day, it looks like I have to wait a few years to know more. If I remember right, listening to Mervin with Mom, this gray chest of mystery must hold a very big story. Sounds like one about an accident, fighting for lives, and families sticking together. There's more to Mom than I've ever known before; I can't help but wonder how much more.

# Paradise to Paradise

They say that we are "The town that fell into the sea." I see newspaper headlines, and I hear people talking about it. In fact, it's all the adults talk about these days. Basically, because of our last, big storm, our land can no longer hold us. The sea lives too close now. It has gobbled up too many houses and is now telling us to go away.

People scramble to find ways to keep their homes. Some just leave them behind to be washed away, burned, or buried. Others are moving their homes to solid land in Cape Meares, by tractors, trucks, or boats.

Moving a whole house? I had no idea any such thing was possible, but it's happening.

The House of Hicks is said to be "the best house in Bayocean." It has a neon sign on the front. It sits way high upon the hill near the leftover parts of a grand old hotel. The Hotel Annex—that hotel is from history; it's been closed and gone for a really long time now. There's only a ragged wall there and a slope that the boys slide down using cardboard as sleds.

Not too long ago, I guess the House of Hicks had a butler in it. Bubby and the other boys went there for a friend and had to wait by the door as the butler announced their names. From what I hear, they have to cut the House of Hicks in half before they can move it.

Mr. Bigley is still working on breaking his house down. Board by board, one at a time, he numbers them and makes a little note next to each number. This way he knows exactly how to put his house back together again. He loads each board onto his tugboat and barges them across the bay to safer land.

Day after day we move away—each family finding new ground.

One time, I got to go on the tugboat with Suzanne and Mr. Bigley to collect some things. It was a beautiful afternoon skimming over the calm bay. I remember pilings and blue heron standing tall near the shore, the gulls greeting us on the other side. It was kind of a special trip because it was my last Bayocean adventure, walking around on the streets, entering deserted buildings, and a final night of camping on the bay. I knew it was a special day, so I took it all in: I visited the Dew Drop Inn, Twitchell's Hotel, and the house that Dad bought us.

We left our house behind; I guess it wasn't worth moving. We managed to find one in Cape Meares that will hold us just fine, for now. Still small, but it's built on ground that won't go away. It took a big coat of sheep dip to get it clean enough to move in. It was pretty dirty, but, otherwise, it's not too bad, 'cause I still have the ocean down the road one way, and the bay down the road the other. There's also a dike and swimming hole across the pasture, just a small hike from the house. There are still plenty of places to explore in Cape Meares. Most important is that we are safe, I guess.

Mr. Twitchell is the only one left in Bayocean. He doesn't want to let go and is refusing to leave. In my imagination, he lives alone now, at the end of that long hallway. Rumor has it, he's lost his wife. That makes us sad, we haven't seen her in a while and we really liked her. But, I guess she's yet another thing he's hoping to keep. The kids tell stories that he's rolled her up in one of the big hotel rugs, keeping her for his very own, never to let go. Like Bayocean, she's something that he plans to hold on to forever no matter what the cost.

Again, I listen closely, laying or standing within ear shot of Mom and Dad's card games. Adult players exchange the latest gossip.

"By all indications he loved her," says Mrs. Luck.

"They say he's lost it; it's all very sad," says another, tossing cards across the table.

"Did you see? Official people are visiting him—forcing him to pull away."

Despite the disturbing rumors, they speak highly of each of them. Most find it in their hearts to celebrate the Twitchells and the way they cared about our little town. The adults go on about how the Twitchells' store was one of the most successful in its prime and how his real estate efforts with the cabins had been a thriving business for years. And, of course, they mention the Twitchells' home, their beating heart: Twitchell's Hotel, where the doors were always open.

# Monster

Dad's had a hard day of work, I can tell—he smells like beer.

Tonight, at the kitchen table, all of us quiet, the sound of scraping forks against dishes, the only thing we hear.

After a while, he brings attention to the floor. I look down. There's a pile of dog crap right next to my chair.

"Look at that!" he shouts.

I flinch.

"Pick it up!"

I don't dare look him in the eye, but I wonder if he's serious.

"Elin! Pick it up, now!" he yells. His breath so close, his words land in beer puffs on my face. I can't believe he's making me do this. Setting my fork down, I slide my chair back.

"Bare hands." he says, low and hard.

Bare hands?

Fearing the usual dinnertime backhand I move toward it. Glancing at Mom, I notice she's stopped chewing, a look of exhaustion hangs across her face as she shifts her eyes another direction—they are distant, like they've left the room without her. She swallows hard, then sets her fork down.

"Now!!!" he yells. I duck under his shout.

Sliding down from my chair, I reach slowly. As I connect with the pile, I turn away, ready for the stench, the softness, the goo. But, to my surprise I find the pile to be hard. What? Surely it hadn't been sitting there for long; one of us would've noticed it.

He bursts into laughter. "It's fake. . . . Gotcha!"

He throws his head back and releases what seems like a gut full of the funniest thing he's ever seen. I'd like to say it's a mean laugh, but it's not. It's a regular laugh, which, in a way, makes this hurt even harder. There's a ball of emotion strung tight in my throat. This is not funny, and I'm still confused in my crouch, not knowing which way to move next.

The others laugh, too. I'm smart enough to know that they laugh because they have to. Upsetting, yes, but I'm okay if they play along as it may keep his mood on the lighter side. I'm also smart enough to know that their laughter is about surviving him, about not getting hit themselves.

Bubby and Carp look at each other as they finish with their stupid boyish snicker; I'm still down near the floor, in my place, right where I belong, crouched, holding make-believe dog shit—it might as well be real.

# BABE

## Cape Meares
## 1953

My big brothers still slug me every chance they get; it's fun for them. Their way of putting me in my place, I guess. They watch Dad hit me, so why not? I know right where I stand; I've always known it. So, I keep distance between us, most of the time anyway. Despite all their meanness, I still try to join them in their adventures; sometimes it works, sometimes it doesn't. I notice that the older I get the more it does. I get to visit them when they are busy building something big or for swims with friends at the dike across the pasture. Otherwise, how else would I learn how to create or what trick to try next? They still have their moments though, where their punch throws hard and fast out of nowhere. Gosh it hurts, but it doesn't matter. I'll never give up.

Bubby has a horse now, which means I'm willing to take a slug or two more, just to hang around them. Her name is Babe. Well, we call her Babe. Her original name was Jet. In a way that name fits her better, because she is jet black in color and she moves really fast. Like all of our pets, she just showed up out of nowhere with Dad; I couldn't believe my eyes. All those hours playing make-believe with Stickhorse, now I'm standing right next to a real, live one. And she's ours.

I like her eyes, her lashes, her mane. At night and in school I try over and over to draw her.

Her feet and hooves are to be watched closely; as beautiful as she is, she can have a nasty attitude, bigger than all of us combined, and will kick up a storm without warning.

Bubby is more than willing to let me ride her. I think he finds it funny that nobody can stay up there for very long. The moment we're slung across her back, she throws us off and as far away as she can.

"Whoa, Babe, steady, steady." I say, standing beside her, holding her reigns. I look her in her eye and run my hand down the soft length of her neck.

Surely she'll warm up to me. I can't get enough of her and will find any excuse to get to know her better. I keep in mind, though, that it was only a few days ago that Niecie climbed up with Bubby's help. Certainly unlike Niecie to try such a thing, but somehow Bubby talked her into it. She sat calm for a moment or two, right there in the slope of Babe's back. Before she knew it, Niecie flew straight into the air, flipped a summersault, landing square on her butt. She hit the ground so hard, the wind knocked way out of her. Once she caught her breath, she swore she'd never try that again.

Babe is mostly Bubby's responsibility. He even put together enough money to buy her the new bit and reigns. She has a saddle, but you have to be really strong to strap it on. Babe doesn't like her saddle. She runs away for hours or days at a time, dragging her leather straps through the wet and the mud. Twice now, Babe has been lead back home by the same barefoot lady that lives in Oceanside twenty miles away. We think there's another horse there Babe goes to visit. Mom shakes her head knowing how far the lady has come to bring Babe back to us and tries to give her a little something for her trouble, hoping she'll use the money for some shoes.

# Spell of Nine

I'm eleven, going on twelve now, and very happy that I broke the "spell of nine." The family talks about the "spell" like it's something scary and serious. The story goes something like this. Age nine is the time when our family members find the biggest, hardest things happen to them. Mom, for example: I guess when she was nine a train hit her? I don't know, nobody has told me the whole story yet, but that sounds pretty scary to me. Niecie was nine, riding a bike, with Carp on the front handles one day. She couldn't wait to share a giggle with our neighbors about the curlers she set in Carps thick, red hair. He looked so funny, they were laughing all the way there. But, then Corpy, our dog at that time, tripped the bike and broke Niecie's leg. Bubby was nine when he fell backward on a double-edged ax and sliced his hand and wrist so badly they had to drive him to Washington, a whole different state, to get it fixed. Then there was Carp. When he turned nine he rolled into a ditch, playing hide and seek, and ended up with a rusty nail in his butt.

I guess I'm the lucky one, 'cause nine was no problem for me.

# Bats and Bedtime

I know that it's time for me to become a young lady, but I find this challenge to be one of my hardest. I am feeling a little bit grown up and stronger than ever, but there a few things that still make me small. It's mostly during the night that I feel like the smallest, the weakest of all.

Even though Niecie is so much older, we've slept in the same bed my whole life. But not for long. It's time to make things different, I hear Mom and Niecie say in their talks.

"We're moving soon, to the Lighter's house. You'll have your own room there,"

Mom tells her.

I've tried and tried, with all that I have, over the years to wake up dry. I know that it upsets Niecie when she wakes wet because of me. I don't blame her, and I wish I could fix it. I'm afraid that this is just another disgusting thing out of my control. I've tried every trick in the book: staying awake late, running out to do my business right before sleep, even avoiding too much liquid at dinnertime—nothing works. I guess I just get too lost in my sleep to know what my body is doing. I can't wait to deal with the problem on my own, without Niecie getting wet and being upset.

—

Finally, I have my own bed now; we've moved down the street to the Lighter's house. The boy's sleep on one end of the attic, I sleep on the other. It's just us and the bats and bugs that live up here.

We climb a ladder, attached to the wall, straight up from Niecie's room. Up in the attic, we are separated by a big board that sits in the middle. Nobody ever comes up the ladder, except for the boys and me.

Once in a while Bubby goes after a bat flying around the room. He whacks at it so hard I want to put my hands over my ears. It all makes me shiver. To me, the bats are exactly like mice with wings. They get in by crawling down between the space in the wall and the chimney and then they fly around the ceiling all clumsy. I always worry that the bats will tangle in my hair while I sleep. It's easy to tell when they've snuck in, though, 'cause it's impossible for them to stay sneaky—they always end up fluttering around in a flurry. Bubby slings his pillow at one, or he picks up his cartoon board and whirls it around the room till he traps it. I always think he should be careful with his cartoon board; I like it a lot. He's filled it with drawings from the funny papers. Not only does he draw the funnies, he paints them, too. I never tell him so, but I think his cartoon board is pretty neat.

The bats aren't the only things bothering me, there's the smell. I don't really notice it unless I've been out in the fresh air all day. I think otherwise my nose must be used to it. It smells like pee. I'd like to blame it on the boys and the bats, but I know better.

Although I'm relieved that Niecie no longer has to take part in my nightly problem, I'm still really upset with myself for it. For years I had no idea I was different from anybody else, I guess I thought everybody in the whole wide world wet themselves. But, now I know I need to find a way to stop it. It should be as easy as those words that people say, "Mind over matter," but no—no matter what my mind says, it doesn't work that way.

The mattress is wearing through, and I can see a couple of the springs have rusted too. Mom gave up long ago on my bedding. I guess I can't blame her.

# Take Him

I'm still enjoying pet beings much more than human beings; we have plenty of them: a rooster, chickens, rabbits, dogs, always a dog, Babe, and now Dad has shown up with a skunk.

The skunk is tied in one of the cages out back; again, a mini chain link around his neck. I'm not sure why the skunk came to live with us, maybe he got hurt and needed some healing. He can be nasty, but so interesting to look at. Funny, though, no matter how nasty he is, I still want to give him a hug.

There isn't a day that goes by that I don't think about King. Sometimes, in the distance I see a dog jumping and playing on the beach or down the road. My heart hopes he may be better and finding his way home. I still ask Mom about him. Her latest answer is always, "Maybe he's resting somewhere." He must be really tired. How much rest does he need?

For now I just reach for my glass ball that reminds me of him. I'll play with it on my own, think about him, and hope that he's safe.

—

Dad works for the Pacific Bottling Company, in Tillamook. He works like a dog and drinks like a fish. We go in, with him, every Friday so Mom can pick up his paycheck; she has to in order to keep food on the table. Otherwise, a lot of it disappears in drink; he loses himself in the fun, and gets too generous with his friends. You can tell all the men see him as a manly man, the biggest, outgoing, funnest man of all. They enjoy his humor, and I can see that the women always want to be close—too close.

—

I can hear Mom pulling open the front door.

"Yes?" she says. I know there's wonder in her word, because she's my mom. I know every feeling she wraps around every single one of her words.

"You want me to what?" I hear her question.

I step into the room curious to know who's there, to get closer to the conversation.

There stands a woman looking at Mom; I can tell she needs something. Maybe she's a new neighbor, looking for a cup of sugar? Do we know her?

She looks a little emotional, even desperate, like her talk is about to make her cry. There's really nothing that stands out about her other than a full figure and dark, shiny hair.

"I want Perry," she says.

What? Did I hear that right? Did she say she wants my dad?

Mom, takes a step back, drapes her arm up across her chest and stands calmly listening to her. The woman goes on, "Evelyn, please just let him go. I want him. We need to be together. He'll be happier with me."

I'm half expecting Mom to throw the door shut, slamming it hard in her face, but no, it looks like Mom needs to hear more. Amazed at her patience, I'm realizing she could be even more stunned than I am at what is being said on our front doorstep.

Maybe Mom is frozen in disbelief? She hasn't moved, or said anything.

I walk around to the side of her, still giving lots of room for her to ponder the offer. The woman just keeps on, like it's a possibility.

After a while, Mom says the very same word that she said when she opened the door in the first place. "Yes."

Yes?!

This time her word felt final, like she had just made the day of a sales person selling their cleaning supplies or encyclopedias.

"Yes, please take him—he's all yours," she says, then promptly closes the door.

Later, while trailing some oats for Oats, the rooster, I think about how Mom is, her proud, quiet way. I imagine not many women could hold themselves up to a conversation such as the one she had earlier today. Other than the mumble on the way back to the kitchen, something about having the woman "get in line," and the fact that she tossed a question in the air—"Does she think she's the first?" she didn't miss a beat. Even if Mom thinks Dad is the hardest part of her life, she has kids to raise, a household to keep together. The fact that she said the simple word "Yes" shows me that she's probably one of strongest people I know. Her strength may be on the quiet side, but she's solid as a rock.

—

Mom is still the post mistress. After the water broke through, the US Mail people just picked up, and moved the post office from the vacation cabins in Bayocean into a small building in Cape Meares. The building sits on the corner down the road from our house. I visit her most every day that she works there. Lots of days we have fun talks between happy customers. Sometimes she sells hot dogs on the side to make a little money. She slips me one here and there to sooth my hungry tummy in the afternoons.

---

Today I fall into the post office door, stumbling; my clothes are still damp from my swim at the dike. My hair is still wet, but has finished dripping and hooks slick behind my ears. I shiver a little telling her my story. I'm sure she can tell my shaking comes from a combination of the chill of the day, the events that took place, and the look on my face. So far, she's not a bit concerned; Mom's only half listening, glancing at the newspaper.

"I dove in, sweatshirt and all. That's all good, nothing new, but, then a mud sucker went up my sleeve!" I reached for my arm. "Those sucker fishes are prickly!"

Mom, pulled herself from her newspaper stare and laughed. "What? Oh, for cripe's sake." She stops reading and reaches through the cage she sits behind.

I love to hear her laugh.

"I felt it go straight up! Still underwater, I quickly grabbed it from the outside of my shirt, getting a handful, it just wiggled in there. It was pokey!"

Together we pull my sleeve up to take a closer look. Mom runs her fingers from under my elbow, then smoothed them across the turned up, underside of my arm.

"I was way under when I felt it. I held tight till I was able to get some air, then flipped my sleeve inside out to see what it was. That fish couldn't get out of there quick enough!"

We both get the giggles. My body shivers along with my chin.

"Man! Swimming can be hard when you don't know what's up your sleeve!"

I think Mom is beautiful when she smiles, even more so when she laughs.

I don't dare tell her how curious we are about the dike itself. The swimming hole and fish that join us, yes, but the dike is another story. Us kids can't help but watch and try to understand the workings of it. We are not even sure why it's needed or what it does under there. Maybe the underwater door helps control the tides coming in from the bay side? Maybe it was built there to keep the pasture from flooding when there's too much water? We're just not sure.

The underwater door is sort of a gate turned on its side. It's kind of big, and you never know when it's going to move, stay open, or decide to close. We talk about how we should try swimming through, underneath it, to the other side—the bay side. The handful of us that are brave enough to try it, are certainly smart enough to know that if trapped by the door, you would be done for. Still, we spit the words while treading water; words like "dare" or "double dare you" float across the water in spit and ripples. Then one or two of us dive down to take a look.

Under water, my arms move like the grace of a bird, back and forth; my breath held tight in my throat, I blink a few times to see better. It's hard to tell the difference between open and closed through the murky water. I decide, watching shadows and counting on the feel of the push and the pull of the current seems the best way to know.

If the boys do it, I'll have to. I cringe to myself.

And so I tread and tread, wondering if I should be the first to go.

# Luck of a Snitch

In the still of the afternoon, Carp yells, "Elin is stealing bread out of the kitchen!" I slow my chew and kill him with my dirtiest look. He has what Dad would call a shit-eatin' grin on his face. Sure enough, Dad shows up, looks at me, points straight in the air, sending me up to my room. I feel lucky he didn't pound me.

Darn, I hope this doesn't mean no dinner tonight, or worse. Maybe I still have some punishment coming? My throat tightens a little just thinking about it. If only I can find a way to get Carp back—my mind is busy thinking, as I scramble up the ladder to the attic. Hate it when there's meanness in the air. It changes everything from light to dark, in an instant. I was just HUNGRY for goodness sake. Just when the usual pee smell hits my nose, I realize there's something different about it. I look around the room and each side of the board in the middle. There's a crackle sound. My first thought is a bat or some other furry thing, but crackling is not a normal sound that bugs or critters make. Soon I realize the house is in trouble.

"Mooooommmmm, Daaaaad! There's smoke up here, noises too!"

"What? Elin, what did you say?" Mom is shouting back from another room of the house. I hear her as she comes closer to the bottom of the ladder, her fingers reach up, hanging from the highest rung within her reach. Even though she usually refuses, I'm sure this time she might climb up to see what's going on.

Nope. She just stands there. "There's fire sounds, and it smells like smoke!" I shout down to her. Mom runs to the other room.

"Perry! The house is on fire," she yells.

I hear the water turn on in the kitchen and Dad busting out the back door. Carp calls for Bubby; they fly up the ladder to see for themselves.

"Water!! We need water!" Bubby yells. Mom returns to the bottom of the ladder. She's holding a full dishpan in her hands.

"Here!"

Bubby reaches down. I think she might find a way to reach him with the dishpan? Maybe by stepping up a rung or two? But, again no, she keeps her feet flat on the floor. She decides to throw the water straight up into the air, not the pan, just the water! As if Bubby can magically catch the flying water in his arms, then somehow, run it over to fix the problem. Bubby looks at her, his hands barely wet; he's puzzled.

"Mom? Was I supposed to catch it in midair?"

Mom drops the pan, putting her hands on each side of her head. She looks as puzzled as Bubby does.

Dad yells up from outside, "Here, take the hose!"

Bubby climbs out the window. Carp, not knowing which way to go, dropped to the bottom of the ladder, his feet and hands touching maybe one rung or two on his way down. I think his feet are running before they touch the floor. Soon the roof and chimney are covered with a blanket of wetness.

Tonight, I'm not in trouble for eating the bread. In fact,

I haven't even been backhanded, slapped, or hit in the head. The excitement of the day and stories of flying water have been the talk of the dinner table. Mom still wants to place her hands on her head, embarrassed, I think. She's laughing about it now, though. Bubby still looks puzzled.

As for Carp? Well, I guess I'll let him off the hook this time. That lucky snitch saved the day.

# Ickiness

Our neighbors live just a few feet away, to the right of us, if you're facing the front of the house, that is. I know they can see me, 'cause a lot of their windows face mine. Most days I'm okay with that, but not on this day.

Today they get to see all of what makes me disgusting. It's not fair. Everybody has ickiness about themselves; you're not being a truthful person if you think you don't have something icky about you. Some people are just better at hiding it then others. Heck! Up until these past months, I felt my problem was normal and really nothing that a good spit bath couldn't fix. I think Mom had a good idea when we were smaller, though. She used to lay hay as mattresses. Hay is much easier to toss and replace when it gets full of pee. Plus! What neighbor would bother to watch hay being tossed from an attic window?

I pull at the smaller pieces first. The mattress falls apart easily because of the months of dampness. I begin throwing the bigger pieces out my window. That first big piece falls hard. The plan is to let it land on the ground below, then I can just carry the pieces over to the garbage pile in the backyard. It's easier then dropping them down the ladder into Niecie's room and then dragging them through the house. Besides, Mom says, "It wouldn't be sanitary, would it?"

As I drop each piece, I know the neighbors must be getting an eyeful; they must know I'm out of control. They see me, all twelve disgusting years of my smelly dampness. Maybe they are trying to look away because they think I'm embarrassed. But, I just know that they can't. They are at least staring from the sides of their eyes. How can they resist?

I keep at it—tearing, ripping it apart chunk by chunk, pulling at the soiled cloth and cushion; white bugs and more rusted springs than expected.

I've been sleeping with bugs? There's a turn in my stomach, but I keep at it.

Stopping to take a look at the crumpled mess below, I try to tell myself that this will be the very last time. That I am strong enough to figure things out. I can do just about anything else that's tough in this world if I put my mind to it, so why not this?

Tonight, I'll try something different. Maybe better thoughts before sleep? Or, nothing to drink after lunch?

One last look outside, to make sure the coast is clear, I dump the last, few big pieces.

"Done!" I say under my breath. I wipe my hands of it. Now, down I go to finish the job.

# Bark

"Chittem! Let's go, Carp!" Bubby yells, slinging the gunnysack over his shoulder. Bubby looks back at Carp for a moment, then turns to head out.

"Chittem, chittem, chittem," Carp repeats, his shoulders teeter-tot up and down with each word. He then steps up after him, the sun bouncing off his shiny, red hair; must've been swimming earlier, it looks so clean.

"Here." Bubby throws Carp an extra sack. Bubby then quickly runs way ahead of him, Carp tries to catch up. The moment Carp gains on him, though, Bubby takes off again. It happens over and over. I watch those very same shoulders droop when he realizes he might never catch up to his big brother. Carp goes on trying, though, till they run out of sight.

I'm never sure where they go to peel the chittem. Tried following them once, but I couldn't catch up with them myself. One time I caught them in the act just by accident. They didn't even know I was there. I was out in the forest, exploring on my own, when I overheard them. There was Bubby chipping away with his tool. The very same tool I saw him pounding with a hammer, earlier that morning. He was busy banging away, flattening the round end of a bottle opener, making the metal sharp and thin as a blade. I can see why now. The tool has to be sharp in order to slip along the tree trunk and bust away the bark. Bubby pushes it in, then he works it around, till the bark pulls loose and falls off.

The boys peel and dry chittem bark to make money. They bring the bark home, stuffed in gunnysacks, and then lay them out on the roof to dry. They can sell the pieces wet or dry, but dry is best, cause they get more money that way. From what I hear, they get five cents a pound wet, and seven or eight cents a pound if they take the time to dry them. And so they dry them, then find a way to take the bark to town. There's a place in Tillamook that will pay for things like skunk cabbage root and chittem bark. They say they use them in medicines; I guess the roots are used for headaches and other aches and pains. And the bark helps people go to the bathroom a bit easier. I think the problem is called "constilipation." Something like that. I don't know; I've never tried either before. I do know that Bubby and Carp will do just about anything for money. For years, I've watched them search for nails in used boards. When they find them, they pull them out. If they are bent in any way they pound them straight again. They get one penny for three straight nails. Bubby and Carp are so good at this, we never have to buy nails to build something new.

# LIGHTHOUSE

## ELIN—TWELVE YEARS OLD

It's warmer than usual in Cape Meares today, even the ocean and cheering seagulls think so. What's in the air floats light in a sweet breeze. I stand tall on solid land, just before the line of the sand, and I look straight out into the sea, far at the horizon. I know there's a curve to the Earth way out there, because they say so in school—otherwise, from here, it just looks flat to me.

To the left something catches my eye. A mist? A spray? A whale?

The mist moves near the steep rising rock that holds the lighthouse on top. I can't see the lighthouse from here, but I know it's there. This I can prove because I've seen it and explored it for myself many times.

Just a two-mile walk to the lighthouse, with friends, and your view of life can instantly change. It's all up hill on a gravel road to reach it, but it's a journey worth every step; life feels different up there. The feeling you get has a lot to do with hearing the echoing sound of the ocean that high up—the slamming sounds of powerful water, the sway of the trees in the sea breeze. Us kids have crawled every inch of that rock on top. We even explore the cliffs. Scooting onto our knees, outstretched, holding tight to the roots, we lie there very still, watching the massive waves crash hard against the rocks below.

It sounds like thunder, or maybe the rumble of a train just before it hits.

There are the days we see whales traveling, searching for food and cool waters. We stop to play on the nine-in-one tree—it easily holds all of us at once. Shaped just like an octopus, there are trunk-sized branches for each of us, where we get to lay our lazy heads, lost in story. Stories of Indians laid to rest there, where their ancestors placed them, leaning them onto their very own trunk-sized branch, letting their bodies find their way back to nature.

I'm convinced that our lighthouse is a magnet of some sort; people big and small can't help but gather there. I think the building the light lives in is shorter than most lighthouses are. I always imagine all lighthouses as tall and skinny, but, not this one. It doesn't have to be tall, 'cause the rock it sits on is more grand than any rock I've ever seen or climbed before.

Our lighthouse is basically just a bright light, behind dusty glass, upon a wooden box, that sits on what seems to be the top of the world. It can see everything from there: the ships, the boats, the whales.

I climb up the quick ladder, spit on my hand or use my sleeve to clean the glass for a peek inside. Shadowing my eyes with the flat of my palm, I can see better that way. The light is so big, I wonder how it is they were able to get it inside where it lives.

Sometimes I wish it were night so that I could see the bright of the light. It's okay though, a visit in the day is always good. Better than good, in fact—amazing. 'Cause way up there, where I can stand high in the sky, I swear, it's the curve of the Earth I see out there.

# All Grown Up

Niecie moves out today, which means her tidy ladder-drop room will become mine. I wonder if there was an argument, if Bubby was considered first, 'cause usually I'm not the one that gets to have anything before anybody else.

I heard Mom talking with Dad in the kitchen last week. "Perry, she's getting older now, becoming a young lady. It's time we give her some privacy and something of her own, don't you think?" she said. "Besides, the boys can take over the attic for themselves."

I notice she likes to make things his idea, things go much easier that way.

It seems this time her talk with him worked in my favor. Shortly after overhearing them, a plan was set in motion.

"Elin. Time for you to have your own room," Mom says as she smiles a little, her eyes light up. She seems as happy as I am about it. I'm almost afraid to believe it.

Moving in, I lean Stickhorse in the corner and hang King's glass ball from the knob on the bed stand. Plopping down on the freshly made bed, my mind instantly goes to whether or not I can keep it that way: freshly made, unstained, unsoiled.

I have to—I need to this time.

Even my position at the dinner table has changed. I sit near the opposite end now; closer to Mom than Dad. Mom made that happen, quietly, I'm sure. Time at the dinner table is still tough, always a strain, but a little better these days.

Growing through to my teen years, girlfriends become more and more important: the secrets, the confessions, the companionship. I'm almost surprised at my sudden interest and attraction to boys. All my life boys have been nothing but a nuisance, a bother not unlike the worst rash you've ever had in your whole, entire life. Other than competing with them and following in their exploring footsteps, they would have absolutely no place in my world if it were up to me.

Kind of happy and a little proud of myself, I've been able to rid most of my ickiness. Unravel the part of me that has been wound so tight I could hardly move—flinch, yes, but not move, freely and fully relaxed. No more wet beds, no more loss of body control without my making my mind up to do so. Also smarter than I've ever been before. I'm hit less. I just don't make myself available for it.

This all means even more freedom, maybe some overnight slumber parties with lots of giggling girls, more activities and finagling more time away from home.

# MINE

CAPE MEARES
1953

I've become a master at escaping the house, especially on the weekend nights. During the daytime it's easier to disappear, staying away through dinnertime, not so much. Trick is, plan a slumber party for Friday or Saturday night; get permission during the day and then bust out early.

This week Friday works for our group of girls. We are all ages, shapes, and sizes. Most of us have known each other for years and everyone feels like family. Mom is quick to say yes today, so I set out before Dad gets home from work—perfect.

Tonight, right in the middle of a great big giggle, us girls are interrupted by a *BOOM.* A sound you can't ignore. You feel it almost as much as you hear it. We stop to look at each other, around the room, then up at the ceiling.

"What was that?!" we say together.

"Was it a boom? You know, one of those sonic ones?" the youngest of the group questions, following her big sister over to take a look out the window.

Funny, what do they expect to see? It's not like a boom

shows up in front of your eyes. It's just a sound in the air that happens now and then.

"I don't know, sounded different this time, more like something closer, to me," says another. She hesitates, but then takes a peek out the front door.

We go back to our games and skits and giggles, leaving it up to the adults to figure it out.

The night grows late. We decide to set each other's hair, then hunker down for some rest. All I can think about now is staying dry. There are only a few hours till daylight, so I bet I can make it. In the lull just before sleep, I think about that sound. It's true, that boom was a little different than the big sounds we've heard in the past. It was eerie, but then booms have always sounded eerie to me. I think it has something to do with how the adults react when it happens. How it throws them into conversations about war times. I need to remember to ask Mom about it when I get home tomorrow or maybe try running it by Bubby; he always knows about these things.

The morning comes early. I'm relaxed and relieved. I smile to myself, but then I quickly hop to my feet and head for the bathroom. Carefully tiptoeing over sleepy, curved bodies, heads covered in rag curls, I'm just tickled with myself! I can't help it, cause I'm dry as dry can be. This happiness comes from knowing that I've finally reached a point where I don't have to let myself down anymore, where others might view me differently. Where that pit of disappointment I get, when I lose control, just might visit me less and less from here on out. Can't get too confident, though. I know what happens when I do.

On my way home, I swing in to see Mom at work. The post office seems busy today and extra interesting because there's some gossip going on.

Mom finally nods my way, reaching her hand my direction under the postal cage. Her way of showing me that she knows that I'm here, but is clearly not finished talking with her customer. I watch them carry on. She mostly agrees silently, but you can tell Mom's eyes are wider than usual.

Suddenly, I pick up on what all of the gossip is about.

A mine?

They are deep in conversation about what rolled up on the beach yesterday. Us kids saw it lying there, but left it alone. It looked kind of oblong with poky things coming out all around the wider part of it. Lots of weird things roll up on the beach, though; all sorts of objects are discovered there. People always pick and poke, and this time it was no different.

"Late in the evening, it just exploded! Right there!" the customer said with disbelief.

"I guess it rolled around in the waves for a while when the tide came in, lapping it back and forth, then, BOOM! There she blew. Did you feel it, Evelyn? I can't imagine anyone not feeling it!" The customer doesn't give Mom a chance to respond, she just goes on and on.

"They say windows shattered as far as five miles away, across the bay, in Bay City!"

Mom eventually jumps in saying that it scared the dickens right out of her. The house and windows shook, and Bubby couldn't believe his ears. She tried to get him to stay put, but Bubby just had to go check things out. I imagine he took off like lightning. I think Bubby likes to protect Cape Meares; plus, he's always curious and wants to know.

"Yes," the customer said. "I think a lot of people needed to go check it out for themselves. I'm sure Bubby wasn't alone out there."

Mom and her customer go on talking. I decide to stay put and listen for a while. They talked about how mines show up on the beach from time to time. How people skirt around them and get suspicious. And so they should, I guess. This time they had to stop kids from climbing all over it and hitting the pointy things with sticks. A few adults put their heads together and decided that notifying the Coast Guard was probably the smartest thing to do.

"Thank goodness they did," Mom said, raising her arms high in the air to make her point.

The Coast Guard showed up and immediately shooed people away. They tied the mine to a log to keep it from returning to the sea, then roped off the area so that nobody could get close to it. Somebody from the Guard stood post and watched.

"Makes you wonder how many more are still out there, shallow in the water." Mom's customer thinks out loud, her head turns toward the sea. She pretends that Mom has responded, adding, "Yep, the war has been over for quite some time now, but it sure continues to scare people."

I know better than to interrupt, so I decide to skip out to let them finish their conversation. Just before I put my hand on the doorknob to leave, I turn to look at Mom. She gives me a smile and a low wave—the heal of her hand propped on the counter.

Because the beach, and the actual spot that it happened, is not far away, just a block or two, I feel the need to check it out for myself. There's still a rope there and lots of chattering people, but I guess a bomb going off on sand, in shallow water, doesn't show much damage. I see a difference in the color of the ground, and the bank close by, it seems a little black, but that's about it.

When I listen to others at the location and about town, I hear about the young man that stood guard. How dark it was outside and how he had just been out to check on the mine because he had thought it had moved. Sure enough, I guess it had. Just as he returned, clearing the safer side of the rope, it blew. HE RAN, startled and stuttering. They say that he was beside himself with fear. I can't imagine how he felt so close to it all.

Mom lifted her line in the sand for me a year or so ago. I think once the wild waters finally took our Bayocean, and after moving us to safer ground, she felt a little better about giving me freedom to go there, letting me satisfy my beachcombing desires. Besides, I'm old enough now. But today, I finally get it. It's not just the undertow and the ocean's massive power Mom was concerned about. It was also the mysteries that lie beneath it. Turns out, she's been right all along. I should have known it my whole life—how important it is to give our ocean the greatest of caution and respect. Now, it's clearer than ever before, the fact that I need to be happy with my touch at the very edge of it. As much as I'd like to think of the ocean as a safe place of my own, it's not, and it never will be.

# High in the Sky

I see this move as a final one—much more permanent than any of our past homes. Bubby finally talked Dad into buying a piece of land not too far from the Lighter's house. Together, they've built a brand-new, much bigger, house there. There's an inside bathroom, lots of bedrooms and two big bay windows in the front.

I've come to realize that Bubby and Carp can be very clever boys. Bubby is more like a man now, tall, catching up with Dad's size, and Carp is not far behind him. It looks like each of them will easily pass Dad up.

I watched Bubby fight Dad once—now that was a sight to see. I think it boiled down to differences in opinion over how to correctly build a house. Bubby takes carpentry class in high school and knows a thing or two more than Dad knows about building, and I think it ticks him off. Dad likes to take short-cuts; Bubby likes to do it right.

Anyway, whether it's a house, a trap, a raft, or whatever, Bubby likes to build and Carp likes to help. I'm best at watching and trying things out on my own, of course.

The latest creation is as amazing as I've ever seen anything built before. Bubby, Carp, and a neighborhood family friend, Verny, have decided to build a swing. No, not a simple rope, with an old tire hanging from a shady tree, that would be too easy. More like the biggest, baddest swing you've ever seen in your whole life!

One day, after returning from a favorite, peaceful spot watching hundreds of pollywogs turn into frogs, I saw them putting it together. A large cable slung high over the limb of a huge tree.

Wow. . . . How did they get it up there?

I'm not sure how many feet of cable it took, but I'm positive it goes way taller than any house I've ever seen! The cable itself is wide and round; it even fits big in the boys' hands. The seat is a thick board with a hole in the middle, the cable runs through it with a knot tied on the underside. There's a small rope attached to the knot so that the seat can be reached from all different areas of the slope below it.

For days I watch them, climbing up the hill, cable and the swing in hand. Up to the mossy-covered fallen tree that lies in front of its stump, which sits in front of a great, big tree full of needles. I see getting to the jumping point is a task by itself. The swing doesn't just come to you—you have to go to the swing; no biggie, I can handle that. But, then there comes the leap. I study the trickiness of it: how you have a choice between the mossy, fallen tree or the stump above it, as a jumping point. How your hands need to grasp a few feet above the seat, and how you have to scooch them up the cable to give yourself enough room to jump on.

Every jumper hesitates; they gather a breath and some courage before they try it. I can see already, in your gut, you know you have to just go for it in one quick motion or you will tumble down hard, landing splat onto the thick brush that grows on the slope below. That throwing your legs over the board and then wrapping them around the cable as quick as you can, has to be the first thing you think about. It's then, and only then that you can, relax. Relax?! Maybe not, 'cause once you're on, you begin to feel the thrill of the ride. It swings you down, then up, way over the slope, the overgrown brush, the electrical wires, and the road below.

Bubby nudges anyone that stands around watching or looking at it.

"Go ahead, try it," he says. "Here, Elin."

I suppose he might enjoy the thought that I may fail, tumbling hard down into the bushes—I'm sure he would get a kick out of that. Can't let that stop me, though.

Anyone brave enough to step onto the mossy fallen tree, let alone the stump above it, pauses to concentrate, and I'm no different. Some people chicken out, not me, I just have to do it.

"Okay," I say to myself, setting my mind just right.

Pulling air deep into my lungs—ready, set, go!

My first ride over the tree tops takes my breath away. I can't believe it. This must be what flying feels like. I've dreamt about having the power to fly. About how wonderful it would be to take off through the air and go far, far away. Not in a machine, never a machine, but just me and the wind. This is about as close as it gets, I think. The cars below must see us high in the sky! With each sway I can hear the creak and pop of the cable pulling at the tree above. There's the fluttered feeling of my stomach as it takes a bit to catch up with itself, like it's been left behind a split second more to savor the moment.

Finishing the ride can be as tricky as starting it, so I'm cautious all the way to the hop off at the end.

I did it; I can't believe I did it!

Mastering the swing surely makes me one of the bravest, toughest of all. Just like my brothers. That's okay in my book.

And just when I've mastered keeping up with the boys, they step it up a notch—that's just what they do. Bubby decides that he needs even a taller platform. Yet another place to jump from that makes this thrill even better. He figures building a platform above the stump, the one that sits just above the fallen tree, is the best place for it. And so in no time, he's put together a super launch built with two-by-fours.

"This'll make the ride even better!" he says proud as punch.

More and more kids are drawn to it—adults, too. Even though the swing is built just a trail walk from the house, Mom won't come see it. I think the stories keep her away; she may be afraid to go there, to witness her children flying high in the sky. I know she appreciates our freedom and very much enjoys hearing about our adventures, even if we live on the edge of the Earth sometimes. I think, when we talk about it, when our eyes light up, she sees some happiness there and refuses to take it away.

# Winds of Gayle

Babe is in her stall, well, her half shed-half stall, I should say. I wonder what kind of mood she's in.

"Whoa, Babe," I say quietly, running my hand along her side. She makes her horse sounds and flips her tail. She's pure black, her shine so black it's almost blue. I can see that name "Jet" all over her; she's always been Babe to us, though. Maybe that's what makes her a grumpy horse. I certainly don't like it when people call me something other than my own name.

"Let's go, Babe," I say, pushing my words up toward her ear. She flicks it, like there's a pesky fly nearby; her eye looks at me sideways.

Leading her out through the yard I see Mom pulling dead leaves and flowers from a bush next to the house. She looks calm, in her own world. I've noticed her growing interest in all things green and the beautiful colors that bloom from them. She stops a moment to look over at me.

"Careful, Elin. You know how she can be."

"K, Mom."

I'm quick to decide that the abandoned house on the other side of the neighbor's place down the road, might be the best plan for mounting her. I've left the saddle behind; it's heavy and way too hard for me to cinch her up by myself. I'm just not strong enough, and Babe fights the tightness by pushing her belly out. Few things are worse than a loose saddle on a horse; things can go from good to bad really fast; so bareback, it is for me.

Holding her reigns in my hand I lead her up to and alongside the porch of the abandoned house. The porch sits a few feet up from the ground making it much easier for me to mount her from here. I park her for a moment to have a little chat.

"Can we make it work this time, Babe?"

I stroke her back lightly, then gather the reigns above her neck. Holding tight I give it everything I have, swinging myself up and over, landing in the slope of her back.

I'm ON. First try this time—I'm ON! Before I can blink, she takes off; I hang on for dear life! I know Babe means business all too well. She removes whatever comes close to her, always, and so she runs fast and hard, slowing only to kick things up now and then. But, I'm onto her. I'm ready this time. She cannot shake me, and I am tired of being tossed aside!

I hold tighter, knowing that if I just hang in there, strong with all my might, that I can show her that I'm good for her, that I am someone she can count on. If she would just let me belong with her, then she'll understand—she'll get me.

Babe zips off the road onto the pasture, still in a fit, but slows her run to a trot. Her head is tossing back; I try and calm her. She takes off again. This time crossing the pasture. Not far from the swimming hole, she slows to a walk. Just when I think things are going the way they should, she throws a buck that would be impossible for anybody to hang on to. Doesn't matter who, how strong, or what size you are: Dad, Bubby, Carp, anybody! I catch a thought midair that tells me I'm done for—I'm through. Landing hard, I feel something under my back.

Uhhh! What am I doing! Letting my limbs fall limp, closing my eyes, I lay still. I'm not ready to know whether she's broken me.

"How much abuse can you take from one horse?" a voice questions, standing over me. I see her now, above my head. Squatting down, she leans over and looks at me like I'm an idiot. "Enough is enough, don't you think?"

I realize it's Gayle, one of the neighborhood girls that usually only speaks with Niecie; her age is somewhere between the two of us, so she's older, at least couple years or more. She and Niecie aren't that close cause there's a wild side to Gayle; Niecie is opposite of wild. They've stayed cordial friends, though. I'm surprised she's even talking to me. Her sidekick is a tough-looking, dishwater blonde even smaller than Gayle. I'm younger than both, but have easily passed them up in height. I've seen Dishwater around before, but never heard her talk. She's just standing there, staring at me.

Still upside down in my view, flat on my back, I realize Gayle might stick around. Maybe she's checking to see if I'm okay? Maybe she's just bored with nothing else to do? Dishwater is still peering at me from behind her.

"What do you think, Elin, want to take a break from all this horsing around?"

Gayle grins, then exhales a cigarette puff, rounding her lips, forming a couple of smoke rings. Lying here I see the smoky O's float away, distorted, vanishing into the sky. There's something cool about her, some wisdom. Like she already knows what she's in for in life. She seems more grown up than all of us put together. An afternoon with her just might do me some good.

Finally pulling myself up to a sit, "Okay," I say, counting on that single word to make all my bones stay in their right place. My lower back commands a hard rub from my hand, my other hand shoves the small log aside that broke my fall. Boy, I'm going to be sore tomorrow. Both hands on my back now, my eyes search the pasture—Babe is long gone. I'm sure that was her plan all along. I'm also sure that Bubby's just going to be thrilled with me.

I decide to shake it off and join Gayle.

"Want one?" Gayle holds out the pack of Winstons, balanced on the flat of her palm.

"No, thank you," I say.

Not a chance. Last thing I need today is more pain; I'd get my butt kicked for smoking.

"Come on, this way." Gayle uses her cigarette hand to motion toward the ocean.

After a short walk we come upon a huge, gnarled log, a gigantic root lying on its side—the best of driftwood. I swear it's bigger than a car.

"Here we are," she swings her hand toward it.

There's a bright-blue nylon scarf blowing in the wind tied just above the entrance; I duck in.

"It's not much, but I call it home," she says, attempting a good tummy laugh, but with Gayle, her laugh comes loud from her throat, catching you off guard sometimes. One of those laughs you can hear a few blocks away; you always know who it is. Of course, I know she's kidding. Dishwater knows, too. She turns herself to squint at the ocean and takes a drag from her cigarette.

"Nice view," I say. "And, listen, it's like we're tucked inside a seashell."

I think of the hundreds of times I've held shells up to my ear to hear what's inside.

"Yeah, it sounds like the ocean, but to be honest, maybe like the ocean trapped," I add.

"I know what you mean, I think it's the way the wood is shaped," Gayle brushes the arch above our heads with her fingers.

She runs them up, across, then down the roots on the other side. The wooden ribbon of color makes me think of Stickhorse.

Should of rode Stickhorse today, instead, I think to myself. I'm feeling the soreness setting in and more stiffness in my back.

The three of us fit snugly in Gayle's gnarled fort; with any more visitors, it would be crowded in here. All of us face the water, chins on our knees. I run finger lines along the sides of my feet in the sand, pushing in deep enough to feel the wet, left-over high tide that slid in, then back out again just a few hours ago.

"So, Elin, besides the horse, how's life treating you? You having any fun?"

I'm not sure what she's getting at, so I shrug.

"I make a point to have a little fun every single day." Gayle says, angling her chin up like she's thinking, planning the next fun thing right this very minute. I can see how pretty she is. Her beauty hits you as an afterthought, though, certainly not the first thing you notice about her. I'm jealous of her confidence, her breeziness, how she tells the world SHE belongs—not the other way around.

"Your hair is looking cute these days, your body, too. Vah, vah, vooom!" she says, her elbow nudging me, I topple over to the root side, but catch myself.

"Bet the boys are starting to pay attention." She adds, checking my figure from head to toe.

"Life sure gotta whole lot more fun for me when the boys started watching," she smiled and flicked her ashes.

Again, I shrug, still not sure how comfortable I should be, opening up with her, and Miss Dishwater over there.

There's a side of me that has hoped very few had noticed the recent changes my body has made. As I go about my life, my head can hardly keep up with it. It seems I shot straight up overnight, then shortly after, straight out, if you know what I mean. It's all a bit confusing, if you ask me.

I decide to turn the table and put the subject back on her. "What about you, you have a boyfriend?"

"Yeah," she says, at the tail end of a smoke trail; her eyes are smiling. I see there are lots of words behind them, but I can tell that her sudden quiet means she's not willing to share them right now. It's okay.

My stroll home is chilly, sore, and gray, but all is good. I've learned some things: that you can't force yourself to belong where you shouldn't be, and that when you open yourself up to new possibilities, you just might gain a new friend. I may have lost Babe along with a bit of my pride today, but I'm happy and thrilled that Gayle blew my way.

# Nice Boys

He looked at me and smiled. Surprising, 'cause I just planned on staying on the sidelines to check things out. I guess he's a brother I've never known about.

What a shock it is to meet a family member that I didn't even know existed. Sure, I've heard his name here and there, but never put it all together.

I wonder what Mom thought when she first found out.

This does explain some of the comments I've been hearing from Mom. Things like: "Perry, is he planning on staying here for long? What do you think he needs or wants?"

Later on, this very same day I heard her in the kitchen with Niecie, "Well, he can't deny him, that's for sure; he looks just like him."

I can see what Mom is getting at. He's a grown adult, tall, has dark hair, and looks exactly like Dad, only his features aren't as sharp. They're soft and more settled, and his smile looks like he means it. I really don't like my dad so I'm pretty sure I won't like him either. That smile could be made out of nervousness or his plan to set a charming first impression, only to reverse it into something ugly later on down the road. Few boys have treated me in a nice way; I don't expect him to be any different.

I remember the very first boy that was nice to me; Sammy was his name. I was nine or so, and now that I'm older, I know what it was—a crush. He visited Cape Meares during vacation time right after all of the hustle of the big move. We were about the same age. We would play-act skits under the trees and run around with the neighborhood kids, but for some odd reason, we couldn't keep our eyes off each other, brushing our hands every chance we'd get. His touch felt like some sort of sparkling moment. We would find excuses to hand each other something just to feel that spark again and again. I remember reaching out to him, exchanging sticks and ferns; we liked to create things, lay a fern roof above our heads propped up on a couple of tree limbs, then we'd sit underneath them for a while.

One time, we wove together a beautiful fern door, climbed down inside the hollow of the big tree stump and pulled it shut. Just a green, fern-stick door between us and the world. We sat alone together; he leaned in for a kiss—my first kiss ever. I never told anybody 'cause I was afraid to.

I've always known, there's no such thing as a nice boy. But, now, once in a while, I catch it. I see that very same spark between a boy and a girl. How the boy will steal a touch or he looks at the girl with moments of gentleness.

After a while Sammy stopped coming to Cape Meares. I'm not sure of the reasons. I never forgot him, though, and I'm guessing I never will.

I discovered another nice boy on the bus ride between here and our school in Tillamook. A seven-mile ride, each way, that was better because of him. He would offer a seat, or move over to make me more comfortable

Maybe I have it all wrong in my mind—could nice boys be everywhere?

This being a brand-new, big brother, I wonder: is he a nice boy? Not in a crush way of course, but in a human way? In a way that could turn into a friendship?

I can tell the family doesn't feel he fits right. Like there's something a little off about him. So far, I can't see it myself. I hear words like "peculiar," and there's some eye-rolling going on behind his back. Except for the fact that he's a bit more hyper than us in his movements and that he's quite a bit older and already has a family of his own, I don't understand why they feel the way they do about him. I still can't believe we didn't know of him before, but, I guess it was a big secret that my dad was married to another woman when he found Mom. Makes me wonder how Mom felt when she learned about it all.

Has Mom always known? I wonder, did Dad tell her when she fell for him in the prune orchard?

My new brother certainly makes things lighter at the dinner table; his expressive hands and lively words have lifted the normal heaviness to something bearable. So far he's at best a good distraction.

After dinner, a few of us head out for a walk toward the beach. Midsentence, New Brother scoops up a football along the way. He topples it back and forth between his hands. Lobbing it over to me, I fumble a little, but then I'm quick to get a grip. Half shocked that I'm included in this game of catch, I twirl the ball between my fingers for a moment before tossing it back. Funny how just one, small gesture can instantly bloom a friendship. I decide right here and now that there is something nice about him. That he may be different, but different may be okay and good.

# Two Years Later

# Like Water

Cape Meares
Late Summer, 1959

I see his fist coming and duck; instinct I think it's called. Although, I immediately regret it, because I know ducking just adds fuel to his fire. I believe anybody would do the same thing, 'cause I think it must be an automatic reflex preset in your body for your own self-protection.

Dang it! There's no question things will get much worse from here. He has a handful of my hair, the other hand is revving up plans for my face. I know this story; I'm sick of it.

"Perry!" Mom said, annoyed. She said just that one word though, she knows better than to say more. By her saying his name alone, I know she's at least trying to get him to hesitate, to rethink his actions.

I decide to fall to my knees. On my way down to the floor, his hand misses the middle of my face but catches my forehead.

Ouch!

Without meaning to, his hand gave me the momentum I needed to roll away.

My feet find the ground and without a second thought, I take off running. It feels odd to run from him, but it also feels right. When I was younger, even a few months ago, I couldn't dream of such a thing, but this time I have to.

Running hard and fast, there's no way I'm slowing or looking back. He could be on my heals, eager to finish the job. I don't know if he's there, and at this point I really don't care. Veering off the road, sprinting onto the meadow, reaching the other side, I decide to go for it—the swimming hole, the dike. Surely, if in fact he is behind me, he wouldn't dare go in after me. Come to think of it, I've hardly ever seen him in the water.

My feet hit the edge of the muddy grass, and then I'm in, head first. The sudden shock of cold yanks at the air in my lungs; I manage to keep most of it, though.

Under now, I see the sliver of light that glows through the murky water. It's the ray between shadows that shows when the dike is open. Us kids have learned over the years that there are two indications to look for when tackling this mission: that ray of light and the direction of the current. The current is pulling at me, so I know this is my chance, an invitation to conquer and leave my fears behind.

I can do this.

And so I do. A sense of peace washes through me. I've always felt that way surrounded in water. Sometimes, I just want to stay here, to disappear in it. I know that I can't, but I want to. Just as automatic as ducking, my hand begins to guide me, my body sliding along the dike door. Turning myself just right, slipping through the ray of light to the other side. Even though I feel this is where I belong, instinct, once again takes over.

Nose first, I pop up through the surface; new air fills my lungs—I made it!

I glide for a moment then flip over onto my back, I just

want to be still, to push myself to relax, to steady my pumping heart. I let the water hold me, hug me.

"Okay, Elin. We have to stop meeting like this," Gayle says, startling me out of my thoughts. She's standing on the upper part of the dike. Letting herself down for a sit, she motions to the swimming-hole side.

"That was impressive! I haven't tried it myself. I usually only see the boys swim through—whoa, wait, what the—" Gayle stops midsentence.

"Elin, you sure know how to take a beating, your forehead! There are three, no four fingers. A hand print?! Last time I looked, horses don't have fingers or hands for god's sake."

She tips her head, "Looks like the stamp of a man's hand to me."

She said it like she knew what she was talking about. I want to ask her why it is I hadn't seen her in a while. It's been at least a couple of years. I almost asked her sidekick, but never got around to it. I did hear that she left with a man. That she may have even had a kid or two, but I didn't know whether to believe it or not—now's not the time to ask her.

We stay quiet for a bit, both gazing at other things.

Gayle has made herself comfortable, her legs crossed at her ankles, her usual cigarette playing back and forth between her hand and her lips.

After a few minutes, she asks, "What'd you do to deserve that?"

I searched my mind for a moment and realized that I didn't have an answer for her. At least not one that made any sense. What am I supposed to say: Because I exist? The fact that I breathe? Or, that my hair isn't the shade it should be? Who in their right mind would believe those are the reasons? But, it's the truth.

"He just always does," I say, dipping my head back letting

the water lap over the marks, hoping the coolness will erase them. My tears slip into the bay, so hot, they must be warming the water they float in.

"Well, that's your sign, Elin, don't you think?"

She gives me time to hear her words, then adds. "It's like water, we need it right? But, when things get dangerous, we get out."

# Graduation Day

1960

I've been sick for a couple of weeks now, dragging on with the most sluggish of head colds and fever. Today, still feeling like somebody took a baseball bat to my head, I need to get myself together as I expect this to be one of the best days of my life.

The family has always gathered for graduations, so I know that I can look forward to seeing everybody there. They've all left home but me: Niecie long ago, Bubby not far behind her, and Carp joined the Navy. He's back now, for a while anyway. Each of them busy pulling their lives together with others, even new babies on the way.

Mom is getting herself put together for the big day. Dad seems in a halfway good mood; he's whistling. He's been at me lately to find a job. I've been looking off and on, but so far nothing promising has turned up. I use to help Niecie at the bakery in town, that was well and good, but nothing to count on for the future. That's okay by me; it was hard to ignore the mouse droppings in the powdered sugar anyway.

I think maybe I'll get this day behind me, shake this sinus nightmare, then back to the job hunt.

My cap and gown drapes, pressed on the wire hangar, all white and silky. The crook of the wire twisted then hooked onto the curtain rod allows the material to hang freely. The window is cracked; the air giving it a little movement. Setting my white pumps below the billowing cloak brings it alive, like an invisible person inside is beginning to appear. I've decided on a classic form-fitted, pale-green dress to go underneath it. It's the kind of dress that takes its job seriously, snapping your shoulders and hips into place the moment the zipper has finished its glide. Once you're in it, you can't help but feel put together—feminine. It's a far cry from my tomboy, ragged hand-me-downs of my younger years. Also, a nice change from my good ole standby, reversible skirt that swished its way through high school. Sensible was its first name, plaid on one, side plain on the other. I could wear it at least a few times a week, with my white bucks, and still make it look like a brand-new outfit every day. I would've loved a poodle skirt, but only a handful of popular classmates were lucky enough to wear those.

My hair style is all about the smoothed perfection of an under curl and getting the bangs just right—every single hair in place from the bang at my brow to the tight pageboy curve that all of us seem to be shooting for. I keep my makeup light and fresh.

In line, my stomach flutters. We stand, single file strung from the entrance to the Theatre, through the hallway, back into the gym; the boys in red, girls in white. Voices humming throughout, all 125 "Cheesemakers" eager and ready to cross into lives of our very own.

"Elin! Look at you!" a gal behind me says out loud. Oh no, what now? I turn to her.

"Oh, my, and your eyes! They are the exact same color as your hair. You look beautiful!"

"Thank you," I say, feeling a tad more blush blend into my cheeks.

I guess I've never considered the brown in my eyes as matching the red in my hair, but they do. Turns out, they are both a shade of auburn. And, here's the best part: there's at least one person on this planet that thinks I am beautiful.

Hard to see, leading up to my turn at the stage, but to my surprise I catch them all out of the corner of my eye, even New Brother. There they are, my family. I wonder if each Cheese-maker has the mixed feelings that I have. I care for my family, of course, but, how is it that we grow past so many years of turmoil as full-grown adults and still care about each other? Is it easier than I think it is?

A diploma and a handshake, and then I'm ready for adult life? Just put it all behind me now? I'd like to think it's that easy, but my mind is betting it's not.

Later, at dinner, New Brother was his cheerful, expressive self. He insisted on paying and congratulated me on a job well done. He went on about some ideas on where I could live and work.

"Heck! I think you should go to beauty school!" he said, getting a good look at my face.

Really?

"The thing is, you could do whatever you want, Elin," he went on. "See that phone booth out there? If you ever need me, I'm just a dime and a phone call away."

# Last Hurricane

"I'm sorry, honey," Mom says. This time I think I see a tear in her eye. She sighs, that all-familiar, worried frown spreading up across her face.

"How do I do this? Where do I go?" I say, frustrated. Stacking and stuffing as fast as I can, there's no time to stop and acknowledge her. Besides, I can't handle even an ounce more emotion right now, especially not my dear mother's. I keep moving, packing, throwing my hands in the air.

He's still raging, slamming something in the other room. I feel lucky he didn't slam me out of my morning sleep.

"Mom? Where am I supposed to go?! He hasn't even given me a chance to figure things out. My head—I still feel like it's going to burst. I just graduated a few days ago!"

She's at a loss. I know it; I can see it.

"Why does he do this? He pushes everybody, every one of us away from him!"

I want to call him names. I want to use every filthy name he's ever used on us, reverse them, throw them right back into his face so hard that they stick there for everyone else in the world to see. I'd just as soon beat the living shit out of him than anything else, but I know that's just not possible. As tough as I've become, I would surely lose.

And then, I feel it deep inside—a collapse. My heart breaks knowing I'll never belong in his world, I never have, and I never will.

Moving about the room collecting myself, I quickly grab up the suitcase handle, step out of my bedroom through the living room. Wait. A vision of King's glass ball pops in my head. Dropping the case on the floor I run back to my room, slip my fingers through the net, yanking it from its place on the knob of the bed stand. Seeing Stickhorse in the corner, I pause a moment; deciding to leave the rest of my childhood behind, I make my getaway.

Mom follows onto the front porch; I can feel her behind me.

The ground below my feet looks a little different as I walk away, suitcase handle in one hand, the dangling net that holds precious glass in the other. I try not to look back, but I can't help it. After all, it's just Mom left standing there, watching her youngest, the last of her four children walk away.

Her hands lay limp on the skirt of her dress. *How does she stay so calm?* I wonder.

I decide to stop a moment, to look at her. She holds my gaze with a heart as only a mother could. I WISH she could be stronger, I WISH she could stand up to him, I WISH she could defend herself and those that matter to her most.

Will she be okay? Does she know how much I adore her?

With a lingering turn, I walk away. The dark, cool shadow of tree limbs overhead soon brightens to the sparkling, vast waters of Tillamook Bay. I stop again, to take it all in, letting the suitcase drop at my feet.

How can I leave this behind? My place, my adventures.

Scanning, I can still see a bit of it—Bayocean. It's right over there. Yes, the water has battered it, reshaped it, broken it down until it could no longer stand on its own, but I can still see her beauty, her toughness, her light.

"Shotgun!" I hear voices down the road. "Nobody rides shotgun today, everybody in the back," a voice of authority nips the debate before it could even get started.

A carload of Boy Scouts have finished their adventure for the day. They are throwing sticks, rocks, and shells into the trunk and are piling themselves in for the ride home.

I'm thinking, that's a lot of boys for one back seat. I watch a moment as they tumble over each other, finding a comfortable spot to sit.

"Everybody in?"

The troop leader does a walk around the car, closes the trunk then stops to look back at me before setting himself down into the driver's seat.

"You need a ride, Miss? We're headed for Tillamook."

"Yes, thank you," I say, quickly using my palms to dry my face.

"Hop in. Hope you don't mind a car full of rambunctious boys. You okay? Something you want to talk about?"

I look around at all of their faces, each boy sitting up eagerly awaiting my answer. For boys, I notice that they are quiet and well-mannered—there's even a note of concern.

The troop leader puts the gear in drive. I turn myself calmly facing the road to my future.

"No, it's just time for me to go."

# PART THREE

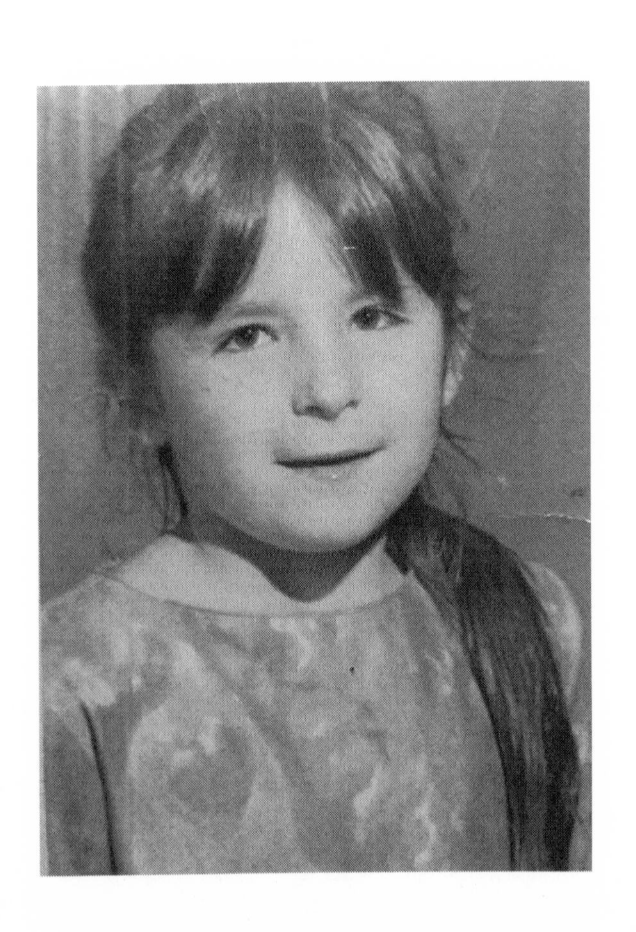

*Touched by confusion, he's sly.*
*Fear creeps through her bed; something's sad in her head.*
*Frozen, she shivers.*

# LU

## Age Six
## 1967

His hand is sliding, sneaking under her tummy.

She's sleeping. This strange, man thinks she is, anyway. He should realize, he should know, she's holding her breath.

She does her best to pretend and freezes. If she moves, she fears he'll hurt her.

She wonders what it is he's looking for, why is it that he needs to touch her there?

The sounds are unfamiliar, uncomfortable, then quiet. He disappears. She breathes, sinks under cover and fades away.

---

It's morning; her Mom's mood is light. Should she tell her? Will she get in trouble? Before she knows it, the words fall out.

"Mom, he touched me."

"WHAT? Who touched you? What do you mean? Where?"

Her mom's sleepy, morning eyes grow big. Pointing, she tries to answer all of her questions at once.

"That babysitter's friend. I dunno his name," she says. She tries to remember—she thinks it starts with an E.

"What do you mean, she had boys here? God DAMN it!" Her mom stomps away.

She wonders: Is Mom mad at me? She feels like throwing up. Maybe she shouldn't have told her.

—

Big words everywhere—"pressing charges" and "see a judge." What does it all mean?

They say her mom is doing the right thing by putting her six-year-old on top of the Police Chief's desk. The chief is a gentle man. He makes her feel safe. They talk about private things. It's easy, like she's telling about doing the dishes or sweeping the floor. Her mom is on the other side of the wall; the chief made her sit there. She hears them, though—she's crying.

—

"They say this is too much for a little girl to handle in such a public way!" her Mom shouts, releasing her smoky drag. She slams the car door; her eyes are red and angry. She raves on. "I just want to KILL him. His punishment will be some sort of quiet record in some fucking cabinet somewhere. It's all a bunch of bullshit!"

*Her name is Lu. She is six years old. Whom can she trust in this big, scary world?*

# Happy Camp

## Lu, Age Seven
## Happy Camp, Oregon

Silky, soft bits and pieces fall through my fingers. I sit curious, pulling my palm closer to my nose. Where do these pieces come from? Why so tiny? Where do I come from? Some are brown, some beige, and some white. This is not a regular child's sandbox. My backyard is the ocean, but not in a fancy way; we seem poor, really.

My mom's name is Elin; she has five kids: there's me, Mick, Charlie, Lacy, and Shay. I'm the biggest—the one mostly in charge, especially when Mom's sleeping, when she's not in the same room, or when she's stepped out of the house. We live in a shack above the beach in a place called Happy Camp.

Is there any happiness at Happy Camp? Yes, I think so, at least now and then. On the days between watching Mom getting hit and her madness with the world, we have long car rides, singing, middle of the night feedings, and stomping on the beach with jellyfish, driftwood, and my little brothers and sisters. Yes, a tiny bit happier in this shack, than before, where the bad touching happened.

I'm seven now. Bigger. I try not to think about the touching anymore. Feeling safe with people is hard, though; I flinch sometimes. People say that I'm shy, but really I just don't want to talk, and I certainly don't want to be touched.

My mom treats me like I'm her best friend, always sharing her feelings. Even though I'm much smaller than her, I can see how one minute she's weak and the next she's strong. It's so confusing sometimes. She seems in hundreds of pieces, then before I know it, she raises one big fist in the air with ugly words. I know when she's afraid too, sometimes I see her flinch.

Mom has beautiful eyes and pretty legs. I think her body is not too sexy, but, maybe just sexy enough? I understand that men like sexy, that stockings and fluffy hair get their attention. She hardly ever shows off what's good about her, though. She only puts herself together when she has to. I've heard her say, "I'm an independent spirit." That she doesn't really care what people think.

"If they don't like me, well screw them!" I hear her say. She says it all the time.

She's kind of like a boy sometimes. She's tough, and she can fix cars when they don't run right. But she's especially like a boy when she does things out loud with her words and her body—never holding back with all the noises a body can make. She can be really funny, laugh-till-you-cry funny. She has days where she's high and low at the same time. She likes who she likes, and will have nothing to do with people she doesn't like. She calls herself an "atheist." I don't know what an atheist is, but I know she is one, because she says so. She loves all kinds of animals, every kind—sometimes I think more than she likes her own kids. She's honest, more than honest, and she can be kind of selfish. "Generosity for the Underdog" is her motto. What's a motto? What's generosity? I have no idea, I just know that these are the things that she says.

Mom calls herself an "open book," sharing all sorts of stuff whether you want to hear it or not. She tells me everything. Lots of it I don't understand, but I listen as if I do. Some of it makes me afraid inside. She tells me that lying and keeping secrets is just plain wrong. She says that she likes to tell the truth no matter what. Because I'm the oldest, I get it; I know it's mostly adult talk, though. That's okay, I get to know everything about her life and about each of our father's lives—except mine. I can never know enough about mine. I've never met him before.

The men rule over her, always. She takes what they give her, even if it's mean. After all, just like anybody else, she enjoys a full tummy. I think she's always looking for love, too; just like food, she can't seem to get enough of that either.

I see her worry about food. Whether or not there's enough for all of us, for her. We also need milk for Lacy and Shay. A lot of times I think she goes from one pounding person to the next just for food and a roof over our head. She only stays for so long under their hitting hands, though. Then there comes another man, another explosion. She starts over; we start over.

—

"Lu! Come here! Get over here," I hear him say, as I climb my sandy beach steps.

He tries to make me move faster by fluttering his hands. He's down on one knee on the path below the shack above the beach. He looks skinny and angry, his bulging arms open and ready for me to walk into.

"Lu, no!" Mom's crying high up, near the door of the shack. He's beat her up, again. I can tell by her tears and also by the thick, ripped sweatshirt that she's holding across her chest. Some of her hair is stuck, slapped over her face, and she has red marks. Mom is hurting . . . again.

"Don't you move, Lu! You stay right there!" Her words are wet.

Bulging Arms is yelling, too. "Get over here, Lu, now!"

Mom cries, "Luuuuu! Don't you move!" through clenched teeth.

I stop to look at each of their faces, my head going back and forth; I'm realizing that I need to make up my own mind. I have to do what Mom says—no choice. Does Bulging Arms really think I'll go against her? This is not a time for me to be bashful; I shout up at Mom, "Only halfway!" holding my eyes on hers for an extra moment or two.

Mom is still sobbing. I take a few steps his direction, one eye on Mom.

"What . . . ," I say to him. My eyes now looking straight into his. "What do you want?"

He begins, "I love you kids, but . . . I can't . . . I just can't," he points both hands at her and moves his head from side to side, like he's given up. He then turns and walks away, just like all of the others before him.

---

Our shack is a mess, the refrigerator is down on its side, it looks odd lying there on the floor. There's nothing, not one thing in its place.

Like seagulls, looking for scraps, we pick about the room putting our lives back together. Mom's still stuck in her hiccup cry.

A sound comes from the front door. A surprise sound of breathing in backwards. Our neighbor Gayle steps in, her eyes are as big a saucers. She's one of Mom's closest friends, so there is no knocking, ever. She's shaking her head.

"Elin, you know what you have to do now, right?" her stare holds on Mom, waiting for a look or a nod.

"Look at you." Gayle's chin pulls in, like she's looking over glasses that aren't really there. I've seen this look on her face before. She uses it when she's making a point with her kids, when she wants to know what they're up to. Gayle lifts a chunk of the thick, torn sweatshirt, dangling at Mom's chest, and pretends to put it back in its place.

So, that's what friends do—pretend to fix things. I like that. It didn't fix the shirt, or her hiccup cry, but that's okay. It helped the look on Mom's face a little bit.

Gayle pulls her sleeves up and joins our flock, busy putting the shack back together.

---

Bulging Arms returns. I think he's drunk. He's no longer allowed to break my Mom, so he's breaking her car windows. People have always teased Mom about our car; it's big like a boat. They call it her pink Cadillac. It's a Pontiac, but, I guess that doesn't matter anymore, because our pink Pontiac Cadillac no longer has a single window. I'm not sure if it even works anymore.

Can cars even go without windows? The sound of glass shatters the late night at Happy Camp. It's one big bash after another. I think he's getting Mom back for standing up for herself. I guess it helps him to throw gigantic rocks and swing big sticks and boards. Not small rocks, like most boys throw or skip, but huge, two-handed rocks. I guess those rocks make his point better. Each broken window says to her that he no longer cares—that he's all done here.

The police show up. Lots of nodding. Their big lights and uniforms. They are taking notes. It seems all police do is wear their uniforms and take notes, put their notes in a file—in some stupid record somewhere.

I look at Mom, our protector, then at Mick, Charlie, Lacy, and Shay. She's alone again, what are we going to do?

I'm worried, but I know in some way, every man that

breaks her down seems to make her stronger. I watch it happen every time. I almost understand it, but not quite. There must be something thick around her heart, layers and layers of old sweatshirts maybe? I think she's tough. But, way deep inside her, she's our mother; that's all she is, really. Sometimes a bartender, sometimes a waitress, but still, mostly she's our mother. Tough is just who she is. She's hard on us; she even hurts us sometimes, but, we walk by her side, live in her moods, move with her changes—good times and bad times, we trip along with her like the sandpipers do, looking for bugs.

Maybe that's how we become strong, too? We grow up, wrap something thick around our hearts, and keep moving?

Us kids hunker down in the big, pink car with no windows, speeding with the wind toward Tillamook, or maybe it's Dallas this time, for a visit with a friend or a relative. I try to ask her, but we can't hear each other in the car unless we stop at a stop sign; the winds are the only thing your ears can handle. I know enough that with Mom, in a car, you never know where you're going. Lots of days, she just likes to drive for the fun of it. We even get a little lost here and there. No worries though, she always says she's like a hound dog, that she can sniff her way back if she needs to.

I soon realize that we are headed for the grocery store, where, on the road near the parking lot, people slow and look at us in a funny way. Sometimes, shouting comes from the car driving next to us. My brothers, Mick and Charlie, get up on their feet, so they can wave and smile at them. Mom takes their looks and comments with a laugh or a joke, her finger and her long, red hair flipping in the wind.

I can just hear them now, "We saw her again, today, that crazy mother with all those kids." They go on, "You know the one, the redhead that drives the pink Pontiac Cadillac with no windows."

# Sweet Scavengers

## Happy Camp

My thumb is in my mouth. It finds its way there no matter how hard I try to keep it out. Every night I slip my hands under the small part of my back before I go to sleep.

"I'm in first grade now; it's time to stop." I say to myself, again and again.

I hate my thumb. And, so, night after night, I lie uncomfortable, hooking them at my spine.

—

"Shhhhh, Lu," I flinch.

"Mom?"

"Ssshhh. Lu, wake up," she whispers in the night.

All is dark and calm in the shack above the beach. The lazy hush of the ocean is the only sound in the house. The room is chilly; my thumb is damp and cold. My sleepy feet hit the floor. I always notice tired feet forget how to walk, or is it more about blurry eyes? Blurry eyes without feet and tired feet without eyes, either way makes it hard to walk straight. It takes me a minute to get them both going the right way at the same time. Tucked away, in the corners of the room are my brothers and sisters deep in their sleep.

Mom digs for the last few pieces of Wonder Bread. She digs way past the red and blue balloons, the white part of the bag is pulled up above her elbow.

"Here you go," she says, handing me a slice.

Her pointer finger bounces lightly on her lips, "Quiet," she says, moving toward the front door. I can hear the air dancing with the trees as the door pulls open. A salty mist blows across my face.

"Shhh, look!" Mom points.

Letting ourselves down easy onto the front step, we sit. Below us, up on their hind legs, are three raccoons. They're just sitting there, straight up like puppy dogs, waiting. I can see they are a little nervous; they look ready to scram if they need to.

Mom leans down with her snack. Sniffing whiskers and twitching noses come closer.

"Watch their little fingers," Mom says. "Look at their front paws; their hands, they look human."

I decide, they do have fingers like real hands do, and they work just like mine do, too! My other favorite part is the sparkle in each of their pitch-black eyes. It's like someone put it there, like it's fake or magic. I see the magic in my mom's eyes too.

"Mom? Who's my dad?"

I know it's okay to ask this kind of question in the middle of the night, because that's when she likes to talk about these things. I also know that each time I ask her, she tells me a little more than the time before.

She taps a pack of Winstons on her knee. Using her teeth, in one quick swish of her chin, she strips the plastic wrap away. She then whacks the open end of her freshly opened cigarette pack against her hand. Tugging at the cigarette that sticks out the most, she pulls it free and places it on her lip, in that spot, the very same spot every time. I've watched it thousands and hundreds of times, but, it's what comes next that I find most interesting. One-handed, she opens the book of matches, and her thumb snaps a red match ball across the scratchy part. FLASH! It pops bright, ready to light her torch. Sucking her cheeks in two or three times, she pulls a great, big breath. Here it comes—her dream-spell face, the face she makes when she's having something delicious.

Happier now, she goes on to explain that my dad's name is Kim. I keep thinking that Kim is more of a girl's name, but she tells me that boys can have that name too; that he's a handsome man, half Apache Indian, the other half, "White or something, I'm not sure," she says. And, she goes on saying that he's a very nice person.

"You would like him, and you look just like him, too," she says, waving smoke from my face, like she needs to double-check that I still do.

She always ends our "dad talks" the same way.

"You are too young to know the whole story; I'll tell you more when you get bigger."

I quiet down, but still, I wonder if Kim knows about me. And if so, what does he think? Does he know where I am? Why not come see me?

I also wonder about Mick's dad and Charlie's dad, too. She does say that one was mean and sneaky and the other went to jail. I'm not too curious about Lacy and Shay's father; he's the one that likes to crash great big rocks into windows.

I tell myself that one day I'll get to know everything, maybe even everybody, but tonight is more about the ocean breeze. About sitting in the moment, sharing magic with critters, and learning as much as I can.

"Do you still like any of them?"

She snarls a little, flicks her cigarette ash downwind, then brings her face back to happy again. We go on feeding our furry friends.

I think Mom might be in her idea of heaven, these moments spent inhaling, talking, and feeding her sweet scavengers.

# LIFE

Some driftwood chunks seem as big as houses at Happy Camp. Us kids pretend to be in love there, raising our own families. We play, cook, and clean in the hollow part, inside them. Tall trees sway above us, all rough looking because of many hard winds. Some days are clear and blue, but most days are damp and windy making playtime tricky. Sometimes the wind picks up so hard and fast, it throws handfuls of sand in our faces. It's okay though, we just turn our backs for a second to let it pass.

There are waves and the water from the ocean, but I think our beach, in real life, is named Netarts Bay. There are high tides and low tides just like any other beach. Now and then, a whale or walrus rolls up dead, right up near the edge of the waves. It's exciting to see such a big sea creature up close. Sometimes the eyes are closed and sometimes they're open. I like them better closed. It just lies there rotting under flipping and diving seagulls. Eventually the creature disappears. I'm not sure how, maybe a tide or a storm takes them back where they belong.

Relatives show up at Happy Camp Campground, just down the way. They camp there past the big pile of driftwood. It's fun. Usually they are resting and relaxing after a big day of crabbing. I watch as Great Uncle Elias tosses live crabs into an old, boiling barrel of water.

Is it seawater? I keep meaning to ask somebody. Nobody talks about how scared the live crabs might feel just before they splash in.

I don't know Great Uncle Elias as much as I know my other Uncles, Bubby and Carp. He's my mom's uncle from Grandpa Perry's side of the family. What I do know, for sure, is that he has a wife with a perfect, flower name—Rose, and a crazy fun family, with bunches and bunches of kids. The fun side of Mom fits right in with them.

Some of our other relatives live close by. Not too far down the road, in a place called Cape Meares, lives my Uncle Bubby and his family. We don't get to see him much as I guess he and his lovely wife are very busy building things, and raising a big family of their own. I always think about how much I would like to play with all those kids. Mom doesn't say much about him. There are times I hear things about how Mom thinks Uncle Bubby and his wife are checking up on her.

Uncle Carp lives far, far away, somewhere up in Washington. He also has a wife. She has something extra sweet about her, like she's been kissed by kindness. You can't help but see it, there's a brightness that shows from the inside out through her eyes. There are more kids to know there, too. I always think, maybe someday when we're older, we'll get the chance to know each other better.

When I see Uncle Bubby and Uncle Carp, I think both of them tower above everybody else in more ways than one. Their height, yes—you can't miss them, they are taller than anybody in the room no matter what room you happen to be in, but also there's the goodness about them. I think it's a goodness that goes even higher than their tallness.

Mom's big sister, Aunt Niecie, is the closest of them all. Even though she lives an hour and a half away, in Dallas, near Grandma Evelyn and Grandpa Perry, she stays close with Mom—always there for her. It's funny how my uncles feel like gentle giants to me, but Aunt Niecie, being the oldest of them all, is the shortest by a long shot. So much so, that the family pictures make me giggle a little. It also makes me realize that people come in all shapes and sizes, that it doesn't matter how tall you are or what age; it's what's inside you that counts. I always think that you have to look through people to know who they really are. And when you're busy looking, be sure to ask yourself, "Can you trust them? Can you love them?"

When it comes to my aunts and uncles, I think, *Yes, I get to adore them.*

Our tummies sore from laughter and fun, with family, it's time to head back to the shack.

I notice our wet evening has asked the slugs to come out to play. They line the path between our shack and Gayle's house. They are kind of big, and they have long antennas that help them know where to go. Mick puts them head to tail, in single file, like they make us line up or stand in school. And, then Charlie follows him, eating them one by one.

"Damn it, Charlie. Not again!" Mom runs for the shack. I know what she's after. She's getting the salt, the Morton's kind, where the girl on the side has a nice dress, holding an umbrella.

Mom pulls open Charlie's three-year-old mouth and pours the salt in straight from the spout. She always thinks that the salt helps, because the slug slime shrinks when it hits it.

"Careful, Elin, salt doesn't kill just slugs," Gayle says, letting herself down for a sit on her back doorstep, near the slug trail. She strikes a match, lights the end of her cigarette, then sets her chin on the bottom edge of her palm.

"That kid'll eat anything," she adds, laughing her big, Gayle laugh.

Sometimes it's sad at the shack: fights with a man, weird babysitters, the scary howl of a windy night. I'm especially sad when Mom forces us to eat. Mick gets upset when he has to eat slimy spinach that comes from a can. She'll spoon feed him, if he won't do it himself. He gags it down along with his tears, or she'll make him sit, forever, until he finishes. She looks so mean, but there's also what looks like panic in her eye—a never enough food panic. I think sometimes her meanness comes from being tired and not knowing where money or food will come from next.

The shack is always happy when Santa shows up. This past Christmas he brought us some things. I just know he enjoyed the large, colorful bulbs that glow in our tree as much as I do. I think he must love seeing all of the trees around the world. Sometimes I lie under ours, my view going straight up; I get to see what the presents can see. I like the shiny ornaments, all different shapes and sizes. They get to shine with the lights and breathe in the pine smell all day and all night.

Mom always makes the holidays special. Our gifts are smaller than some people's, but that's alright with us. Santa gives us the best gift of them all, because he's the only one that can afford them. And, the food at Christmas is special, too—the powdered milk is not my favorite, but the rest is delicious.

Our shack can be a really happy place on the weekends. Especially when there are no men around, and life is calm and relaxing, everybody busy doing their own thing. There are many days that Gayle's house feels like another room attached to ours. Just steps away, we go over for play and have laundry time. We are lucky that Gayle and Mom are best friends. Gayle has a piano, and she sets up art time in her kitchen. They practice at seascapes with oil paints and face portraits with chalk. Mom takes a break now and then to plunk "Moon River" across Gayle's piano keys. I think the piano music and sound of the sea, just outside the kitchen, must help them create such beautiful art.

I like to listen about the times when they were kids, in Cape Meares, learning from and watching artists that lived there. I see the look in their eye when they speak of a woman named Barbara. About how interesting and talented she was. How she did Mom's portrait and had Mom try her hand at some art of her own when she was younger.

On the happy weekdays, there's a bus that picks up Mick and me for school, across the street by the great, big ditch. It pulls up, we climb on and leave for the day. We get to learn and play with others. I was shy at first, but after some time I finally warmed up. I even look at the teacher now when she calls on me. Yesterday the teacher clapped with us when the school announced that girls get to wear pants now. The news blasted over the big horn in the corner. Now, we get to play upside down on the monkey bars without our underpants showing. That's the best part.

So, yes. There's some happy life at Happy Camp in the shack above the beach. The question is: How long will it last?

# The Ax and the Owl

Bay City, Oregon
1969

We had to move. Bay City is where we live now. I really miss the shack, the backyard beach, and Gayle. After all, for a while there, I had a great big sandbox with no sides built on, practically all to myself, and Mom had a protector—her dear friend close by if she needed her.

I'm never sure why it is that we have to move all of the time. Maybe she follows a job, a man, or the next place costs less dollars than the place we live in now.

The name Bay City doesn't really fit this place. I think it should be Water Town or Bay Street. There's really nothing here, a couple of roads, a store, and a few neighbors. That's all.

I'm not used to the new house noises. Mom says, "It's just settling down for the night. The wind cools the house off, the cracks and creaks come from old wood."

I can tell, though, she's listening, too.

Different from our shack on the beach, this house seems bigger, and it has a huge, empty, hollow space underneath it. Anything or anybody could live under there. Probably just critters and insects looking for shelter from the wind, but, when I hear things, my mind creates scary people and big monsters, maybe even a ghost or two. I'm not afraid of ghosts, though, no matter how scary they are, they can't touch me. Ghosts are much less scary than people and monsters.

Tonight the bay winds kick up blowing through the hollow and up against the windows—more cracking, more creaking.

There's a rustle at the front door. I close my eyes hard.

"I'm okay, I'm okay, Mom will protect us," I tell myself over and over. It all just makes me want to suck my thumb.

I need my thumb less and less, but it's times like these that it wants to creep back in.

Lying on my tummy, my head on the pillow, I pull my thumb away, then turn my head toward Mom.

I keep my eyes on her face. I know I'm okay if she stays relaxed.

What's that?!

A sound out of place—this is not good.

She looks up from her book, her eyes search the room, she then looks down at me. She's probably wondering about my brothers and sisters, fast asleep, in the next room; I know I am.

A loud pop yanks her out of bed.

"Shit!" her eyes flash. "What the hell was that?"

Flying up into a heavy tiptoe toward the window, she peeks, then moves toward the bedroom door.

"That's it! I've had it. I'm sick of this!"

Faster now, she flies through the living room, grabbing an ax by the handle.

Holding the ax close at her side, she slowly turns the front doorknob.

First she looks through a sliver of an opening, then one, big strong pull, she throws the front door wide open, leaping onto the porch.

"You want to screw with me?! Come on! Try it!" she yells.

I wonder if somebody is standing there; is there a person in our front yard? Maybe a monster climbing out from underneath the house?

"You'd better get the hell out of here!" she warns.

She's holding the ax high in the air, high enough for a burglar and for the neighbors to see.

There's no reaction from the outside, just more wind. Her hair flies up, then settles.

Staring into the dark, she stands there listening harder. She steps back in, locks the front door, then moves through the kitchen to the back of the house. I poke my head around the corner to watch her. She touches the lock at the back door, pausing there for a moment, she checks the back window. Still holding her ax at her side, she's listening. Not quite satisfied, she quickly moves toward the silverware drawer. She reaches into the drawer pulling out a handful of kitchen knives, some big, sharp ones, too. Then, I watch as she makes her way back to each door.

"This should do it," she says with a grunt, sliding her knives in, slipping the blades between the wall and the wood that frames them. Her arms are strong, so the knives go right in. She's not happy till they are tight, the thicker part of the knives jammed hard, flat against the door.

"At least this way we can hear them if they try to get in," she says.

I feel a knot relax in my stomach; nothing can get us now. All is calm. We drift off, safe and sound.

Night after night I find myself listening for things that go bump. I'm never sure what's out there, or whether or not we are safe in any way after dark. Most of the time I feel safe in the daylight, as if life truly is brighter once the sun comes up. But, the black of night is just plain scary.

---

On this bright, new day, the front door flies open for different reasons. Mom has a big cage.

"What is that?" Mick asks. Us kids gather around.

"This is our new pet, he's hurt," Mom says. "At least I think it's a he. He was hit by a car."

I imagine my mother chasing an owl in the middle of the highway.

"He's our pet for a little while anyway, at least until he gets better."

She mumbles to herself about how legal or illegal it is to keep an owl, in a house, held in a cage. I give her a sideways glance. Still, I can't get enough of him. I'm fascinated by our new, wild pet sitting inches away, right here, within my reach. Face to face, eye to eye, we just look at each other. After some time, I shift my stare away from his serious glare.

"We shouldn't say anything for at least a while until I check into this," Mom says.

How could I not tell anybody? It's an OWL, for goodness sake!

I soon realize, he's just another mouth to feed amongst this wild bunch.

And so we live, side by side with Screechy. Now a full-on family member, with housing, feeding, and cleaning demands.

---

"Charlie!" I said, "PICK, now!" I use my harshest whisper.

I'm careful not to say it too loud, as I don't want Mom to know Charlie is goofing off. He just can't pick like Mick and I can. He's little and can't pay attention—much too young to understand how to clean a house.

"Here, sit like this," I show him. We scoot, one knee up and one knee down; we are human vacuum cleaners. Little hands full of lint, the teensiest leaves and twigs, food crumbs, and feathers. Company may be coming soon, so getting the carpet as clean as possible is a must.

"Come on! Move!!" Mom shouts from the kitchen. She's busy swiping, cleaning food crumbs off the seats of kitchen chairs.

"This place is a pigsty!"

There must be somebody important swinging by, as she can't seem to clean fast enough. I'm hoping all of this effort is for Grandma Evelyn and Grandpa Perry. I want to show them our pet owl, how I can read now, and do a handstand against the wall. Sometimes I can pull my legs away from the wall and balance without anything helping me. I'm sure they will be proud and surprised. I have a killer backbend to show them too.

Whoever it is had better be important, it's a lot of work being a human vacuum cleaner.

My escape outside came earlier than I thought it would. What a relief. Cleaning seems to last forever, longer than anything else I can think of. There's a ray of sun and some blue in the sky. I slip around to the back of the house. The wind catches me turning the corner. I can't help but bob and weave between sheets and towels clipped high in the air to dry. They are fresh from the bathtub, now dancing free in the wind. Laundry always makes me squint my eyes. They automatically turn up to the sky, checking for dark clouds and rain drops. If I think I see either, I need to run in and tell Mom right away. It's kind of a pain when the dry laundry gets resoaked by wet weather.

I always like the wooden pins that hold up the laundry; they seem handy. They squeak open, then pinch hard at the shoulders of shirts, belt loops of pants, and corners of sheets, towels, and washcloths. When there's no laundry, they perch there like good little birds, all lined up, waiting for the next batch. I like the way women clip them to their blouses, aprons, even hold them between their teeth just before clamping them over, snug to the wire they stand on. They hold so tough not even the big winds can take them away. Sometimes I see them being used for other things: clipping what comes in the mail left on the counter, or clamping onto a damp, dangling towel at the kitchen sink. I've even seen them used as toys; it seems one always hangs off the end of Mick's nose, fingers, or chin. I see one lying in the grass nearby. As I bend to scoop it up, I hear a car door slam out front.

Who's that?

The clip mindlessly finds a place on my sleeve. I pick up my step and turn the corner to see who's here. Life lifts instantly. It's Grandma and Grandpa! And, in their arms they carry fruit crates. Apples, maybe? Peaches or plums? I can hardly hold my excitement. My heart leaps out of my chest knowing this is going to be a wonderful evening.

Grandma Evelyn is wearing light colors: a blouse, white, with tiny pink flowers, a baby-blue sweater draped over it. Her slacks barely touch the bow tied at the top of her shoes. She wears a smile, too. She's warm as sunshine.

Grandpa is balancing a crate and scrambling after Charlie at the same time. You can tell he's happy to see us all, not by what he says—it's something about the fun way he's moving his body. It just never stops darting from here to there; he's everywhere.

---

"Well? What do you think you'll do Elin?" Grandma questions her while sipping water from a yellow cup. We must be out of Pepsi. I'm not sure what they are talking about, but it must have something to do with Mick or maybe the owl? I heard Mick's name in the middle of a serious sentence. And then I heard Grandpa ask if the owl is better. I decide to grab a book from the corner and walk over to Grandpa.

"I can read now, Grandpa," I say with a grin.

He looks at me surprised, then slaps both hands down on his lap.

"Well, then here! Let's have a read!"

The book is half my size so he helps me hold it as I climb up. We open the pages together.

"Once Upon A Time," I read, then look for his response. "You CAN read!" he says, then helps me with the rest of the story.

I'm sad to see them leave—lump-in-my-throat sad. There are always the bye-byes, see you soons, and see you later, alligators." All said in the most wonderful way, but it doesn't help much or make the time pass any faster till the day that I get to see them next.

They pull away; Grandma's kindness and Grandpa's whistle in the air.

—

We wake this morning and to our surprise we have an empty cage? Screechy has squeezed his way through a small broken square. I guess it was just big enough.

Eyeing the small gap, he must of pushed his bird body really hard to get through it. Must've taken him all night, but he did it! This makes me think that he's a bird in disguise. That maybe he's just a big, fancy rat with wings? Screechy has escaped! Now what do we do?

He's found a new spot, comfortable, on the top center of the living room curtain rod. It's a grand perch. He looks a little ticked off, but proud of himself. Come to think of it, all owls look proud of themselves, both in real life and in storybooks.

Now, for us kids, the trick is to get from one end of the house to the other without being attacked by this wild animal. His stare feels even scarier now.

When we slowly step across the living room to the kitchen, he watches our every move. I can't believe my eyes as his head turns all the way around to see the car pulling up out front, then quick, he whips it back around to watch us run.

"Wow, it's true, look! Owls can twist their heads in a full circle," Mom says in amazement.

We know who's out there. Our friends have arrived to help us catch him. Us kids are shut away, in other rooms, during the ruckus of the final catch. Darn! I wish I could see. The laughter alone would be fun to watch.

Soon, Screechy is tucked back into his cage. I look around the room. I can see our future all over the floor, that our super-human vacuuming skills will have to kick in soon; there are feathers everywhere. Stories about this exciting day, and sounds of our pet owl echo throughout the house as night falls.

A few weeks have passed; Mom is planning one of her driving days. This time, we are also on a mission: first, we place Screechy on top of the shed out back. Second, Mom hitches the front of his cage wide open, inviting him to return to the life he was meant to live. Screechy just looks down at her in his serious, funny-owl way. Third, we leave.

"Say good-bye, cause he might not be here when we get back," Mom shouts loud enough for all of us kids to hear. We each say our good-byes in hopes that he goes back home, all better now. All of us turn to give him one last wave as we set out on a lazy, afternoon drive. Maybe we get to have a picnic today? I can't wait for the bologna sandwiches and tall, frosty bottles of Pepsi goodness.

We decide to sing "Found a Peanut" and "The Skunk Song" on our ride to nowhere.

*"Welllllll, I stuck my head in a little skunk's hole*
*and the little skunk said, well bless my soul!*
*Take it out, take it out . . . "*

Charlie throws his hand in the air when he sings. Lacy watches, her lips catching up with the words a split second after ours. She thinks she knows them.

Mick, Charlie, and Lacy pinch their noses, squeaking out the last words, "I removed it…a litttttle laaate."

All of them giggle, I'm sure, imagining how it would be to have their little heads sprayed by a big, stinky skunk.

All of us know that Screechy will be moving on today, much healthier and smarter about how little humans live. Five sets of eyes leaning, poking at him for weeks now. I think, he must have found us just as interesting as we found him.

"Our Screechy is still a little broken, but better able to handle life on his own now," Mom mumbles as she picks up speed on the highway, flicking her cigarette butt in the wind.

Upon our return home, sure enough, we find an empty cage. Screechy has moved on.

I look high in the trees above us. I can't help but feel that he's sitting up there somewhere, no longer with his piercing glare, but with a better understanding of the world he lives in. I imagine him watching over us, a bit wiser, and forever thankful.

# Sleeping Giant

She's raging, again. Oh no. Why? My insides crumble. One moment she's resting, snoring, the next, she's twisted herself straight up onto her feet so fast her head spins along with the room. Her face flushed red, it looks angry and tired; sleep lines have pushed deep into her right cheek.

Our hearts are racing. I quickly hush the others so that she will stay calm. My urge to calm HER is just as important as it is calming her toddlers, but I choose to duck instead. She's screaming, swinging. I don't dare cup my hands over my ears for fear of more—even the little ones know not to do that.

"WHO DID THIS?" she screams.

I stand frozen.

One of us has been up to something. We have awakened the sleeping giant playing too loudly during her nap or maybe someone has touched or moved something they shouldn't have. Calm down! Talk to us! I want to say. My mind begs her, *Please, just talk, maybe whisper; we can hear you better that way.*

She rages on. "FINE! I WILL get to the bottom of this.

You'll all get it, till one of you tells me the TRUTH!!" She adds, through her clenched face. "I DON'T CARE WHAT IT TAKES!"

We stand, shoulder to elbow, to shoulder, lined up—trembling. She glares, her jaw tight. She storms away. We don't dare move.

The clinking jingle sound of the heavy, bronze buckle is coming from the bedroom. Watery eyes look my way, back to the bedroom door, then up at me, again—sweet little eyes looking for me to save them. Returning in a stomp, she's serious we know because of the leather she holds, but also because she's moving too fast for the room she's in.

"WELL?!" she demands.

Not one of us has an answer for her; all we think about is what she's holding in her hand. It's the monster of all forms of punishment. Even cutting our own switch from the forest or her quick, flashing slap is better than The Belt. Sure, there are belts, all sorts of them. But, she is holding in her hand THE Mother OF ALL Belts. Its worn, brown leather, has two long rows of bronze colored, metal rings that line from one end to the other. Rings that stick with you, like an octopus has sucked on your skin. The buckle itself could be a weapon. It lies across her palm, eager to make her point.

It's long, it's wide . . . and it hurts.

# Mick

Bay City, OR
1969

Today, like most days, I play with my brothers and sisters. Charlie and Lacy are in the front yard; Mick lobs a ball over their heads, it stays up there, in the air for a moment, then lands softly in my hands.

Mick and I are very close in age and have a really big love for each other—there's something dear between us. Sometimes all we have to do is meet with our eyes to know what the other is thinking. I hear the word ornery when people talk about him. I think it means that he's everywhere and into everything at once. He's more ornery than I am, but somehow we meet in the middle with a great big sister-brother bond that can't be broken.

Into the forest we go, slipping down the bank rolling onto a floor of pine needles. The trees tower high above our heads, outstretched limbs overlap each other making a ceiling of fluttering leaves. We dodge, bob, and sway through lean, twiggy trunks. Mick, naturally tries to climb anything he can. Hopping, jumping, his body full of fidget, half of the time he doesn't know which way he's going. I smile.

He is funny—so very funny, swinging from limb to limb. We stomp out a living room between the trees, and continue carving out an area for the kitchen. Rolling in logs for furniture, sticks and broken tree parts become a broom, a spoon, a hair brush. We gently push sharp ends into the soft earth, all in a row, building pretend walls between rooms. A stump makes for the finest of dining tables. Pinecones, leaf pieces, and tiny twigs are placed on slats of wood for lunch. After finishing our earthy meal of make-believe perfection, we dance breezy throughout our leafy living room. We swirl in smells of wet pine, crushed leaves, and fresh dirt. Holding hands we face each other, then push away. Together we stomp and shout "Fe! Fi! Fo! Fum!" our voices big, echoing high up into the trees. A deep, strange voice shouts back, "I SMELL THE BLOOD OF AN ENGLISHMAN!" Stopping our dance, we share eyes of terror; it's obvious we have awakened yet another sleeping giant. Our happy, make-believe world has disappeared. We break into nervous giggles, turn and hit the ground running, heading back to the bank as fast as our legs will carry us. Mick's ahead of me as I slip, slamming to my knees at the base of the bank. He turns, reaches down for my arm. We scamper up together. Safe now, we turn to each other for a big laugh and sigh of relief.

Arm in arm we head back to reality.

—

It is nighttime. I hear her sobbing. Heavy heart sobs so deep, I can tell it hurts. She's in that way, taking short, hiccup-type breaths in her cry.

"Mom?" I know better than to get too close. That mixture of fear and worry stirs inside me. "Mom?"

She can hardly hold her head up or down, she moves it

side to side, swaying in her pain. Her tearful face looks lost. I slip away to give her space, setting off to check on the others.

"Lu!" she sniffs. "Lu, I need you!"

My stomach jumps.

"Please." She reaches for me, and I go to her.

"Oh, Lu, we lost Mick," she says, hardly able to finish her sentence.

"What?" My stomach drops. There's an ache in my throat.

"His daddy took him." She's shaking; she's breaking. "He promised to bring him back! He promised Mick everything under the sun. Everything a little boy would ever want. How can I compete with that?" She looks me straight in the eyes, "How do I get him back?"

I'm shocked by her words.

"Please, honey, I need your help."

My chin quivers. I reach up to rub it, but then I tell myself that it's time to be strong.

She's crying, shouting after me. "Run! Hurry, Lu."

And, so I run.

It's dark. A black, starry night outside, my eight-year-old legs run franticly for help. I can't get there fast enough. Finally, pounding my fists on a familiar door, they answer.

"It's my mom." I shout, catching my breath. "She needs help."

"Please!" I say, through tears, "they took my brother."

# Months Later

# Wee Little Cousins

## Grandma's House—Dallas, OR
## 1970

Her hair is golden, flashing; her skin is kissed by the sun. Her existence is no-nonsense, strong, opinionated. There is no winning, after all, she is three years older. She's my cousin Bea Susan.

I see a dream room. A beautiful little girl's bedroom, in order—perfection. Delicate trinkets placed carefully on the dresser. Clouds of powder puff and perfume float in the air. Colorful, posters hung with care—adored. Bedding for a princess complete with stuffed pillows and talking dolls—pure comfort.

I'm holding an apple-sized lump in my throat; I have to leave.

Again, I have to leave. . . . Really?

My mind begs quietly, *Please, let me stay just a while longer.*

This feels like the opposite of my life—it's quiet here; there's a togetherness. It's where to be when things get hard. Maybe it's the normalcy of it, the sense of safety? It isn't just my cousin Bea and her room, it's my Aunt Niecie, my Grandma Evelyn, my Grandpa Perry, this charming small town—the community, busy and healthy. Life's heartbeat of goodness seems to happen right here.

*Please, I don't want to leave.*

Tears stream quietly, as I'm whisked out of town.

---

Weeks later, it's dark. I smell rain. I smell earth.

I'm groggy from the night drive but excited about my return.

"Come on," she says, "let's go play!" Cousin Bea Susan seems excited, too. We get lost in hours of play.

I adore Grandma's backyard. Organized patterns of blossoms sprawl past a small greenhouse. Gorgeous fuchsia baskets sway, wispy above our heads.

"Pop one," Bea says. "Pop it!"

I follow along, popping one fuchsia pod after another. There are shades of pink, yellow, and purple everywhere. Faces of pansies dance happily under an oversized cherry tree. We find ourselves masters at dodging bees, buzzing circles around apple trees.

Roses guard the front entrance. The milk has arrived. Cold, thick glass tucked neatly in the box on the front porch. I slip my hand through the metal mail slot built in the front door.

"Who is it?" I hear Grandma say. Of course she knows by looking at my fingers, but it's the game we play.

I can't wipe the smile from my face; I'm finally here—I'm back.

There's always the smell of fresh, crisp cucumber in the kitchen when it's lunchtime at Grandma's house.

First, a competition to see who can get their hands the soapiest. Fluffy clouds clean away the wonders of the backyard. Water drops race up, tickling the underside of my arm as I reach for the towel to dry.

Time to sit. We are served. We eat quietly. We lock eyes.

Then it happens. Somehow, my lima beans magically turn into cottage cheese, then something mystical turns cousin Bea Susan's cottage cheese into lima beans! It is our pact, our little secret. The first of many.

There are the giggles—all out, pee-pee-dance giggles, the kind that brings good tears to your eyes.

"Today we skip!" Bea says.

"Wait! I'll be right back."

I hear her push open Grandma's front door and beg, "Can we go around the block, PLEASE?"

Cousin Bea Susan returns, chin-up, grin on her face, taking obvious pride in her top-notch convincing skills; off we go, skipping along, chanting "Don't step on a crack, you'll break your mother's back!" Kicking pebbles and pinecones along the way.

Around her I have the pleasure of being the youngest. In the real world, I'm the oldest, responsible for a lot of my brothers' and sisters' needs and happiness. Cousin Bea Susan is more like a big sister than a cousin to me, and I know that she holds my heart just as much as the others do.

Cousin Bea is a trickster at times. "Close your eyes," she says. "No really, close them. Don't peek!"

A hint of something touches my lips. What is it this time? A green bean, fresh from the vine? Oh no, a potato bug?! Or yes, yes, yes a sweet piece of candy?

"Okay, bite!" she says.

I bite. Oh! Hot! Hot! Hot!! A dastardly belly laugh follows. She's done it again. A pepper, a hot pepper, of course. You would think I would learn by now. Maybe I don't want to.

The back room, past the kitchen, at Grandma's house is tiny. It has a small bed and canned peaches that hide behind a curtain in a closet. The smell in the air has leaked in from the garage; the dirt floor is covered in sawdust. Grandpa Perry likes to build things out there.

My bed lies under a small curtain made of plastic bubbles. We like to pop those too, just like the fuchsias outside. Sometimes, I lie there sleepy in the morning wondering what might be hidden in the wooden chest, against the wall, beside the bed. It's red with grey chips, or maybe it's the other way around? I'll have to ask Grandma for a look inside, one day. There must be something special in there. Sometimes we lift the top, just an inch or two, for a look inside.

"Quiet. Let's peek!" says cousin Bea. I know I would eventually peek on my own, she just gives me enough courage to do it sooner rather than later.

There's what looks like newspapers, letters, maybe a scrapbook. Also, a few bobbles. A bracelet, a looking glass? I hope soon to get permission to explore this treasure chest even more.

The attic can be a fun place to see. There's a train up there. Grandma sits in her favorite spot in the living room just below it. Little tracks fit together, and black train cars glide along them. It's really the only thing in the room. There's a few cardboard boxes, but that's about it. It's dusty, and the entire room, and what it holds, seems to be the exact same color. The natural wood and rafters are the same tan shade as the cardboard boxes. The only thing that really stands out is the train itself. One day, I asked Grandpa where he got the train. He said it came from Grandma's father, that they've had it for a very long time. They just keep adding to it, expanding it with more tracks and cars.

---

"But I can't swim! At least not like you can," I say, upset, knots in my stomach.

Cousin Bea Susan glides under the water near my feet; she

grabs hold and yanks me under. Panic sets in. Off she goes. I'm okay with being left behind. I cling to life at the side of the pool, regrouping, spitting, gathering air for the next round. A little playful sibling rivalry? Possibly. Since she is an only child I can imagine she might crave somebody of her own to pick on. I realize I might have cravings of my own, too, maybe seeking someone older, more kidwise, to come along and toughen me up.

As time goes by, we grow. It's late summer. Waves of heat blur views of the valley. A hint of grape rides the warm afternoon breeze. We are barefoot, always barefoot. Hot pavement—too hot for tender toes. Heading home, snug under one arm, we carry neatly rolled bath towels. Each towel contains a wet, chlorine filled, sun-faded bathing suit. A must-have in this hot, sleepy, little town.

The Dallas Community Pool is the place to be. Announcements, competitions, and friendships flourish here. The vending machine snack hardly touches the oversized hunger pang growing during hours of hard swim and play. At the end of the day, our faces are tight, our eyes are red, we are beat. Exhausted. Sleep will come soon.

Grandma Evelyn's tiny home shelters artful decor and a settled comfort. I hear musical, ticking chimes announcing the time. Velvet petals float, arranged lazily in a glass pitcher. Grandpa arriving home evident by the unmistakable squeak and slap sound of the back-door hinge. He leans in for a quick, playful smooch. Grandma shoos him away. She's giving him a sideways glance.

Grandpa turns my direction, "Hi, squirt," he says.

I stand guard with a big, bashful grin, steady, ready to flee from the whisker burn headed my way. I reach over and pull hard. . . . *SNAP!!* His suspenders are my only defense within reach. He lunges at me, pretending to give chase.

My heart jumps! More giggles. I head for the backyard.

There she is, my sleepy cousin, resting in the grass. I lie beside her, stringing a daisy chain in the making, listening to the winged flutter of a robin collecting dinner and the sound of crickets breaking into song as the evening sets.

I reach for her hand. She knows. I know, too. I have to leave.

Again, I have to leave? Really?

I close my eyes and say to myself, *Please, let me stay just a little while longer.*

# Evil Lurks

Tillamook, Oregon
1970

I've arrived home from my third-grade class. We live in Tillamook now. Turning the doorknob I can already feel that things aren't right on the other side. It's hardly ever this quiet with a house full of kids.

I step into the sadness. Things are worse than I thought.

Little Lacy glances over, her droopy, swollen eyes are wet and glossy. Her pudgy fingers pulled in tight, just as her jawline does when she's angry or upset. Her lips are swelling with emotion under a dewy-eyed, heartbreaking stare. She's physically hurt; a big sister can tell. I make my way over to her.

"What happened?"

Through hushed cry, choppy breath, and plump tears, she explains.

"He burn-dded me." Her tiny hand is wrapped in cloth. She raises it, carefully.

"How?" I whisper.

"Ober dere." She sobs, nodding toward the wall.

Where? Oh no, the electric wall heater?

Her breathy sentences skip and interrupt, each word forces her chin to jerk in an upward motion. My heart drops. The always-scary heater sets flush into the wall. It has coiled, red-hot wires covered by a heavy metal grate.

"He pushed me hhahhand." The word hand comes from her gut, loud with emotion and three-year-old confusion.

"Shhhhh . . . let me see." I whisper back. The fleshy back of her round, little hand is painfully branded with the crisscross shape of the grate that covers the bright-red coils.

My throat is filled with anger; I swallow. I just want to scream at this shifty-eyed, teenage boy to GET OUT! For now, I focus though, listening for his side of the story.

"How did this happen?" I ask him, careful with my tone. I'm very cautious; I wonder if I'm next. Even worse, if I push too hard, would he choose to harm the others? Has he already harmed the others? I glance toward Charlie—he's okay, and am now scanning the room for Shay. All the while, I'm waiting for his words.

Where's Shay?

I find her in a corner of another couch sleeping. This is a nightmare. Fearing more of one, I keep the peace.

"Here, Lacy, lie down." I pat the cushion. She swings her legs around and places her head against my jacket. She props her healthy hand under her burned one for support.

"I'll get you some water."

I head toward the kitchen, dribble some water in a small, plastic cup—the red one; it's her favorite. Taking it to her, I keep my eye on him. He's squinting with guilt.

My tummy hurts. It's partially the situation, but, I know it is hunger too. Lacy has closed her eyes so it's back to the kitchen for me. Our donated food only lasts for so long. Mom says, "Saturdays are commodities days, so soon we'll get more."

All the good stuff goes first. For now, there's plenty of canned beef; I'm not interested. I settle for raisins, reaching into the box for a dry clump.

Above the sink is a latched cupboard. Tugging at the latch, it swings open. I catch a waft of dirt, moss, and damp—the smell of a rainy day. The cubby acts as a fridge, a box that keeps things cool, not cold. Nothing there either: a butter stick, some Velveeta, and mustard. I don't bother checking the cupboard under the sink—it's mainly storage for a sea of Pepsi bottles. A nice collection—looks like lots of glass money under there.

The next cupboard over holds the powdered milk. My nose wrinkles, the fake milk just doesn't compare to the small carton of silky, white goodness that I consumed for lunch, earlier at school. So, I dig for more raisins, I'm tugging at the moist ones near the bottom when I hear Shay.

Baby Shay wakes with a whimper, and I go to her side. She's still the tiniest thing I've ever seen. She seems underweight, but I guess she's not; she was just born that way.

Shay is my sweet, delicate creature. A live doll that I've added to my small, raggedy collection of cloth and plastic ones. Mom lets me help with her a lot. She is a quiet baby, patient, nothing bothers her. Most of the time, she just watches her older brothers and sisters, happy, her eyes following, trailing each of our movements. She smiles easily. She's almost two years old now, but looks half the size she should be. Her tiny body is just built that way.

She smells wet, her cloth diaper is soaked. I sort through the pile of laundry across the room for a dry one. There's a sudden yank at my hand.

"I'll do it," Evil demands. I shoot him a stare, each of us holding a side of the diaper. I'm no match for him, so I have to let it go first. He picks her up and makes his way to the bathroom, shuts the door behind him, then locks it. The heavy, clunk sound of metal doesn't feel right to me. Why lock a door to change a baby?

I place my hand flat against the wood, near the knob. Waiting there quietly, I listen.

Charlie is up to something, around the corner, in the hallway. I can hear him voicing car sounds over the small wheels of his dump truck. I walk over to see what he's up to. I'm almost there when I hear her cry. It's like a surprise cry. It's coming from the bathroom; it's Shay! I run back.

"Hey! Open the door! OPEN IT! I'll show you how to do it right!"

Shay cries out again.

My mind is crazy, wondering what to do. I turn to look around the room. Maybe I can get in somehow?

I just know he's poking her with safety pins. I need to help her! He's hurting her. He's doing it the wrong way! Could he be touching her?

I'm always so very careful when I change her. Careful to push the tip of the pin through the cloth only until it touches the skin of my finger, I then move my finger to the side, flip the sharp point up toward me, or the ceiling, and then, only then, I push it through and safely clip it into place. Doesn't he know how to do this?!

I beg "Please!! Let me in! Stop poking her!" My heart is broken. I try the knob again. Why won't he open the door? What could he be doing?

Poor Lacy, now Shay?

That's it!! Mom's going to hear about this!

I hear the toilet flush. He throws open the door. "Here!" Evil says, tossing Shay into my arms. She seems a limp banana peel, thrown out. She folds herself into me, her face buried hard at my shoulder—quiet.

# The Big Cheese and Mother Bear

Tillamook, Oregon
1970

Mom is parallel parking her great big, banged-up car in front of the Big Cheese. Her palm slides flat against the steering wheel. She turns back and pauses. A glow-tipped cigarette hangs with ease between two fingers; she takes a drag, then checks and adjusts the rearview mirror.

"Sit down, Charlie," she says, cranking her neck to see. She needs to tuck the car in just right.

"I can't see through your fat head Charlie. DAMN IT, MOVE!"

I'm in the front passenger seat. Shay is lying across the seat between Mom and me. Lacy is busy in the back with Charlie; she's on her knees, tummy flat against the back seat, her forehead down, knowing better than to be in the way, but ready to spring back up on her feet once the car is parked.

Mom throws the gear shift into park, then pulls her keys.

"I'll be right back," she says, jumping out of the car, cigarette in hand, she enters the bar side of the diner. She must be after her paycheck, I think, while running my fingers through the knots behind the back of my neck.

We sit a while; Charlie and Shay nitpick in the back. Charlie's heavy hair still shows the flat of sleep on the left side of his head. Lacy is dressed, as usual, like a rag doll. A few strangers glance at us as they walk by. Mom pushes the bar door open. I hear her long before I see her laughing. She steps out, her head turned back finishing her conversation with somebody inside. There's music and sticks hitting pool balls in the background.

"I'll grab the kids!" she shouts.

"Come on, kids. Let's go have some burgers."

The Big Cheese is a favored spot for the locals. People say that it cooks the best cheeseburger in town. Us kids agree—there's nothing like it. We shuffle inside. A man sitting belly up at the counter tosses a comment over his shoulder.

"Well, if it isn't mother bear and her cubs," he nods a wink toward Mom. We clamber into a booth. Someone has slipped a nickel into the jukebox. The air fills with music, *"Jeremiah was a bullfrog. . . . Was a good friend of mine . . . !"*

I can't help but sing along. Lacy and Charlie feel the same way.

Charlie shakes his moppy head, and Lacy wriggles in her seat.

"Look!" Charlie shouts, lining his finger alongside his nose, pointing it toward the upper wall of the cafe. There's a shelf there that holds a miniature band, where a tiny drummer sits—a monkey slamming tambourines, keeping the beat. The jingle, jingle, bang, bang tickles out some laughter, especially with the kid customers.

The waitress walks over to us, pen and pad in hand.

"Elin, look at all of these well-behaved kids. What's your secret?" You can tell the waitress is raising her voice, on purpose, so that all can hear—I wonder if Mom will answer her honestly: that mostly it's her heavy hand that keeps us in our place or maybe the answer should be that we are simply afraid of behaving any other way. We hardly make a peep in public; it can hurt otherwise. It's easy to behave here though: it smells good, there's a lot to look at, and people seem to be happy.

I've always liked this cafe; it is shiny, silver-trimmed—maybe something out of the '50s? The adults say that it was fun in the '50s. If it looked and smelled like this back then, well, I can see why they say so. The cafe has slippery seats in the booths, squares on the floor, and padded bar stools all lined up. I imagine all those poodle skirts that Mom and her friends talk about, sitting there, high pony tails and ankles crossed near the floor.

Our waitress returns holding a tray full of red-checkered, paper-lined baskets, piled with warm, glistening fries and beautiful melt-in-your-mouth cheeseburgers. Mom finishes her talk, then snuffs out her cigarette, adding it to our ashtray centerpiece, already filled with six or eight lipstick-stained, leftover butts from the people before us.

"Scoot over turkey toes," she says, sliding in next to Charlie, joining us in the feast.

Paydays are good days at the Big Cheese.

---

Lacy looks a little like a rag doll most days—darling, but a mess. Her nickname is Pig Pen. When she eats, she squeezes it first. Doesn't matter what it is. It's like a test for her, or maybe she finds it easier to eat whatever it is, all smashed up like that. Every sandwich squishes between her fingers, and her mouth is always too full.

Today she's laughing with Mom. It's morning time. Mom is poking at her ribs, tickling her arm pits and all around her ball of a tummy. A quick dash from a poke and Lacy lands on her bottom. Her joyful play suddenly turns to tears. Something's not right.

"Oh, Lacy, you're okay," Mom says, "It wasn't that hard of a fall." Lacy continued to cry. "Lacy! Stop it now! Get up."

She slowly gets up. She's holding herself, though. Her hand is cupped in front of her pants.

"What's the matter? Are you hurt?" Mom decides this isn't like her after all. "Let me see," she says, looking down the front side of Lacy's pants.

Lacy cries, "He punched me!"

Mom jumps up to take a closer look. Poor Lacy is black and blue where black and blue shouldn't be. Mom looks at me in shock.

I know exactly who did this; there's no question in my mind. It looks like Evil did even more damage than the burns on her hand that day, on top of whatever took place behind closed doors in the bathroom with Shay.

"He punched you?! What else, Lacy? Anything else? WHAT else? Please tell me." Lacy doesn't have to answer her.

Mom sucks up the room like an inside tornado. We hold on; it's loud and angry. "That's it! I'm going to kill him!"

---

I guess Evil is out of our lives forever now. Mom hasn't gone to jail, so I know she didn't kill him, but I'm sure he received a good piece of her mind. Knowing her quick tongue, I can only imagine how that conversation went. She might've even reported him; I sure hope so.

I don't understand where my mom finds her babysitters. I can only think of one that was nice and took care of us well. She was even funny sometimes, always finding little games to play or creating something silly to eat in the kitchen. She and Mom are still friends, I think. There was a time that she lived with us, I'm not sure why. Her name was Margy Ann. Other than her, all other babysitters have been something to be afraid of; forcing us to sit on couches for hours on end, not able to move, or, we've been yelled at, physically hurt, and abused. Is this just part of life? Are we supposed to feel pain and fend for ourselves? One day soon I'll be old enough to take care of us all; that day can't come soon enough.

# Scarlett Tears

It's movie night tonight—a special evening planned at the Tillamook Coliseum Theater. It's just me and Mom, and she is so excited.

My first impression of Scarlett O'Hara is how spoiled she is. Sure, she's every bit as beautiful as a movie star should be, so why is it that she bugs me so much? I think it may be that squeaky, pouty whining thing she does.

Her dresses are gorgeous, the parties are full of boys that flirt, and there are lots and lots of happy, giggling girls. The staircase is as grand as I've ever seen in all my life and the curtains! Wow, the curtains! So, I wonder, what is there to whine about?

Mom has always wanted to share this movie with me.

"It's called *Gone with the Wind*," she says. "You're going to love it!"

She thinks it's the best movie she's ever seen, and for the first hour or so, I understand the reasons why. The big screen above shows pictures so beautiful that I want to melt into the red velvet chair I sit in. There's stunning land and houses, fancy dresses, lacy fans, and pretty hair. The story has a lot to tell about family, boys and war. And, even though I'm one of the youngest in the theatre, I understand most of it. After all, I've seen my own mom with some of the same fits over a boy or two.

Scarlet fancies a man named Ashley. She even tries to steal him from somebody else. I think the name Ashley is much too pretty to be a boy's name. The movie goes on getting a little scary, and soon they have no food. There's love. More war. And then there comes a little girl; finally something I can relate to.

Other than the rich living part, the maids and the massive house, turns out, it's a story about a normal life, about people, and what they mean to each other. But, here's what's different: Scarlett's little girl has everything—well almost. She has a beautiful mom, a handsome dad, and a pony—a pony that accidentally kills her. This is a shocking detail of the story that I didn't see coming. It breaks my heart into a thousand tiny pieces. I just can't believe after all of the hard work, love, war, and tears, that the little girl dies—why?

Leaving the theatre, I can feel my heart in my throat. I want to be a big girl and keep my tears to myself, and so I swallow as hard as I can and keep my chin up.

"What did you think, Lu?" Mom questions, still excited about her favorite show.

I can't answer her, for fear that everything will spill out at once. All I can think about is little Katie or Cat, as her mama, Scarlett would call her. About how everything slipped away between Scarlett's fingers no matter how hard she tried—even her sweet daughter.

I get the message that there's no room for being spoiled, always thinking about yourself. How that is no way to act to get what you want, and Scarlett probably paid in the end by behaving that way.

The words, "Frankly, my dear, I don't give a damn," sit hard on the front of my mind. Rhett was so angry, as I think all men are. Just like in real life, he left her, frustrated, cussing without a care.

# CHARLIE'S WORLD

THE GRAY HOUSE—TILLAMOOK
1970

Charlie appears confused. His head is darting up, then down all throughout the gray, two-story house. He's peering under the couch, the bed—everywhere. He's upstairs, and then he's downstairs. Charlie's hunting for something.

"I know he's not outside," he's saying to himself. He? I wonder, as I finish changing Shay's diaper.

We live on one of the main drags in the heart of Tillamook; it's where they make the cheese. It's a busy street. Sometimes we just hang on the front porch—a cement slab high enough that our legs can dangle. There's a tree in the front yard. It's small, but big enough for Charlie to climb. He swings up the trunk without effort, living up to Mom's early-on nickname for him as a baby. She talks about the day he was born. She's always saying, "He looked just like a baby orangutan with his thick, dark hair, red patches here 'n there."

Charlie is strong and wiry. He has a serious, brooding look about him, but is always quick to smile. There's never a dull moment in a day full of Charlie's shenanigans.

Finally, I need to know. "Charlie? What are you looking

for?" He stops and turns my way. He pushes his four-year-old fist in the air, and beckons me with his pointer finger. I follow him. We enter Mom's bedroom; his head leans forward, looking into the corners, and cracks where the wall meets the floor. He drops to his knees, cheek down, his hand reaching under the bed.

"I can't find him," he muffles, as he pulls a shoe box out from underneath. "Look, my snake is gone."

I jump to my feet. "Charlie! You brought a snake in the house?"

"Yeah, well, he's my new pet," he explains, pulling his palms and shoulders upward.

"But, Charlie, you keep him under Mom's bed?"

"Sure. Why not? Mom likes pets," he says, looking up at me like I'm the crazy one.

Now on the bed it strikes me that the snake could be IN the bed, under the covers or slithering through the bed spring coils.

"Charlie! We have to find it!"

I'm thinking things could get a little touchy, getting Mom involved in the search to find Charlie's newest critter, depending on her mood. She does love pets though, and might find this amusing.

Finally, I give up. "Mom! Charlie lost his snake!" I'm afraid to step off the bed.

"What?!" I hear her in the other room. "What the hell?" she yells back, now off the couch, heading our way. She drops down and takes a look for herself.

"Charlie, how big is it?" she asks, I note a slight irritation in her voice. Her neck is strained; she's grilling him while checking the springs. "Damn it, Charlie! Why under my bed?" She's laughing now—thank goodness.

"You'd better get your ass movin', find him, and get him out of here!"

"K, Mom," Charlie sighs while checking a nearby shoe.

---

It's summer outside. The dew on the grass sits heavy and sparkles. I've already enjoyed part of the morning right here, in our side yard, the shaded, nontraffic side. The water from the grass seeps thick between my toes and fingers as I flip over, onto my feet, out of a perfectly good backbend. It seems extra dewy, and the cooler temperature on this side of the house stings a little.

Walking on my hands, I'm now skilled enough to search for sour grass at the same time—something to get the juices flowing. I usually bite or gnaw on it first to get it soft, then I let it slide between the side of my tongue and my gum; it makes my glands move. The earthy goodness is best followed by the blossom tips of white clover. The truth is, all I really want is a handful of salmon berries—my favorite. Those aren't found in town as much as near the ocean, though.

Still hungry, always hungry, I decide to go inside, but first I kneel in the slice of sunshine lying across a dryer patch of grass, where we find most of our four-leafed clovers. They are supposed to be good luck. Luck always comes in handy. While nudging a daddy long leg along his way, I find one! It's perfect, larger than normal. I admire the matched perfection of all four leaves. I count them, landing a light fingertip touch on the top of each leaf. If only there were five. But then, I reason, convincing myself that the fifth leaf is missing. Just like in our family, the missing leaf is Mick. I push my thought aside and stick another piece of sour grass in the corner of my mouth. I hold my clover of luck up against the sun; the leaves are mighty and they glow.

"I'm keeping this one," I say out loud to myself. Each petal of the clover represents Shay, Lacy, Charlie, and me—strong and together.

I decide to sit a minute on the porch slab, setting the clover on my knee. My hands relaxed behind me, my head back, I can see some moon left in the sky. I wonder, how is it that we get to see both the moon and the sun in the sky, at the same time? That seems kind of lucky, too, if you think about it.

I look at it hanging there and wonder about the men that walked on it. Not too long ago we got to see them on Grandma Evelyn's TV. They say that those men stepped in a place that no other man had ever stepped before. The one man, named Neil, saying special words inside his space suit. Something about, "One big step for mankind."

My stomach growls; I get myself up, catch my four-leafed clover, and head for the front door. Maybe, with all this luck, I'll find some toast.

This morning has certainly been a lazy one. Nobody is moving, really. I find myself a tad bit irritated as my toast is stuck in the toaster. Guess I need to dig it out. I walk over to grab a knife.

I'm struggling with the toaster, when I hear Charlie. He's started his play on the stairs, like most days. We have crazy stairs. Sometimes we slide down them on our butts fast, slamming our tail bones one stair at a time. It's always entertaining, and extra funny if you use your voice all the way down; Charlie does it all of the time. Hours of vibrating, vocal fun spent around these stairs. They are wooden, slippery, and they take a sharp, right turn at the halfway point—an interesting design. There are hardly any railings; our house is a hodge- podge of wood, nails, torn linoleum, and old paint. It's all very tricky for kids.

The stairs are the hidden, centerpoint of the house. Life mostly rotates in a circle outside the walls that surround them. Tucked in a center hall, they feel like the best inside fort ever. I think that's why it's Charlie's favorite spot. I can hear him coaxing.

"Here, sit here."

Lacy comments back. I can't quite hear what she is saying, though.

"Come ON! Get in!" Charlie commands. His tone is eager, not angry. Charlie's convincing is usually successful that way. I hear Lacy count, "One, two, frrrrreeee . . . , go!" The sound is more hollow than the usual thump, thump, thump of tail bones and butt cheeks. There's an extra bump and then a solid boom ending in a tumbled mess!

"Oooooowwwwwwwwwweeeeee! Ow, ow, ow!" Lacy's cry cuts though the morning sleepiness. Adults come out of the woodwork for the rescue! I see some of Mom's friends stayed too late to leave last night. So there's some extra help with the situation.

I hear "What the hell? It's too early for this crap." And, "Way to go kid," said with rolling eyes.

"Ohhhhh shit! This is serious," Mom says. "Charlieeeeee!"

He's hopping up and down, with that cringing look on his face.

"You sent her down the stairs in a cardboard box?!"

"What are you, an idiot?"

There's no question this time, a trip to the hospital is a must.

---

Relatives have dropped in this afternoon, lots of goodies in hand. Exciting, because it's Uncle Elias, Aunt Rose, and their big collection of kids. Uncle Elias is round and loud. He pushes his sentences; he throws them at people in a good way. His laugh is really big. It seems everybody is wearing jeans, sweatshirts, and cigarettes. The smoke fills the kitchen.

They talk a little about Lacy and Shay's dad. About what happened with him and how Mom is getting along on her own. Also, how Mom's last name is Kennedy, the same as one of our president's name. They look sad though, because I guess Mr. Kennedy, the president, got hurt.

"Right through his head," one of them said. "It's still shocking to this day."

They said that his wife tried to crawl out of the big car when it was happening. I guess being a president can be dangerous. From what I hear, everyone seemed to like him, though, so it always makes me wonder why they hurt him in the first place? Maybe someday I'll understand these things.

"Wow! It's hot in here," Mom says. "Too many bodies." The back door, off the kitchen, swings out.

"Careful!" she says. "There are no stairs. Do NOT step out, it's a reallllly big drop." The kitchen explodes with laughter. "Well, especially you Lacy. You're banged up enough!" Mom adds.

Lacy stares up with her three-year-old, Kool-Aid stained grin; her sling is snug, in place, already busy repairing her broken collarbone.

"Charlie, no pushing!" Another burst of laughter fills the room.

"You kids go out on the front porch. Go on! Get outta here, go play!" Scrambling, we file out of the hazy smoke– and adult-filled kitchen—thick, plastic, Kool-Aid cups in hand.

As we sit, feet dangling, watching the cars drive by, there's a sudden yank at the front door.

"Here ya go!" Uncle Elias steps out onto the porch and hands each of us our very own, whole Dungeness crab. He's passing them out like a deck of cards; a bit like Santa, I think: big, jovial, arms full of generosity.

"Here! One for each of you. Just break 'em open and eat the meat. It's good; eat all of it! Use a rock if you need to." He goes back in for more.

I run my fingers across the brown shell and between the pinchers. It's lined with hairy bumps and tiny nodules. Charlie is staring at his crab. I see the wheels in his head already turning, no doubt thinking of ways to use every part of it. He's clicking the pinchers together, pretending the crab has captured his nose. His cross-eyed imagination is now in overdrive.

Lacy just holds hers; she's watching everybody else, not sure where to begin. A rock is a must for her. Cracking and eating crab with one hand is not an easy thing to do.

It doesn't take us long till the pieces of shell begin to fly. One sits like a barrette on Charlie's thick, bed-head hair; he doesn't care. Lacy gives hers a great big whack! Small specks land and dangle in mine. A shell hits my cheek. Using the back, dry side of my hand, I swipe it away. Everybody is happy. Our white slips of meat sit rich and salty between our lips and on our tongues.

# Color Me Orange

Wilson River—Tillamook, Oregon
1970

An orange glow spreads across our grubby cheeks, chins, and noses. Our faces lift high toward the sky. We can't hold back our squeal and dance. We are playful, almost drunk with happiness.

"Again, again!" we say together. Our small fists clamped tight around the edge of the cloth, we form a circle.

"One, two, threeeee!" Our arms toss up, outstretched, throwing high to the sky! We let go of the glowing cloth, run toward each other, laughing, huddling, watching as that color hangs in the air above us. The parachute does what it's meant to do—it floats, then falls closer.

"Here it comes!" we yell, crouching together. It falls to the ground, wrapping us in a gentle, silky soft hug.

Today, "Mother Bear" and her "cubs'" are going camping. Housing our campsite will be our splendid orange-and-white parachute. Staked out and up the chute easily provides enough room for a bear and her cubs. A light breeze offers assistance as we fluff, unfold, and measure. This magnificent piece of silk becomes our home for what seems like a week, maybe longer.

Wonder Bread deliciously cradles our hot dogs; the mustard and ketchup drizzle and drip. Surely it will stick around as it dries neatly in the corners of our mouths and front of our shirts.

Charlie attempts a dive into a bag of marshmallows. Mom's paw rips it from his grip.

"Give me that! You little shit," she says, a slight irritation crosses her brow, as she finishes her sentence with one of our visitors. She pulls at the bag, her elbows outstretched like wings, and the plastic gives.

Charlie can hardly contain himself. He's hopping. One hand cupped over the front of his pants.

"Charlie!" Mom yells. "You need to pee?"

He's on his tiptoes, back arched, his face looks a little like The Joker on Batman cartoons, pulled back so hard he has a double chin. His head sways side to side; he's eyeing the bag. Mid-answer he changes his mind; his head now urgently bobs up and down.

"Go then!" she shouts." There's a perfectly good tree right there, hurry up!"

He scrambles over. He's within earshot.

Thick, switch-sized, branches have been collected and whittled—our roasting tools. There's a hint of hot-dog flavor on the tips.

"Charlie? You done?" Mom asks, checking on him. He shows up, exhaling his pee-pee stress. "Come 'ere Turkey Toes."

He wipes his hands on the belly of his shirt. I laugh a little.

She tries to show him how to brown the marshmallow sides, patiently, slowly. I follow her lead. They turn a perfect golden brown at first, but if you're not careful, in a flash they become marshmallow torches, bubbling black and burnt! The taste of oozing, smoky sugar melts, swimming in our mouths.

We slide them on, stacking one, then two, three, and four at a time, then slip them off the hot, sharp sticks. First devouring the crusty shell, then the gooey middle. The stickiness collects sugar dust and dirt in the crevasses of our fingers.

There's word in town that mother bear and her cubs are camping down at the Wilson River, "First parachute on the right; you can't miss it!" they say, laughing at the directions upon their arrival. Word travels fast and rambunctious company arrives deep into the night. They carry six packs: Pepsi and beer—lots of beer. From the looks of things, I think there must be lots of bar people missing from the Big Cheese tonight. Our outside kitchen is THE place to be. Oddly shaped rocks circling hot, orange flames. The spark and pop shoot high into the sky. The dancing smoke swirls, rising up into the darkness. My head rests against a log. The ground is damp. Layers are a must tonight: sweatshirts, old blankets, anything to block the damp and chill.

Lacy stands over me; she's shivering. "Ine code" she says.

I understand her three-year-old language. Her lips are turned down. Mom is visiting with her company, but manages to hear Lacy.

"Come here, Lacy." Mom motions her with quick hands, then pulls her top layer up and over her head. She then slides the large, thick sweatshirt over Lacy's sand-colored hair. Mom's extrabig sweatshirt becomes Lacy's oversized, full-length dress, her round, little body disappearing in it. Her hands reach only halfway down the sleeve.

Lacy heads back to me, dangling sleeves held out. "Boo?" she says, her sweet way of saying Lu, with her brows are turned in. The sleeves drag the ground, collecting, adding more dirt to the mustard and marshmallow. I fold, fold, fold each sleeve, rolling up until her tiny fingers poke through. She scoots down next to me, her little head propped against the log.

"Look, Lacy," I whisper in her ear. "Those hot sparks are shooting toward the stars." My hand guides her eyes. "And, look over there! That's the moon. It's watching over us." Lacy looks at me, her lips turned up now. She settles in, quietly watching the moon and the stars. A floating ember pops! We flinch, then huddle a little closer.

# What Now

Mom is sitting on the toilet; the bathroom door is wide open. She's shouting commands from her throne.

"Go get me my cigarettes!"

Two of us take off on a hunt to find them. We know enough to grab her matches, too. There's no ashtray needed, because when she sits in the bathroom, she flicks the ash right into the sink. Her thumb toggles the butt of the cigarette till the gray falls off. Then, when it burns all the way down, she plops the rest of it right into the toilet, where it snuffs out with a hot *pffft* sound.

Mom strikes a match and holds it up for a moment.

"Whew! I'm rotten today," she says, then quick torches the end of her cigarette pulling a long drag of air. Here it comes again, that look where her face loses every care in the world. Happens every time, like she dreams for a second.

I look at her; there's no such thing as prim and there's no such thing as proper—she just is. She's kind of a mess this morning. I can also see her mood, the one where she needs to talk. It's another look. Not the one where I need to take cover and duck; the other one, where she's upset, maybe a little sick to her stomach. A girlfriend knows, after all, we've been through these sessions before.

She points toward the tub, "Lu, come 'ere, sit," she says, her two fingers and cigarette showing me to the edge of the tub in front of her. She reaches over to the sink, flicks her ash, then puts herself in a forward slump, elbows onto her knees.

"What are we going to do? How should I handle this?" she's half asking me, half asking herself.

I realize enough, in my almost nine years, to know that she's talking about our life here, our money struggles, man problems, the sick abuse from evil babysitters, her health—the usual.

Not long ago the doctor made it so she can no longer have kids. I guess he took everything out that makes children. Something about it not being healthy in there.

Can you take all the woman parts out without replacing them? I'll have to ask sometime.

She looks at me in her tired, weak way. "What do you think?"

My mind wonders if it's time to move, again. If that's the subject she's getting to. Her problems always come back, and there's something always putting us on the move.

There are times I wish she had a man in her life—one that wasn't scary, that could sit and listen for her, a man to help with her big decisions. I stop my head though, as most men make me cringe. I never know what they are thinking or who it is they really want to hurt or touch.

It all just makes me want my thumb. It's been a very long time now since I've tackled my thumb problem, but the urge is still there. I tuck it deep inside my fist. I've noticed the other kids like their fingers, too. Charlie's favorite is his pointer finger, sucked under the edge of a blanket when he's sleepy or relaxed. Lacy and Shay both like their thumbs, just like me. Mick? I'm not sure.

Mom yawns, her elbows still on her knees. She presses her eyes over onto her turned-out palms, seeming not aware of the cigarette that dangles there. She treats it like a sixth finger. Her beautiful, full, red hair hangs in a ratted mess. Her lash laced, classic shaped eyes smudged from rubbing sleep. She finishes her yawn, then out tumbles the words, "I think it's time, Lu—time to move."

—

The evening feels a little better; it's wet outside, cozy inside. There's a quiet hum throughout the house. The small black-and-white TV glows in the living room. The two-foot, rabbit-ear antenna adjusted, readjusted, then propped just right.

"Charlie, hold this!"

Mom has Charlie reach up to hold the antenna. She steps in front of the TV to make sure the picture comes clear.

"Perfect! Charlie, now you just stand there for the whole movie, okay?"

Charlie frowns.

"Just kidding. It should be good now," she says. "You kids are going to LOVE this one!" Mom is rushing around getting ready. She's grabbing comfort: pillows, torn blankets, her cigarettes.

"Lu, Charlie, here run down to the motel and grab three Pepsis and four Hershey bars. This is a special night." Dropping coins in my hand, she adds, "Hurry, it starts in twenty minutes."

We slip out the front door, off the porch, and run down the block.

The pop and candy vending machines are tucked under wooden eaves outside the motel's front entrance. Big, flat winged cars cruise by, their whitewall tires tossing puddles across the sidewalks and into the parking lot. We ignore the whisking activity around us, our wet feet, and our wet heads.

Even though it's raining, this damp, gray afternoon is glowing a little brighter now; this should be a fun night.

I'm on one knee collecting bottles. "Here, Charlie, you hold the Hershey bars, I'll carry the bottles," I say, deciding this is best, knowing Charlie would somehow manage to shatter the glass, the yummy substance it holds, and most importantly, any money we should get from returning our empty containers. We are extracareful returning home. It was a quick, winded walk.

Mom mentions one last thing, just as we settle in for the movie.

"A little Kleenex might be a good idea. Charlie! Go grab some toilet paper, quick!" Off he scrambles, returning with two hands fully fluffed. "Ok, here we go. Turn it up, Lu!"

The stunning vision of wildlife appears before us, I should have known this would be a special night full of animals, furry critters, because this is what makes her the happiest. All walks of animal life send my mother into a trance. Anybody that knows her, knows that. Elsa, the lion, is beautiful, and I instantly fall in love with her myself.

*Born Free* is the name of our movie, and a very special movie it is. The story is about an overprotective mama lion getting shot. She leaves behind three baby cubs. Two of the cubs go to a zoo, and Elsa is the lion cub raised in a regular family's home. Elsa eventually behaves in her natural way, chasing and causing fear. Hard decisions soon follow: Elsa is either to be held behind bars like her brother and sister or released back into the wild. She's released. It makes you cry. The music is like nothing I've ever heard before. It's powerful.

Mom sings along, *"Born free, as free as the wind blows, as free as the grass grows, born free to follow your heart . . . Livvve free. . . !"*

The music allows us to cry. We don't look at each other for a really long time. After a while I realize Mom is in a puddle of tears, Shay is sleeping, Lacy lost interest around halfway, and Charlie is still talking about the mama lion getting shot, way back, in the first part of the movie. My heart is big with emotion. This is more than a wildlife story pressing rules and regulations. This story is more about lessons of love, respect, and graciously letting go.

I think about Mom and her favorite movies, how tragic they are. How they push you through every hurt deep down in your bones.

# Finally Home

Dallas, Oregon
1971

I know that Dallas is close, I see the monkey trees, weeping willows, pine, cherry, walnut, crabapple, plum and maple trees—every tree you can imagine. The radio volume is set low, but the words are there. *"Here comes the sun, little darlin', here comes the sun. . . . It's all right. . . ."*

I find the song fitting. It's happy music, and it adds to the excitement. I can't believe we are finally here. I hope upon hope for good this time. Finally in this town that stills my heart—it's the only place I've yearned for. No more tears when I'm torn from visits with Grandma, Grandpa, Aunt Niecie, and Cousin Bea Susan.

I'm home.

---

Most of the time moving into a new place brings me down. It's a lot of work, all this jumping from place to place. But, this time I'm excited to see our new home, after all, we get to live HERE, in my favorite of all towns.

Thrilled as we pull up to the large green building; there

are schools nearby and we have very close neighbors. In fact, six other families live in our building. One of the first things I notice is that all of us have popcorn ceilings and shag carpet. Everything inside is brand new, and there's even a machine that washes our dishes!

As we settle in, Mom is sharing moving stories with visiting family. She goes on about all of our packing, cleaning, and driving. Heads throw back in laughter when she tells of cleaning the last of the closets. She found a snake skin in the corner. No doubt a gift, shed and left from Charlie's long lost, bed-spring-crawling pet. I'm guessing Charlie should have checked the shoes a little closer that day.

"Not a night goes by that I don't think about that goddamn snake in my bed! We found a few dead crickets, too!" Mom shouts. The room roars; Mom quivers at the thought. She throws her hands in the air, "And, of course Charlie has to pee every ten minutes during the drive. It's okay though, I just had him aim through the board-covered hole in the floor of the back seat. Sometimes that damn hole comes in handy!" Another roar, this time the laughter seems a bit awkward, a few sighs and head shaking at the end. Mom takes a drag off her cigarette, through her smoke, she says, "Oh, Charlie, what am I going to do with you?"

Charlie shrugs and decides to leave the room.

I follow him out the front door, across the parking lot, onto a large field of rocks, dirt clumps, and grasshoppers. He lunges after one. "Whoa! Come 'ere," he laughs. They're too quick for him, like miniature, popping springs, they fly right through his cupped, little hands. He's hopping like a frog after one, then again, quickly onto another.

It's warm out. Mom's always saying, "The sun is much warmer here in the valley, definitely warmer than the coast." She adds, "Dallas can get very hot in the summertime, sometimes, a hundred degrees or more."

I already know this from my past visits with Grandma Evelyn and Grandpa Perry. *That's what the Dallas pool is for,* I think to myself. Fingers crossed, that sooner rather than later, I'll have a return visit there.

Oh, how I've missed this weather and THAT pool.

Setting my pool thoughts aside, I look around the field hoping for a smooth spot where I can stand or walk on my hands, turn a cartwheel, or bounce a high-flying roundoff. Not one smooth spot, so it looks like my upside down days will have to be carefully maneuvered over pavement.

While I'm keeping an eye on Charlie, a beautiful girl with waist-long hair walks up to me. She looks me up, then down with her bright, steel eyes. I'm not sure of her, but I throw her a smile anyway.

"I like your bathing suit," she says motioning toward my middle. "The daisy is cute."

I glance down toward my hip. The large, plastic daisy sits flat against my bright-pink suit.

"Thank you. What's your name?" I ask.

"Breena."

She points at our new building. "I live right there, right next to you."

I can't believe my luck!

"What's your name?" she asks.

"I'm Lu." I say, gazing over toward Charlie. "That's Charlie." Breena squints at him, then watches a moment as he pops up and down with his grasshoppers.

Before I know it, we are turning cartwheels on the pavement together.

I walk away, pleased with myself as it's taken less than a day to make a brand-new friend. She's the same age and lives right next door; she's literally inches away!

Our summer flies by with family, new friends, the pool,

river swimming, and camping under our fluff of orange. Many hot, hot days and evenings result in hose and water fights right here in our front parking lot. All six families join in with buckets, pitchers, anything that can hold water. Pretty smart when you think about it—around fifteen kids and all six cars get washed at the same time.

There are the days that we take drives up logging roads searching for a good swimming hole. Usually it's a last-minute decision; one where we end up skinny dippin' in our underwear. The log trucks barrel down on us. We meet each other, head to head, in a mountain-road standoff. Mom stops, cranks her steering wheel to the right, lining her tires on the edge of a ditch. I swear, if I stick my hand out the window, I could touch the massive wheels of the truck, maybe even a log or two, as they find a way to squeak by us.

Finally reaching the icy-cool waters, she likes to throw the little ones in first. Sink or swim-testing them, she's always nearby to see that they make it back to the surface for air. She pulls Lacy's hands around her neck, wearing her like the sweetest of capes. They bob along watching Shay play in the rocks and Charlie catching his crawdads near the shore.

"Hang on, Lacy," Mom says, diving underwater with her.

I sink myself under, open my eyes, and watch them. Mom looks like she's flying, cloaked with Lacy, their hair waving through trailing bubbles of breath.

---

Occasionally Mom slips two or three of her children in the trunk of the car. Her way of saving a couple of bucks as we sneak into the Motor Vu Drive-In Theater.

"Ssshhhh," she tells them, "I'll pull you out in a minute."

Sometimes, she just hides the littlest ones under blankets

on the back seat floor. We know the coast is clear when we hear the static sound of the clunky, metal speaker as it hitches onto the driver-side window. We huddle in, cozy with our blankets and popcorn.

Things aren't perfect, not even close, but they're better.

We hand the grocery store clerks what looks like fake money to buy our food and hand-me-downs help us dress. Each of us kids has been assigned Big Brothers or Big Sisters. Something about a healthy person for each of us—"A guidance program which promotes growth and mentorship for under-privileged children," they say.

Mom still flies off the handle more than I care for, her backhand and belt way too quick and sharp at times. She says it's for our own good, though, that it's the only way we will listen and learn. I often think, if violence equals learning, than all of us may end up pretty darn smart.

I know that she loves us, but I think more in a smothering way. It's like she needs us in order to feel loved herself. I wonder, *Is needing somebody and loving them the same thing?*

Maybe that's why she had so many babies—so that she can feel more love.

Loved or not loved, this new life seems to be distracting her in a good way, and our neighbors have a lot in common with her. I can tell that some of them have also found themselves under the strong hand of a man, or have hit hard times with money.

---

Mom's in a good mood tonight. "Okay! Let's head next door to Freda's," she yells up the stairs. "We're going to watch Elvis. He's on TV tonight!" she says.

"Lu? You know who Elvis is, right?" I nod yes, look at

her confused, and think to myself: Who on this great big Earth doesn't know who Elvis is?

We enter without knocking.

"We're here!" Mom shouts upward, as we walk in. I run up the stairs to Breena's room where I find her shoving her candy box under her bed. I wonder what it would be like to actually have a candy box—what a luxury; a whole box dedicated to just candy? My mouth waters.

"Ready?" I motion.

"Yeah," she nods, slipping me a piece on the way down the stairs.

Elvis Presley is introduced over his shrieking female fans. His leg moves up and down along with his lip. Our entire bunch sitting in a half moon, Indian-style around the TV, snacking and sipping on pops.

"Well, shit the bed; there he is!" Mom says, turning to Freda. "Look at him, he's changed—he's gotten bigger, much bigger! He needs to lay off all those cheeseburgers."

I notice that he's sweating, sweating a lot.

Mom shakes her head. "His voice though, listen—he's still got it. And nope, I STILL wouldn't kick him out of bed for eatin' crackers."

As he goes on about his blue suede shoes and tender love, I get the feeling his talent is unmatched by anybody else in this big world. He sounds silky, I'm thinking much like the teasing, drippy scarf that he's tossing onto his adoring lady fans.

Many evenings are spent with our neighbor families watching TV, playing games, dice, and the Ouiji Board. We get to see how Charlie Brown and Snoopy stay loyal, best friends no matter happens. How Rudolph can ALWAYS get you through the storm. We watch the *Wizard of Oz*, where we learn that somewhere over the rainbow troubles melt like lemon drops and pretty, little blue birds fly. Evenings turn into days,

days turns into months, then sure as the sun comes up, it's time to move.

In my disappointment, I know that staying in one place can't work, won't work; we never seem to stick. I leave behind yet another set of much-needed friends.

I have had some time with Grandma Evelyn and Grandpa Perry. There isn't a question where I feel most at home, relaxed and secure. I've had a taste of what it's like to trust and feel completely at ease with one another. They just seem to know how to be without all the noise in life.

My visits with them are always too short. Grandma's curious, ready to laugh, sit, and talk about anything under the sun; Grandpa's tucked in the corner of the couch sipping a whiskey and Squirt. I note the way he breathes, his thick brow, and the rigorous bounce in his legs. His one foot rocks up on his heel every few seconds, covered in a thick, black leather shoe. He then drops it flat with a thud . . . rocking it back up again, then another drop. Again a rock up, then plop. I've gathered in the small amount of my years that there's an edge about him. Once in a great while, Mom refers to hating him under her breath. That she can't get over the hurt. She cuts his hair when it gets too long. Though she does him this favor—she will not let her hands touch his skin. I can't begin to understand the reasons she feels such hate for him. To me he's a great man. He's been nothing but wonderful and supportive in my eyes. And in my eyes there have been very few great, supportive men.

Each of our "real" fathers has left us behind. They've either cheated on her, or her face has taken their fist for the very last time. I'm relieved in that, at least this time we aren't moving because of a violent hand of a man, or a sick babysitter. I think this move is simply about brand-new, more-affordable housing.

---

Thank goodness our move has only taken us a town or two away, located not too far from my Dallas.

This complex is quite large. It's white, and offers a roof for around double the amount of families that our last place offered.

Today is spent cleaning and organizing. The smaller kids run things up and down the stairs; the bigger kids handle putting away the dishes. Barbara Streisand fills the air, crooning about lovers being "the luckiest people in the world." As we go about cleaning and organizing, I listen to her words. Her words are touching, but, I'm not sure that they are true, considering my mom's lack of luck and love. I think even if lovers start out lucky, like with anything else, their luck runs out.

Soon, though, there comes music that is more true to life.

"Oooooh, turn it up," Mom says.

*"Draggin' the line, draggin' the line, do, do, do, do . . . beep, beep!"*

Mom's moving to the sound. One hand flat on her tummy, the other in the air, her hips move in circles, her lips are singing, *"IIIIIII feeel fine, I'm talkin' about peeeeeace of mind . . . "*

She looks happy in her head, signs of a fresh, new beginning written all over her face.

---

Now, how is it that I go about collecting new friends?

Deciding the best place to do so is right here in the middle of our complex courtyard, I take my bike for a ride, hands straight up in the air, long, dark hair trailing behind me. Sometimes I make the attempt to turn the bike with no hands, it rarely works ending in a crumpled disaster, sprawled across the cement. I don't care though; I just keep trying. If I can easily turn my cartwheels, flying roundoffs, and back walkovers over cement, then why not ride circles on my bike with no hands?

Thank goodness for my brothers and sisters. Still tiny, Shay sits like a feather on my hip—she's miniature, really; people stop just to look at her sometimes. They're always surprised when she rattles off a full-on adult sentence. She's been known to mimic old-time movie stars like Mae West, saying, "Hey, big boy, come up and see me sometime." Her tiny shoulder rounding sexy under her smoldering words. Lacy is learning her ABC's and Charlie is busy collecting his insects—filling his jars with spiders and releasing them beside screaming girls. Once in a while, we perk up and say what we want to be when we grow up. Charlie says he wants to be a fire truck, not a fireman, but a fire truck, mind you. That cracks me up. Lacy wants to be a waitress, and of course Shay wants to be a movie star. When Mick was with us, I remember him saying that when he grew up he wanted to be an alligator, so that he could finally catch Tarzan. That one always makes me chuckle a little, too. They are forever my friends, and I get to take them wherever it is that we move next, well, at least most of them. I even took miniature Shay to my fifth-grade class for show-and-tell one day—so tiny, nobody could believe a creature so small could talk and sing that way.

Of course, I don't know why it is that I worry about making new friends; it just takes a little time and effort. Most often, all it takes is a smile. Our family is instantly accepted with children of all ages and sizes; there's at least one friend for each of us here.

Hooti is my newest friend. She's a little older than I am and a little bigger body-wise. I think her body is more adult size. Her personality far surpasses my own in the goofy department. She's especially goofy on this late night playing a good game of Clue. Charlie, Lacy, and Shay are asleep upstairs. Other than our pet rat, Timpleton, his nesting efforts, and his random sprints on his squeaky wheel, the house is silent; it's nice. We play Clue at the table in the kitchen till wee hours in the morning. Although I'm no match for Hooti's personality, I give her a run for her money in the games we play.

"Scarlet, in the kitchen, with the revolver!" I proudly announce solving the clue and winning the game—again. She slumps down heavy onto the table, then plops her forehead down onto the back of her hands.

"Uhhhhh! Let's try Masterpiece," she says, while tossing miniature weapons into Clue box.

I hear laughter coming from outside the sliding glass door; Mom's home. She steps in.

"Hi!" she says, grinning ear to ear. I suspect that she's a little bit tipsy.

"Hello!" Hooti says.

I'm wondering who's stepping in behind her.

"Lu, this is G. Louis." His grin matches my mother's—tipsy times two. They look happy.

Mom goes on to explain to G. Louis, that I'm her oldest and that Hooti is a neighbor friend.

"Who's winning?" he asks, still smiling. There's a brightness to his eyes, his cheeks, a little rosy.

A big shout comes from Hooti, "She is, always!" her face showing her silly frustration.

Mom jumps in with surprising news; "G. Louis is taking me flying tomorrow." She follows the comment with a big, "MAYYYYYBE?" And continues, "I still haven't made up my mind yet; I'm such a chicken!" She looks at him out of the corner of her eye while reaching for a glass of water.

I pick up my chin and laugh, kind of. As I remember, during car rides, bike rides, and backyard sessions in ragged lawn chairs, when our eyes were pulled to the sky by a plane flying by, the one and only thing she's ever said is that she would NEVER, EVER be caught up there.

"Those things are dangerous," she would say. "No way I'd be caught in one."

His grin still intact, G. Louis responds, "Oh, you'll fly. And, it'll be fun!"

I watch the two of them banter, and I wonder what to make of them, whether she'll fly, and if he is the next man in our lives.

—

My mother has flown straight into a new relationship. Yes, she took flight that day with G. Louis. And, yes, she flew way out of her comfort zone and has made herself a brand-new life.

Weeks later, I'm doing the dishes when I overhear Mom and G. Louis talking about Dallas.

Pinch me!

What? Could it be true? We're moving back to Dallas? And, to top things off, only a few blocks away from Grandma Evelyn's house? This news is too good to be true!

—

This house is green, and there's only room enough to hold one family. No more complex living.

We live on Oregon Avenue now. My favorite feature at this house is the scallop-shaped front yard, and the fact that we have one. No more flipping my body around over cement; the yard is huge. The house is small and comfortable. A little crowded when everybody is home, but that's okay.

Soon after our move, I'm lying in the side yard, thinking, holding my breath in anticipation. Gently letting it out, I push it against a delicate, cottonlike dandelion weed. The seeds take flight carrying my wish. If dandelions care about floating wishes, there's a good chance Mick will finally come home. There's been word that this may happen, so I've decided to do my part by using my wishing powers.

As I rest on my back in the fresh green grass, one foot propped on the toe of the other, I decide to count the years; it's been six. What kind of life has he lived? Six years away from us is a very long time. Will he be the same? Does he still love us? Will he like G. Louis?

My questions seem endless.

An overwhelming sense of relief falls into place on his first day home. I can see and sense that the changes are hard on him. And it's as if Mom feels the need to "whip him back into shape." She's careful at first, but soon falls back into her old ways. He talks loud and nervous, and struggles a little getting back into the groove. Although, he's a little different than he used to be, I'm just so relieved that he's back. I felt it the moment he arrived. He's still my Mick—my lifelong friend.

Now that Mick is home and Mom's relationship with G. Louis has flourished, things seem to be falling into place. We have settled in as a complete family now, and there's a plan in motion for a small wedding.

# Take Flight

On this day, G. Louis takes me flying. Like Mom, I wasn't sure I'd ever have the desire to leave the ground in a machine. Why would I?

Now that I'm up here, I understand the draw, if for nothing else, the unbelievable thrill of leaving Earth. The patchwork design on the ground is the first thing I notice—all different colored squares, rectangles, even circles, the lines of pavement and the cars the size of ants. The air is bigger and even bluer than when my feet are connected to the ground.

Buzzing along in the blueness, I look at a line of mountains in the distance, the cloud formations, other machines in the air. There's a lifting of spirit I didn't expect, as if life on the ground is suspended when you're high in the sky. Everything behind and below appears to stop, frozen in place, only to move again after landing safe and sound.

Lost in my gaze across our patchy Earth, I feel the plane give a sudden shift. At first I'm concerned, but then I note G. Louis and his smile.

"Hang on!" he says, "It's called a lazy eight."

The plane takes a turn, dropping lazy to the right, circles down, glides upward, then lazy to the left, down, then back up again. We are weaving circles in the sky. My seat feels like it's left me behind. And, my stomach? Well, I don't know where it went. My body is laughing even though I didn't tell it too.

"Here, take the plane," G. Louis says, showing me where to place my hands. I look at him surprised and ask myself why he would trust me to do such a thing—take the plane?

Does he mean fly it?

"You can do it. Go ahead," he says, still smiling. He then shows me again where to place my hands.

I'm flying . . . are we over a rainbow? Way up high, where the pretty, little bluebirds fly? I think so.

He MUST know this is one of the most amazing things I've ever done in my life.

# Grandma's House

Dallas, Oregon
1974

The sidewalks lead easily up to Grandma's house. I'm taking my time, losing myself in the warm weather and the neighborhood. Passing aged, humble homes resting, settled in, one after another, each holding their own in character and modest design. I try to imagine the living activities and people inside them.

Soon, I approach Grandma's house on Tenth Street. I can smell the sticky, aged fruit that's longed dropped and turned to bee sugar under the apple tree. Also, the tall standing rose bushes that guard the small path leading from the sidewalk to her front porch. I lean in for a long, intoxicating inhale. Tinkling chimes ping in the breeze; quiet blossoms hang next to them. She's a master gardener in my eyes—her house always surrounded in beautiful flowers, like a ballerina's tutu, fluffed and delicate.

I approach her door and the dedicated, wooden milk box sitting beside it. There's faint organ music coming from inside. The built-in mail slot set in the front door still makes me smile.

I think about slipping my fingers through, and I wonder if she would recognize them; I knock instead.

"Come in!" In I go.

"Hi, Grandma." We scoot onto the organ bench for my lesson.

Simultaneously, shifting her hands and feet filling the air with glorious music—music she's written herself. She stops, erases, then pencils in a note or two. I glance up at the wall. Just above us hangs an oil painting of resting flowers in a water pitcher, done by her own hand. She picks up the beat, her fingers glide over silky, white keys. I follow them, they are supple and lived in. I'm fascinated by them, and for some reason, in this very moment, I realize how many lives they've touched and just how truly gifted they are.

My struggle to understand and read notes gives way to memory. Eventually I make music. Nothing compared to hers, of course, but it's music.

"Watch," she says.

I know she means for me to watch her hands and her feet, because the music comes out best when they work together. The notes play.

> "*You are my sunshine, my only sunshine.*
> *You make me HAPPY when skies are gray.*"

We sing; I watch her, learn from her; we play on. She gives me cheese, cucumbers, and buttered crackers. We watch TV. We talk about family, school, the world, and how we fit in it. Our lessons together are sweet, full of music, but even more so, full of life and what counts. I walk away, at the end of the day, filled with hope and promise.

# BALANCE

Tightening your core is the secret to being a good gymnast, to having good posture, to trusting your own strength. It seems in some ways that I've been upside down my whole life—balanced in a handstand against the wall shared with Screechy the owl, eventually holding that handstand without needing any help to do so. Soon walking on those very same hands, room to room, across a yard, over cement, down a sidewalk, attempting porch steps and then from one end of the gym to the other at school. My hands then turn around, walking their way back to the other side. Life upside down just feels right to me.

I'm realizing though, through my never-ending passion and research on the subject that tall, lanky gymnasts are not in demand. This point doesn't dampen my spirit, nor my drive to learn more—I keep at it.

Our local library holds only three books on the subject. I check them out time and time again. There's one in particular that I've checked out over and over, my name is listed on the inside cover so many times, they have to add more lines. It's the book that features one of the best in the business, Olga Korbut.

Olga is extremely popular as she springs, bouncy across the floor; her pixielike pigtails and flashing smile capturing Olympic fans all around the world. My desire to be like her is cut short, though, if by nothing else than the way that I'm built. My body is not ideal for tight curled flips in midair. I'm tall and thin, not tiny, and my hands and feet just aren't as quick as hers. Still, G. Louis must be paying attention. To my astonishment, what shows up in the side yard is a handcrafted, homemade balance beam.

The width is built to regulation, the length is just fine, but, here's what makes my balance beam unique: it's definitely higher than four feet off the ground, which means that my handstands have taken to new heights! And, so I practice, I slip, I hurt, I pick myself up, rub my bruises, move past the knocks and slivers in my socks. Maybe not rising to Olympic heights, but high enough. Yes, he's built it tall, so tall that I need to be extra careful not to fall. I raise my arms up, swing a pointed toe forward, then carefully bend a circle through a cartwheel—I balance. Next, comes a split leap high in the air. It's scary up there, so I pause, find my core, and, with everything I have, I trust it.

# Adopting G. Louis

I remember the first time I called him "Dad." To my knowledge, I've never called anybody else that name before. If I have, I was too young to remember it. G. Louis came home for lunch one evening. He works nights for Caterpillar, the place that builds tractors and large equipment. He set himself down at the table in our green house with the scalloped front yard. I was seated at the opposite end.

"Hi, Dad," I said, my heart pounding, not sure if he would accept it, or how he would take my new name for him. I think he froze for a moment, maybe I caught him off guard. Did he hear me? Maybe it was too soon? I wondered. *Does he realize how hard this is?*

Without being too obvious—maybe he needed to take a second or two to think about it. He looked up at me. "Hi, Lu," he said—his face turned bright. Mom also looked up; she knew this was a moment to take note of.

I know I can call him Dad, because he's made himself one. All of our birth certificates have been changed, and we are now legally his, I think almost, if not just as much as we are Mom's.

My birth certificate looks a little funny as it lists my mom as a nineteen-year-old housewife and now shows Dad as a sixteen-year-old student the day that I was born. That makes me smile. Of course, they didn't know each other back then, but it's good to know they were destined to be together in the future. I think that sixteen-year-old boy has saved us.

My Dad, G. Louis, has stepped up, married a woman with five children, and has given us all the same last name. He helped bring Mick home to us, he gave us food, and now helps us with education, assures our health with doctor care, and he watches us, patiently, as we grow into ourselves. He and Mom have their moments of frustration, struggling to mingle their personality differences, paying the bills, and keeping the roof over our heads—it's a humble, but good life and it's because of him.

—

Life is busy, and everybody is working and going to school.

Both Mick and I have paper routes that take us out during wee hours in the morning, what seems like the middle of the night. We go out in the dark and come back in the light. We wear heavy pouches full of rolled, rubber-banded newspapers; our hands turn black from rolling and tossing them. He takes one part of town; I take another. There are others zipping about, but we don't keep track of them. We take off together, then split away onto our own routes, waving when we catch a glimpse of one another coasting through cross streets blocks away. Our bikes crisscross sleepy Dallas most every morning. Sometimes, when the weather gets bad, or when Mom gets a protective, funny feeling, she piles us in her car, and we sling papers from there.

—

We've moved to Court Street into a large, white house that's set on almost an acre of land. It's tucked at the end of a cornered cul-de-sac. Each end of town is within easy reach now, this new home is near the center of it all. The house has big, white pillars, a standing invitation into three levels, if you count the attic and basement.

Us older kids have our own rooms now. The floors are covered in carpet and linoleum. There are large, wooden doors with glass knobs. It all squeaks and creaks—the sounds of a fifty-year-old structure. Finally, we have some elbow room, both inside and out.

The solid-brick fireplace and opposite dining room are flanked in gold sconces. There's even a laundry chute. We now have two bathrooms, a main, full bath, and then one that sits on the enclosed back porch. The porch toilet is only used urgently when one of the seven of us are hopping up and down waiting outside the main one. This home hums with continual human and pet traffic.

Just outside the back door lies a sprawling backyard. Powder-blue hydrangeas hug the cement steps. There's a patio and apple, walnut, and maple trees. The garage is separate from the house; pigeons nest in the roof. They are named and watched closely for personality differences. It's back here where our small dogs, Ziggy and Klinger play amongst the darting squirrels and sneaky garter snakes. On sweltering days, Blue Jays tattle on them, in their questionlike screech, hopping to and from the rugged outside fireplace and the apple and walnut trees. The backyard is alive—this house is alive.

Our dining room and front porch are warm, popular gathering places when company arrives. Laughter, Folgers drip coffee, and Pepsi flow in abundance. Any other day of the week the dining area proves either giggly fun for us kids or gravely intense, it seems nowhere in between. The mood gathers along with the family. Mom serves herself first—always—all the while commanding that Dad gets his fill; we come next. We inhale as quickly as possible, there's no such thing as leftovers. Once finished, we are quick to excuse ourselves. Facing never-ending dishes, after dinner, we then settle onto the front porch. Draped, we lounge on our refreshing, cooling post, we watch the world go by. Friendly neighbors, more pets, and healthy life stir about us.

"Mick, where's the Frisbee?" I nudge his bare leg with my tennis shoe. Mick hops to his feet and walks back toward the fig tree around the side of the house. He finds it there, then flings it high above the porch, the plums, and their purple leaves. The Frisbee hovers, in a spin above the street. I sprint to position myself under it. It's floating, waiting for me; my hand outstretched, I feel the whirl of air as it lands lightly on my fingertips. I turn on a dime, tossing it back knowing exactly where he's positioned his athletic self. His sleek, football-conditioned body is agile and ready. We sling long into the evening under the humming glow of street lights.

Football is our home town's pride and joy. Crisp, fall air is filled with excitement of the big game day. There are pumped football heroes, celebrated coaches, sounds of pep, live band music, shouting sponsors, and proud parents. Our grandstand win leads into lifting one another in hugs and high fives. Our small town gamers and goers exit the stands hand in arm, leaving behind blood, sweat, and tears, painted posters, and fresh mum petals trailing across the field and covered bleachers.

---

Just down the street, in a little yellow house, sits my new best friend. She's visiting her Auntie. Mom takes up an invite and brings me along for an afternoon visit and makeup session.

There she is, Demi. She's tall and has long, dark hair. Her dramatic, lash pointed, hazel eyes are beyond expressive, and that smile! I think it wraps around the world. She's a beauty queen, and, I hope upon hope, a good friend from this day forward.

We spend weeks getting to know each other. By all accounts she's one of the most stunning creatures I've ever seen, but I can already tell that the very best of her is her heart. I adore her, her gentle spirit and wise existence. She's been through loss, heavy change, and yet she's best at uplifting and supporting those that tackle life challenges around her. I admire the closeness of her family; their bond with each other is palpable, exchanging "I Love You's" and lingering hugs before leaving for school or even the quickest of errands. We stay up all night on the weekends talking, snacking, and playing Connect Four. On Sunday's she shares her church with me, her beliefs, her faith—she knows how to pray. She's my touchstone, and I gauge myself beside her in hopes that I sponge even a speck of her shining presence. There's not an adolescent life problem that cannot be solved with my dearest friend—my Demi.

As we enter high school we meet up at our decorated lockers. We talk about boys, classes, and weekend football games. Strolling the halls, pushing one another into walls and trash cans—it's just so funny! We call out to each other above hallway heads, "Linda Lu, Demi Du, and Tara Sue!" Tara is our classic, lovely blonde, seriously smart sidekick. And, eventually, Lena joins the group. Also brilliant in every way, she demonstrates an enviable meticulous nature that I can only begin to strive for. My high school girlfriends are beyond valuable, and they have no idea how much of a reprieve they offer me in my daily life.

---

"AAA, BBB, CCC, DDD . . . Together now!! Mind your fingers. Slowwww down. Somebody is going to get a speeding ticket!" her voice bounces, it's ping-pongy over the top of our heads.

Ms. Warner is our typing teacher. She painstakingly paces in front of the blackboard. Once in a while she stops abruptly, angling her pointer stick straight up and toward the opposite side of the room—a disheveled typing maestro directing her orchestra.

"You!" she shouts. I notice her fuzzy, dark hair; her head appears to float within it. "You there, slow down!" she continues, "Together now, in unison!"

Our class clown sits next to me. I've known him since grade school. Darvin leans over, and says out of the corner of his mouth, "She actually means it? Is she for real?" At first we think it's a joke, her sing-songy way and her strict yet comical manner. "EEE, FFF . . ." She exaggerates her chin; it juts forward.

We are learning on vintage typewriters. The keys require what feels like a two-inch push, which then forces each letter to slap across a tight, black ribbon. The long-armed keys striking print onto barrel-rolled, well-margined white paper. As our letters near the right-side margin, our lever return handles are to be reset in one fell swoop. "TOGETHER NOW! Go!" she says, her pointer up toward the sky. "Whoosh. Excellent!! GGG, HHH," she says in cartoon fashion; I fully expect to see her pop up on Saturday morning TV one day.

Weeks of manual typing skills are honed before we are to graduate to the next room. A much shinier place patiently awaits eager typists looking to learn on sleek, cream-colored, modern electric typewriters. These plug in! And, they practically type by themselves.

Ms. Warner is animated, a perfectionist, and she prides herself in producing efficient, speedy typists ready for all options and choices in the future professional world. We learn to appreciate her, her animated style, and her love of letters.

# We Blossom

His blue eyes and red truck is all I can think about. Sure, there are times I focus on my homework, my family, and my girlfriends, but, those times are few and far between. I'd much rather stay within myself, and think about him. I'm simply lovesick—my mind running thick in poetry and daydreams. I'm struck, hung up in his suspense.

He's teaching me patience, a slight admiration for The Doobie Brothers, but most importantly, how to kiss.

We climb into his truck, it's clean, it's candy-apple red, and there's a gleaming roll bar above us. The tape player sings, "*Minute by minute by minute by minute. I keep movin' on,*" the Doobie's repeat, on and on it goes. The tape soon rewinds, then starts over. He leans in for a kiss. At first it's a virginal kiss, then not so much. I'm still a virgin, in the technical sense, but not in the kissing way. Our passion is undeniable.

Mr. Red Truck eventually slips away, his college future and my high school senior year disrupting any chance for continuing our sweet relationship. At first my spinning head is upset and wonders if it was something I did or didn't do, or if someone better had come along and taken him away. I'm heartbroken, and I don't want to let go. I find myself quiet and withdrawn, aching for the sound of something red, cruising the front of the house. I'm slow to realize, but eventually I do. He has been the very best of first loves: gentle, nonthreatening, and kind. I'm grateful, and will miss him terribly.

I don't recognize levels of popularity as others do; maybe it has something to do with the way that I was raised. I try not to take the high school hierarchy too seriously. Everybody is my friend until they have proven themselves otherwise, and I pride myself in befriending all walks of life and personality types. I even wave hello to my very own brother in the hallways. He waves back; never again will we take our time together for granted. There are hellos for the jocks as well as the nerds. I care just as much about the smart, snooty, and high class as what we call the smokers—the hoods that hang out back, in the parking lot.

"Purely social describes my existence as a senior in high school: laughing with teachers, hanging with Mr. Talker, teasing Ms. Warner, and surviving the always tough, Coach Bovesse. There's even Grandpa Perry. I get to see him maintaining the hallways as he goes about fixing the building. And when I hear the drone of the riding lawn mower, I know it's him outside on the lawn and fields. There are times that I'm deep in a subject, when there comes the smell of freshly cut grass sneaking through an open window. I hear the sound, and I know that he is close by. It comforts me, knowing that he's the one riding just outside the window, slumped there, humming along, the crook of his nose and his shoulders drooping with age. Sitting at my desk, I watch him and wonder what he's thinking.

All in all, I figure that I should have fun while I'm here. My high school ambitions and average grades are tarnished from time to time by hormonal exhaustion, I suppose, or it may just be the long days of school, sports, and work.

I've always worked. Beginning in the strawberry fields, or cherry orchards, around ten years of age, with Mom, or Freda and Breena. At thirteen and fourteen, newspaper deliveries, on bikes, tossing the *Statesmen* and *Itemizer Observer*; Mick and me, throwing at house after house in the middle of the night. In the evenings, two nights a week, I'd teach gymnastics. Assisting with children, showing them how to stand on their heads, tumble, balance, and safely cartwheel themselves into confidence and coordination, even some trust. I took what began as a life upside down, in a constant search for balance, and I turned it into something tangible. I chuckle to myself: You'd think, as serious as I took my studies and practice on the subject of gymnastics that I would eventually secure a spot on the American Olympic Team, but no such luck, not even close. I've traded impossible dreams in for a position with Kids Incorporated. Instead of flipping around under flying pigtails, I spot, and teach other little girls, from five to eighteen, how to tighten their core—how to trust themselves and others, to carry them through to the next step. Later, in high school, my jobs pay a little better. I find work at the popular burger joint known for its special fry sauce, a pizza place, and a jewelry store. Having my own money, independent of my parents', is most important. There's never enough to go around in this big, busy family.

---

It's early; I smell coffee. There's a laugh coming from the dining room area. I know that laugh.

Rolling onto my side, I'm not ready to get up yet. It's Saturday, there's nothing on the agenda, so I take an extra moment to relax, to just be. Adjusting my eyes, I see a pretty day ahead through the sheer of the curtains. Just below, a slice of sunlight cuts across the cedar chest. Different from Grandma's gray chest, this one is bigger, with natural wood colors running through it. Uncle Carp built the chest for Mom long ago; it's special to her. Even though I use the top of it for displays of my favorite teen things, I'm careful around it. Inside holds a tiny red velvet and white chiffon dress, a glass ball wrapped in net, a ceramic baby shoe, a piece of driftwood, a rubber doll, lots of papers, and more, much more. I think there's a piece of everything that means something to her stashed, tucked away, in her box of cedar. The red-and-white dress was something I wore when I was very little. It was given to me by someone dear to her—a brother. I don't see him much anymore, but I remember him as a kind man full of awkward energy, who was always quick to offer Mom a helping hand in rocky times.

Outside the cedar box lives my room. A record player sits on the floor, vinyl singles slung beside it. The Carpenters, Barry Manilow—they sit on well-used carpet along with the rest of my life. I know if I just spring up quickly, and spend a few moments picking up the clutter: my shoes, clothes, books, and papers, that my room would appear mostly clean, but I'm not ready yet.

There's that laugh again. Who is it? My bedroom door clicks. No knock so I know to look down rather than up; our dog, Ziggy, has nudged it open. He saunters his way in looking bored with life—past bored, he looks exhausted. With hardly an effort he glances up at me, then walks right past, head down. He's ho-hum, I think much like Eeyore in *Winnie the Pooh*.

"Mornin' Ziggy," I say, as exhausted as he looks.

He finds a sunspot on the carpet across the room, curls up, and lets a little air out as he sets his chin on top of his paws. He's already fast asleep.

Throwing the bedspread aside, I decide it's time. I'll pick up a few things, get dressed, and take a look out in the dining room. I know they are there because, other than the front porch, the dining room is the gathering place.

—

"Lu! You remember Gayle, right?" Mom says, her face lit up in friendship, caffeine, and nicotine.

"Yes, hi, Gayle," I say surprised, and then I take my seat at the table. I note how instantly comfortable I feel around her.

"Oh, Elin, she's so grown up!" Gayle says. She adds her cackling laugh and a look of disbelief.

"Yeah, I know." Mom nods in agreement.

They go on talking about me like I'm not even in the room. It doesn't feel rude though, quite the opposite. I feel myself flush with the kindness of her words.

"Exotic, that's it, that's the word," Gayle says quietly. Her eyes pour over me.

I'm wondering what she's talking about.

"She has such an exotic look about her," Gayle repeats, then looks at Mom like she's not sure where I came from. I get it—I'm not sure where I came from.

After a while I join her cackling laugh. Gayle fills the room, so much so, that I know the neighbors can hear her; they must be laughing too—she's infectious.

"Let's go out back. Lu, come with. Let's show Gayle some of your moves," Mom says, "You know, Gayle, she teaches gymnastics now."

The air is light, the morning is fresh, and the backyard inviting. I watch them together, friends talking about everything from foliage to property lines, long lost beaches and boyfriends.

"You've come a long way, Elin." Her eyes dialed direct into Mom's. For a moment, I watch them telepathically spin back into another time. Each of them eventually break their dial, though, with a smile, like they've together and forever lightened some darkness from the past.

# SMACKED

I'm basking in the sunshine on the back patio. It's a white islet, bikini kind of day. Giving my towel a snap, I lay it down and begin soaking up the valley sun. Faint sounds of my brothers and sisters move in and out of the house and yard; the dogs are rooting about. There's flapping overhead, as Charlie's pigeons, Penny and The Hulk, hover, just before joining the other winged characters nesting above the garage. I can see Mom's elbow resting on the bathroom window sill, her arm swings out flicking the ash off the end of her cigarette.

"Lu? Can't you find something productive to do?"

I can tell by her tone she's not to be messed with. I gather myself up along with the towel and head in through the basement door, below the bathroom window. Greeted by mounds of laundry, I'm instantly overwhelmed; it's dingy. Laundry for seven is my job at home these days, that and making dinner from time to time. It was a much-welcomed relief when Lacy and Shay took over doing the dishes a year or so ago. I have way too many years of that under my belt.

Walking over to gather a pile from the chute, I begin the sorting process. Mom heads down the stairs.

"You need to get this done . . . now." She can see the pang of guilt crossing my face.

"Okay. I'll finish it today," I say, keeping my head down, sorting. "Mom? Do you think I could go to the movies tonight after I'm finished here? Just a night out with the girls?"

I knew my attempt was risking a snappy "no," as I was just out on a date last night. Two nights out in a row never goes over well with her. Only a couple of months from my eighteenth birthday, I figure it may be time to change such rules; after all, I do my school work, I'm responsible, and I hold down a job.

"You went out last night!" she responds, exhaling; she's frustrated.

"I know, but, the girls want me to go tonight."

"No!! You don't need to go!" she says.

I can feel my face fall in disappointment, then quickly, I put myself in check; she sees disappointment as disrespect. Upset, I brave one last try. "But, why?" Hearing the question and seeing my emotion sets her off. Before I can look up, SMACK!! Her heavy hand lands across my cheek, catching the bridge of my nose. The laundry drops from my hands, I turn the opposite direction, and run for the stairs.

"Lu! You get back here, NOW!"

My heart pauses for a second, then my mind catches up. I'm FINISHED! No way I'm stopping. Busting up the stairs across the house and out the front door, my warm upper lip tastes of blood. I can't stop my nose. The neighborhood watches as I run for the car.

"LU! You get back here, NOW!" she's in panic mode, well into her mission to stop me.

Again, NO way I'm stopping—I'm done. Finally reaching the car, I slide in, slam the door, and start it.

Mom runs in front of it. She screams, "STOP!"

Dad appears out of nowhere; he bends at my driver's side window, tapping it lightly. I roll it down.

Mom is still screaming, "Stop! G, stop her!"

He throws his hand up high, hushing her tone. She holds her stance just a few feet in front of my bumper.

"Please, Lu, don't go. Not like this." Dad says, calmly.

Through tears, I'm deflated. I gesture at the windshield. "This isn't a good place for her to stand right now," I say, shaking, still bleeding. The gear shift is in drive—my foot holds heavy on the brake. He reaches over my shoulder, his hand patting my back. He looks at her, then back at me.

"You're right, probably not, huh?" He attempts a smile, but then his face drops back to serious. "Not like this, Lu."

I put the car in park and pull the key.

"Come on, let's get you cleaned up." I look at him, bewildered. "I know," he says, opening my door.

---

It's evening.

I'm wondering if it's truly a heartfelt apology if I'm forced to listen and accept it, as I sit here, engulfed in the stench of her toilet activities. Taking what's become my normal seat at the edge of the tub, she drones on.

"Mom, can I go now?"

"Just sit there. A little stink won't hurt you. I'm not finished yet."

Her words all sound fine and good, but hardly make up for the action dished out before them. Why is it that I'm not worthy of these words while sitting side by side on a couch with her or while sharing something refreshing at the dining table? Better yet, in public, or maybe in front of our neighbors.

Come on! Announce it to the world. I deserve at least that much!

An apology, in my opinion, should be something clean and pristine, held in the highest regard. Why is it that her apologies are always some sort of a disgusting, smelly secret?

---

Only a few months later, Mick has left us on his own this time. He's a junior in high school. He claims he can't take it any longer. That Mom has hit him for the very last time. He works and shares an apartment with one of his friends.

Charlie flies across the kitchen sometimes; Mom tosses him, he slides, then hits the back door with a thud. Lacy and Shay are slapped and pushed around. Why does she do this? How can it possibly help things? It's hard for us to understand. Sometimes we know we deserve it, because she tells us so. Other times it seeps in, out of nowhere, like the scariest of invisible fogs.

She goes to the doctor and lands in the hospital from time to time. Some kind of mystery illness, where her body wants to work against her. It makes her heart race, her chest hurt, and she sweats really hard.

"Something doesn't feel right, something's off," I hear her say.

She goes on, though, waking from long, midday naps, shaking, flying into a rage after rage.

I don't understand it, and I never will.

# Dearest

## Dallas, Oregon
## 1979

The heavy front door opens loudly; it always has. It's a comforting sound though, one that means somebody's home. You know that it's probably one of the seven of us, but could also be Aunt Niecie or another close friend or relative. This time it's just me.

After a long day of school and work I never know who I might find sitting in the living room. Usually Gilligan is on the TV or maybe the Flintstones—the whistle blowing letting Fred go home for the rest of the day.

Today, the living room and gathering place are empty; everybody's busy doing something. I think Dad's in the garage, Mom is somewhere, maybe grocery shopping or slinging pizza at Angelo's. I hear Mick and Charlie in the basement. I'm thrilled that Mick is back again. I guess there wasn't enough food—he was just too hungry to live on his own. Mom found that funny.

Walking down the hall to my room, Ziggy is in his Eeyore slump, in front of me. I don't dare rush him. He's known for taking your foot off if it comes too close. Finally, strolling far enough, I reach for my bedroom door and push it open. Geez, I need to clean.

I set my things down, drop to my knees, and shuffle through the small pile of singles slung near the record player.

Neil. Yeah, he's always good.

Soon, Neil Diamond fills the room with "Forever in Blue Jeans." I begin to hum, picking things up to the music. Something catches my eye on the bed. There it sits, a letter on top of the sheer silk of the fluffy white bedspread—a gift of feminine softness from Aunt Niecie, a year or so ago. The envelope lies near the matching pillow. Kicking my shoes off, I flop back and put my feet up for a read.

*My Dearest Daughter,*

*No real reason, other than love, for this. Maybe I'm feeling that time is becoming short and soon you'll be on your own. I can remember the fears, but also the elation of freedom of making my own decisions, of coming and going as I pleased. Things will change for you, honey. You will no longer have your clique of friends in school, or your family at home (oh, we will always be home for you, and the door will always be open).*

*Be careful, and take precautions at all times. I know in my leaving home I had great fears, but my leaving was very different than yours. You are much more mature than I ever was at your age. I believe it's harder on me now letting you go, than it was for my parents years ago. Sure, I've shed tears over the thought of you leaving, but that's my priority of being a mother. I never thought it would be this tough.*

*In less than a year, you'll be doing things differently. Whatever you do then—college, work, whatever, just remember it will be a big decision and give it a lot of thought. I'm hoping I'll be making enough money by then to help you further your education. But that's not the most important thing. It's doing what you want to, to be yourself, and to accept people for what they are.*

*Oh, you are so beautiful. I've always been so proud of you. What greater gift could a mother receive than someone like you. You're honest, forgiving, faithful, and have an inward beauty to match your outward beauty.*

*Looking at the years of your childhood, they zipped by so quickly. It just seems now that I missed out on a lot of your growing time. Having the other children kept me pretty busy. By the way, thank you for all of your help throughout the years. I also want to apologize for all of the pain, suffering, and hurts I may have caused you. You were probably never deserving of them.*

*Love,*
*Mom*

I can't believe my eyes—I decide to reread it, and then I read it again.

# My Day

Dallas, Oregon
Spring 1980

My orange gown is pressed, and my cap is tasseled. I am a Dallas Dragon, eager and ready for graduation. It's my day.

The gifts of the day unfold: a phone call from dearest Demi, a dozen flowers from a boy I'm dating. There's the dark, extra shiny curls swirling around my shoulders, the celebrated walk with friend Keith under blossomed arches, the lift from classmate Larry high above the senior crowd. Our chins toward the blue skies above; caps, tassels, and raining mum petals toppling all around us; the gathering of family; the dining table filled with generosity and cheer; and last, but not least, the gift of words—my very own electric typewriter.

Ready to join a night of fun with friends, I climb into my car a different person now. An uncertain life ahead of me, yes, but I know that I'm ready to take it on.

While turning the curve of the cul-de-sac, I look up at the house, at the big window of the dining room, the gathering place still a buzz of late-evening activity and celebration. I stop the car to watch for a moment. The golden glow of sconces lighting loved ones enjoying each other's company: Aunt Niecie, Grandma Evelyn, Grandpa Perry, Mom, Dad, and all my brothers and sisters.

Turning the radio up, I lift my foot from the brake, sing along, and roll away. *"I can see clearly now the rain is gone."* I love this song; I keep singing.

Listening, I then pick up on the words that catch me, that I know I can use in the moment.

*Look straight ahead, there's nothing but bluuuuue sky, yyyyy, yyy, yyy, yyy, yy, y, ies."*

Outside my driver-side window, I put my hand in the air and change the words to my own—I know better, but I'm going to trust myself and shout them to the world anyway,

*"Life's gonna be one big bright, bright, sun-shiny day!"*

I look straight ahead, then up at the blue skies cloaked in a night full of twinkling stars, and I know—it's time for me to go.

# PART FOUR

## FIVE YEARS LATER

# TIME

ANCHORAGE, ALASKA
1985
LU

My flight leaves in an hour. This stuffy uniform still reeks of smoke from yesterday's thirteen-hour workday. No doubt, that today's loads will add a few more layers to it.

"Uck, there's nothing worse than the smell of airplane smoke," I say under my breath drawing up another whiff of my forearm, before straightening the scarf at my neck. Why even have a smoking section. It's a joke, really. I don't know why I question it, I'm bound to smell this way; our hectic flight schedules schlepping oil field, slope workers of Alaska proves hard work. Five or six times a week, up in the sky, all stuffed, shoulder to shoulder, in a tube. I've certainly earned my wings.

Flight Supervisor, Cindy, pokes her head around the corner. "Lu, call home," she says.

What? I think of my three-year-old daughter, Ashlie.

"Your mom called."

"Mom?"

Relieved that Ash is okay, I head for the nearest pay phone down the hall and make a collect call to Oregon.

"Hi, Mom."

"Hi, Lu," she sniffs. "Come home now; it's time."

I tug at the phone, the metal coil is unforgiving, too short to let me sit comfortably, to process her words; Mom sounds tired and upset. I take a moment to collect myself, setting my chin in my palm. Managing my emotion, I'm hoping that Grandma Evelyn isn't suffering in pain.

During my travels throughout the night I think about her life—our lives.

If not for her, not one of us would exist today. I realize that most people can say that about their grandmothers, in fact, all people can say it. But, in our case you can call it many other things: chance, a coincidence, kismet—quite possibly, in this case, a miracle. Perhaps, that's what they meant in the newspapers following her accident. Maybe calling her a Miracle Child wasn't that far off the mark. I'm realizing, in my eyes she still is, and always will be, a Miracle Child.

# Together

## Dallas, Oregon

Her recent months have been surrounded in love, if not expressed in words, than held in an understanding glance, or an offer of physical steadiness in a reach for her elbow or her hand. Her recent days hold quiet conversation, and medical care, allowing her a slow, somewhat comfortable decline. Her hours are embraced in concern: a cloth on her forehead, a soft rub on her arm, quiet words near her ear.

Cancer is ugly, but allows us the process of letting go. I can see it as one of life's most imperfect, generous plans. Grandma Evelyn didn't have this luxury of time with her family, as they instantly vanished right before her eyes. The train then shoving her forward, alone, forcing her to live on. The end of her life is playing out right here and now, with us; she's blessed with precious interaction—time to say good-bye.

I see it in Grandpa Perry, the strain, a softened man's look confronting the unknown. I hurt for him and can only imagine how difficult it would be to lose the person that you've walked through life with. He looks lost, struck—as though he has no idea now where he belongs. I hear his kids kicking around concern.

How he can barely manage making a peanut butter sandwich on his own, so they question how it is that he's going to manage life from here forward?

"Does he even know how to boil water?" I hear Mom ask Aunt Niecie. Mom adds, "Honestly, what do I care? He deserves every bit of misery ahead of him, if you ask me."

Mom has never kept us kids from the love of our grandpa, but there's no question how she feels about him—the word HATE is never far from his name.

"You feel how you want about him," she would tell us. "I can't stand the man."

I've never understood hatred. In my opinion, it takes more energy to hate then it does to understand the reasons behind it. Once you understand the reasons, then it doesn't take much energy to let it go. I think most of the time the reasons have little to do with you in the first place, and more to do with the person or thing you're spending time and energy hating. It's like a boomerang; you can try throwing hate around, but guaranteed, it will always come back to get you.

—

Charlie has his hands full working here at the Dallas Nursing Home. He's matured, growing sturdy and handsome. The tallest in the family now, he's just a hint past his teenage years. I chuckle inside, noting his younger mischievous self and how this group of people, and this work, may be a perfect fit for him. There's a part of me that hopes they are releasing spiders in jars, collecting reptiles as pets, storing them in their rooms for him to discover. The female residents tease Charlie and inevitably grow a crush; he finds humor in their ongoing flirtations. I guess in some way Grandma lucked out in that there was no room at the local hospital. At least here, Charlie can keep a close eye and ensure her every need is taken care of. Even though she's in and out of consciousness, she must know that this is a better place for her final rest. Sure, it can be sad and chaotic here, but, never a dull moment in this big house full of seniors living out there last years, months, days, and minutes. That said, I'm sure taking care of Grandma throughout his workday conjures up mixed feelings for Charlie. He shares as much, during his breaks, taking time for a tear or two. He goes on to explain how he closes his eyes, recruiting help as he continues his mission with the greatest of care and respect. He knows how private she is, and always has been. Surely, in her foggy suspense, she realizes it's dearest Charlie that's looking out for her, and she must appreciate his loving effort.

Outside Grandma's door there's a commotion. As I head to check things out, I'm startled having to dodge a speeding wheelchair; arms held high, a toothless wonder glides past with not a care in the world. A simultaneous scold comes from a nurse's desk. The nurse's shout drifts over as Toothless Wonder flies by; Toothless doesn't mind, she adds her own gum smiling, speedster's victory yelp to the echo in the hallway. The resident has managed to plunge head first into a corner room, grabbing on to a sliding bed curtain.

"Lily! Not again!" The frustrated nurse comes out from behind the desk to attend to her.

Toothless doesn't hear her, though. The daredevil plants her face in the curtain and blows what sounds like her mouth and her nose at the same time, then tucks the curtain in the crook of her arm. She swirls there, spinning one wheel of her chair with her free hand. I can't help but laugh at her gumption. It feels good to laugh. In fact, even her hair has moxie; it brings tears to my eyes. This woman is living her last days in a twisted curtain dance of happiness, and so she should.

—

Back in Grandma's room, my ear picks up on the noon whistle. I think it's been here since the beginning of time; I've always meant to ask exactly how long. It's not a whistle that sounds like it comes from a coach, referee, or musical instrument. This whistle blows more like a siren. Noon every day, without fail, the siren sounds in this little town. A sort of reminder for its people that the day is well on its way, but that it may also be time for: a break, a visit, to have something to eat, or to maybe take a stroll to shake some stress along the way. Telephones begin ringing to check on loved ones if the siren goes off any other time than noon. Because, even one minute before or two minutes after means there's someone in trouble, maybe there's a fire or a heart attack. It's then that we use it as a reminder to look out for one another. I'm warmed by the thought of how a simple sound brings people together—in this case, an entire town.

After lunch we take a seat in the common area, where people wait, relax, and mingle in a room filled with shades of tan, showered in country blue, trimmed in oak. It's busy. Visitors and residents exchange pleasant niceties, greetings, and polite conversation.

A soft-spoken woman approaches with a clock in hand.

"Would you like to know the time?" her sky-blue eyes and inquisitive expression is serious, fragile, and oh-so sweet. She turns the clock toward her face, a studied look crosses her settled features. I see it, the very moment the answer dawns on her.

"Sure," I say. She turns it back toward me, grinning.

"It's 1:30," she says. Her Big Ben alarm clock is larger than the hand that holds it.

"How about you, little girl? Would you like to know the time?" Ashlie smiles up at her.

"Umm, 1:31," she adds, giving the clock a quick wind. The woman continues shuffling on about the room, Big Ben in one hand, her cane in the other.

"Would YOU like to know the time?" Her words carry down the hall as she makes her rounds announcing away the minutes.

Time for some fresh air; we join the relatives outside.

Ashlie scoots up next to Shay, on a bench; she snuggles into her auntie. We take in this fine, clear day. Ashlie soon climbs down and picks up a confident step, forcing a three-year-old tromp across the small courtyard. Her bright-yellow dress, lit up in sunshine, flips forward then back, responding to the jerky, toddler sway in her arms.

"Just a yittle juice, Mama?" her pronunciation is clear, but all Ls become Ys, and sometimes the other way around. She reaches for the cup in my hand, takes a sip, then swipes her mouth with the back of her fingers.

"My yips hurt," she says, the corners of her lips fall down in a frown. Fishing for the Chapstick in my pocket, her lips suddenly turn up—she knows it will taste like cherries. I delicately pat it across her girly lipstick pucker. She holds the pucker longer than needed, then quickly tucks her lips inward for a taste. Happy, away she goes, flitting from one end of the courtyard to the other, the sweetest of social butterflies.

My mind lingers in the past: I'm small, dancing with butterflies in Grandma's backyard. The fresh smell of cucumbers and those beautiful, wispy fuchsias above my head. Where floating humming birds and smiling pansies thrive: the buttercups under chins, the lines of marigolds, the blossomed limbs of a cherry tree where nests of robin's eggs hide. I'm reminiscent of our visits together, our day trips to fresh fruit stands and grocery stores with wooden shelves and wooden floors. Our drives together with Grandpa at the wheel; Grandma's playful shout as the car crosses the railroad tracks: "Lift your feet!" she would say. And, so we did just that, feet up, lifted off the floor, till we cleared the tracks, never fully realizing the significant, heartfelt meaning behind her request.

One more thought dawns on me—her lost family must be eagerly waiting to see her.

I know her story, but I can't tell you the exact moment it all came together in my mind. She never did sit us down and tell us from the first word to the last how things took place. We've had to piece it together over the years, collect it by overhearing bits and pieces at the tail end of adult conversations, or by reading a note here and there. There were hints: the toy train in the attic, stories of an engineer with a big heart, old pictures of a little girl in newspapers, and then there is the fact that I've never seen her behind the wheel of a car.

Just a few years ago, she rode the long journey back to visit the place she was born—Stagebarn Canyon. It had been more than fifty years since her family started their trek toward Oregon, excited about starting their new life. I imagine her standing there quietly, looking up at the protective canyon walls that she knew as a child, wondering how life would've turned out if they had never left them in the first place. Maybe, her hands were in her coat pockets, fingers rubbing the glass that her Papa left her along the tracks that fateful day. Her other hand tucked, a rounded fist, finally relaxed, the size of her solid, mended heart.

---

I return to her room, where I find Mom sitting with Grandma; she's talking to her. A one-sided, peaceful conversation between the two of them. Mom's letting her go. Seeing them together, I think about what it means to be a mother. I suppose in a perfect world, being a good mother is meant as the ultimate selfless role, the most selfless role of all. But for many, I suspect it goes a bit more like this: in order to face unimaginable loss, abuse, and violence, there are the mothers that need to be selfish to survive. Some find themselves empty-handed, continually protecting, repeatedly picking themselves up to face the hardships, only to be smacked down all over again. Somewhere in the midst of it all, there are the moments: an "I love you, Mama" when you least expect it, a child's whisper shared, while wrapped in the arms of a hug, a gentle pat on a hand, or a nuzzle just before an afternoon nap. These are the times where a mother finds the strength to relish her role and discover the amazing joys within it. My heart realizes that nothing grand as a mother can be accomplished by being absent, too loud or too quiet. I think a mother's best role is found in the calm of it—that calm you feel in your core, you can trust it.

My own experience as a mother came early as I've always known it would; a perfect little girl from a kind man. I'm not sure that I'm a good mother by any stretch of the word, but I try. The maternal instinct stuck with me, leaping from all of my brothers and sisters straight into motherhood. Maybe I can't imagine a life without little eyes looking up at me. I try never to touch my Ashlie when I'm angry. I've popped her during a tantrum, or when she doesn't follow my directions. I've noticed, if I let it, hitting happens automatically, sometimes my hands move before my head catches up—that scares me. I tell myself that her face is off limits from this day on, NEVER again. That a bottom side is the only place meant for a swat. But honestly, why violently hit or swat anything or anybody at all? My whole heart is invested in erasing lines of abuse—hard lines that have been drawn for generations. It's time to turn those lines to dust and blow them away.

There's something in the air that tells me not to leave Grandma's side; her room glows, in a haze of pink, as the sun sinks deep into the afternoon. I note how quiet it is, how ironically safe it feels here. I sit, leaning into her, telling her that everything is going to be okay. "This must be scary, but don't be afraid," I say, mindful of the shake in my voice and in my hand as it covers hers. I let her know that it's time. That she can let go now, that she's deeply loved and always will be.

—

So, here we are, together, three bodies—three generations; two of us heavy with emotion and one light as air. Having witnessed her gentle, slow release, there is sadness, of course. But, high on the emotional bracket lies relief—relief for Evelyn—for she no longer feels the physical pain of cancer ravishing her body, nor does she feel the mental anguish of loved ones mourning her departure. She's again, and forever beautiful, but now, no doubt filled with peace. Maybe she's watching, posing painlessly overhead, on her way to a better existence; moving toward her mama's open arms, pulling their shattered pieces back together again. I see her ready for a loving, much-desired reunion with her mama, papa, Sylvia, and Bertha, but first giving us one last look, her hand cupped across her lips as she did here on Earth when alive with laughter, curiosity, or riddled with her sweet, early childhood memories.

I place my hand on my chest—what an honor to know her, to learn from her, to love her.

—

I expect the world to stop, to hesitate its rotation for a moment. Maybe even a second or two? But no. The people continue about their business. The nursing home, still a buzz of activity. Outside, cars zip by containing busy-minded individuals, checking off their errand lists, providing taxi service for their loved ones to school, games, or work.

*Stop!* I shout in my head.

Heartbreaking words sit ready to leap from my lips as we shuttle toward Aunt Niecie's house; I hold them there, so long that it hurts.

Please! Something earth-shattering has happened here!

As I quiet the scream in my head, the lump in my throat squeezes on.

I lean my head back on the seat. Ashlie gets comfortable beside me. For some odd reason, I think of fairy tales and happily ever afters. How I've always known that they are just children's stories, designed to send them dreaming peacefully before sleep. Where hard things happen, but always end shiny and new, no matter what the problem is—we wish it to be true, but it never goes that way in real life, does it?

A single tear escapes; I catch it at the curve of my cheek.

---

Mick is on his way; he should arrive any time now. He's received the same grim update from Mom that I had a few days before. His return home is more difficult, though. He's thousands of miles away, having to arrange leave from his Marine post. Charlie and Shay are here, of course, but I wonder if Lacy has realized the news?

---

"Lu, the phone's for you," Aunt Niecie says, handing me the receiver. I hear sniffling on the other end of the line.

"Hello?"

"Lu, I JUST now heard."

"What?"

"I'm so sad and angry right now, I can hardly keep myself together. . . . Really? She's that pissed at me?"

*Who?* I wonder.

"Leaving a message with my roommate? Hell! My roommate hardly remembered to even say anything, delivering it like an afterthought—basically, an 'Oh, by the way, your grandma died?' Doesn't Mom know that I need to hear these things directly from her? Is she so mad, that she couldn't even bother to pick up the phone and to talk with me, herself? You know Lu, she hasn't spoken to me in weeks. I couldn't take it anymore; I had to get out of there, it was just too much. I guess this is her way of winning—always about who's winning, who's the toughest, never about settling things the calm way. And, now it's too late for me to even attend my own grandmother's funeral? She knew it would be! She did this on purpose!" Lacy cries. "I'm in Nevada, for God's sake, how would I even get there on time?!"

I don't know what to say, but I try. "Oh, Lacy, I'm sorry. I guess I thought someone had contacted you."

I look at Mom across the room. She's busy with her siblings, planning Grandma's last good-bye. Emotions are running high already, so there's no way I'm handing her the phone. Besides, I think Lacy would climb through the line and throttle me if I did.

"You know how much Grandma loved you, right? That's the most important thing."

"I know, but . . ." Lacy let the air out of her chest and sobbed.

"Lacy, please know that Grandma, of all people, would understand—no matter where you are, she'll always be with you."

# Bye-Bye for Now

Dallas, Oregon
1985

Ashlie is on my hip. I look at all of Grandma's children, and their children: Uncle Bubby and Uncle Carp standing above us, their sons beginning to exceed each of their dad's six-feet-six statures, their daughters blooming with hints of their mothers and Grandma Evelyn across their young features.

Grandpa's hands fidget, much like his feet always have, nonstop, his thick brow holds hard in a perpetual worry. I look at Aunt Niecie and Cousin Bea Susan; they make my heart full. I watch Mom and Dad, Shay, Charlie, and Mick; there's a surprisingly close, relaxed interaction between them.

"Quit!" Shay says, blushing, then lashing out at Mick teasing her hair. He's amazed at how much she's grown and how everybody has changed.

Mick is in uniform. He's beyond handsome. His Marine Dress Blues are contoured and striking. The white hat, belt, and gloves punctuate his air of authority. I watch him, arm over arm, walking up the meticulously groomed cemetery slope with

Charlie. Above us tower oak and evergreen trees, all around us, warmth of light and loved ones.

There's a slow saunter in progress. No one is in a hurry, as we are all spent from the tearful service at the funeral home.

We circle around her; her casket is suspended and draped in roses. Delightful words of family and history float about. Precious words, so dear that I want to pick them out of the air and stick them in my pocket, take them with me, and save them forever.

After final words are spoken, Mick steps up. He throws himself into a salute of honor, his hand and elbow sharp, his eyes stern and wet with emotion. He looks first toward her casket, then straight ahead, holding his salute, peering into the future. He snaps his arms tight to his sides, then begins a tug at each finger loosening his bright, white gloves. As he pulls them off one at a time, he draws them in for a kiss, then places them gently—one last gift for her to keep.

Ashlie, still on my hip, places her head on my chest. I drop my cheek down onto her honey-colored pigtails, and pull her in for a nice, long hug. While inhaling her innocence, I wonder if she's grasping the intensity of the moment—the fact that her great grandmother, whom once upon a time won a battle with a train, lost four precious loves, then lived on, replacing the world with four of her own. And, Evelyn's not finished, as she leaves behind an astonishing gift of more generations to flourish.

"Yook, Mama." Ashlie opens her hand; using her turned up palm, she motions toward a busy robin perched high above our heads. Feeling safe, the musical bird braves down a few limbs, pauses for a closer look and a listen, then happily takes flight.

"Bye-bye for now. She fly'd away, Mama!" Ashlie says, waving high in the sky. She turns for my response. Catching the gaze in my eye, a subtle smile crosses her pure, angelic face. I smile back at her, and lean in for a whisper. "It's time to go."

# Acknowledgments

## Thank You

Grandma, Evelyn
Grandpa, Perry
Mom, Helen
Dad, George
My Steve (dear husband)
Daughters, Ashlie & Alisa
Aunt Niecie (Bernice)
Uncle Perry & Family
Uncle Harvey & Family
Aunt Annette & Family
Uncle Elias & Family
Brother, Mike
Brother, Kip
Sister, Lisa (beta reader)
Sister, Shannon
Cousin, Brenda (friend extraordinaire)
Gayle
Gigi Fowler-Hendricks, beta reader
Ashlie Lee, cover photographer

Katherine Marea Photography, author photographer
Susan Jostrom, editor
Brooke Warner, publishing coach
Tabitha Lahr, and Wayne Parrish

There were times when I felt this story wrote itself, but I know better. Without the help of the above-listed people, along with an endless list of awe-inspiring friends (you know who you are), this story quite simply would not exist. Thank you from the bottom of my heart.

# The Cover

The vision of strength and vulnerability featured on the cover is portrayed by nine-year-old Dakota. On the day of the photo shoot, she was the exact age that Evelyn Castle was when she lost her family. Dakota's representation of Evelyn comes natural, as she happens to be a direct descendent of each of the main characters featured. Because Evelyn and Dakota lived a few generations apart, they never had the pleasure of meeting one another in person. Dakota thrives in her education, and, like Evelyn, she shows a love for animals, art, music—anything that has wonder in it. I'm convinced that if they had been given the chance to walk on this Earth together, hand in hand, this world would be even a brighter place to live in.

# About the Author

First time novelist Linda Haas-Melchert resides in Anchorage, Alaska, where she enjoys her family, the outdoors, art, and writing. Her message to you: Take one step at a time, soon you'll be flying!

Contact Linda directly: whispermamawhisper@gmail.com

79301224R00198

Made in the USA
Columbia, SC
30 October 2017